BLACKOUT

ALSO BY ERIN FLANAGAN

Deer Season

It's Not Going to Kill You, and Other Stories

The Usual Mistakes

BLACKOUT

A Thriller

ERIN FLANAGAN

THOMAS & MERCER

Text copyright © 2022 by Erin Flanagan
All rights reserved.

No part of this book may be reproduced, or stored in a retrieval system, or transmitted in any form or by any means, electronic, mechanical, photocopying, recording, or otherwise, without express written permission of the publisher.

Published by Thomas & Mercer, Seattle

www.apub.com

Amazon, the Amazon logo, and Thomas & Mercer are trademarks of Amazon.com, Inc., or its affiliates.

ISBN-13: 9781542039895
ISBN-10: 1542039894

Cover design by Ploy Siripant

Printed in the United States of America

For Barry Milligan

PART ONE

Chapter One

Maris covered the boneless chicken thighs with plastic wrap and whacked them with a kitchen mallet.

"Gross," Cody said over the sound of smacked flesh as she grabbed a cutting board from under the stove. "Are you sure we shouldn't become vegetarians?"

Maris grinned at her daughter as she cracked salt and pepper over the thighs. "No pepperoni pizza? No hamburgers?" She slid the thighs into the preheated oven. "What would you even eat?"

"Flamin' Hot Cheetos?" Cody suggested as she sliced quick, even zucchini disks like they'd learned in the knife skills class they'd taken together at Savory's, their local upscale market. Fountains of Wayne warbled through the speakers from Cody's playlist, a band her dad had turned her on to.

"Ah, yes. A Cheetotarian. I forgot about that nutritional option."

"Good thing you're not coming to career day as a dietitian," Cody quipped, a not-so-subtle reminder to her mother about the school event next month.

"Nothing quite so glamorous," Maris agreed as she shuffled through the junk drawer for a Sharpie to write a reminder for the fridge. She marveled that in the last seven months, the corkscrew had worked its way behind the shamrock-shaped plastic sunglasses, the magnetic notepad decorated with beach balls, and a free back-to-school pen from

Glenn State (what counted as swag for professors). She wrote *Fri Oct 8 2:00!!!* on the summer notepad and stuck it next to the smiley face magnet.

For most of her adult life, when Maris had come into the kitchen to make dinner, her first two stops were always the fridge and the cupboard next to it for a wineglass. She'd drink that first midwestern pour as she scanned the recipe and clicked on the oven to preheat, doing a mental inventory of what she had to throw together in a salad. With a few drops left, she'd top it off and start the first *real* glass, telling herself the other was just the splash they used at restaurants to make sure you liked the vintage.

And for the record, she always liked the vintage. A vintage didn't exist on earth she wouldn't suck down and pour again.

But that was behind her now, seven months in the rearview mirror. Now she made dinner with her daughter as they talked about their days, a scene so wholesome she wanted to rub it in her own parents' faces.

"What about your dad?" Maris asked. "Is he going to find a way to Zoom in for career day?" He still lived in Nebraska, where Cody was born, and while lawyers were just as prevalent in Ohio, Maris thought it was sweet Cody had been so insistent he be included.

"The teacher said she could connect her phone to the overhead. He'll go on before Noel." Noel Hiser was Maris's husband and Cody's stepdad. His ER schedule of 6:00 p.m. to 6:00 a.m. Thursday night through Sunday morning meant he was usually snoring away in their bedroom with the blackout curtains drawn during most of Cody's school days, but he would always sacrifice sleep if Cody asked him to.

"Are you the only kid with three parents presenting?" Maris asked, and Cody snorted.

"Please. There's a kid in my class with five. Three doesn't even make the leaderboard."

It felt good to be joking in the kitchen after weathering the past seven months. Cody was back from summer with her dad in Nebraska, and they were both two weeks into the new school year, a time that Maris had always thought of as brimming with promise. Today had been the first cool day of September, with temperatures in the seventies, and Maris lit a cider doughnut candle on the breakfast bar as she tried to remember where she'd put the papier-mâché pumpkins for the mantel. Probably in the basement behind the enormous spider that Cody and Noel had insisted they buy for the roof last year for Halloween.

Already the chicken was sizzling in the back of the hot oven, olive oil popping in the pan.

She and Cody had fallen into a comfortable routine when school started up where Maris would pick Code up at Horace Valley STEM at the end of the workday and they'd stop at Savory's to pick out a meal for dinner. In the olden days, Maris was sure to go on her own so she could stop for a quick two glasses at the balcony bar.

As Maris sorted the junk mail into the recycling, she asked Cody about her day—who she sat with at lunch, how Ms. Martin liked her Little Library idea for honors ELA—and Cody chatted along, volleying back questions about Maris's most recent article on Vox and her fall classes. Since February, Maris had done damage control on her relationship with her daughter, not wanting to bother Code with her problems, so she smiled brightly and didn't mention the devastating meeting with her department chair, the less than stellar results of her tenure vote. She remembered how her own parents would fight in front of her when she was a child, their problems public fodder. She didn't want to be that person to her daughter.

Her phone dinged with a text from Noel as she was plucking the silverware from the clean dishwasher for dinner. Swinging by Yanni's then home xo. Maris felt a spike of irritation. He'd picked up an extra shift at the hospital, an ever-weary eye toward their student loan balances, but she'd hoped he'd be home for dinner. She wanted to tell *him* about her department's tenure vote—get the bad news off her back—but this was what she got for marrying a saint. He worked in the ER with Yanni, a nurse whose husband was in Afghanistan. She and Kareem were expecting their first baby in a few months, and Noel had been helping with the nursery while Kareem was deployed: painting the walls, assembling the crib. He'd even helped her put together a custom closet from the Container Store, specially sized to baby hangers. He'd shaken his head in wonder as he held his hands six inches apart to demonstrate to Maris how tiny a baby's shoulders would be.

At the time she'd mimicked the width of his hands and held it down to her crotch, saying, "Try telling that to Yanni."

Tonight, she figured his delay would at least give her another hour or so to work, and she texted back the red-heart emoji and the face-blowing-a-kiss emoji, then continued the neat rows of alternating squash, zucchini, eggplant, red peppers, and potatoes as she and Cody stacked the veggies for ratatouille. First on her list was to start her rebuttal letter for her tenure vote, but Maris pushed it from her mind before she could get angry or tear up, wanting instead to concentrate on Cody, the upcoming career day. Right now her advice would be: don't become an academic.

When the timer dinged, Cody reached for the plates in the cupboard, and Maris told her just two. "No Noel?" Cody asked.

"Helping Yanni," she said, and Cody set two Fiesta plates, turquoise and lemongrass, on the table as her mom brought in the chicken. "Cheers," Maris said, and they clinked wineglasses full of fizzy water—she hadn't been able to give up the ritual. Maris took a big drink of LaCroix, the bubbles like small bites in her sinuses. She set her glass back on the table, the bubbles still in her nose, the oregano overpowering from the ratatouille—had she thrown in too much?—and took a

—

—

—

her hands rubbing circles over her cheeks, as if the world had gone from complete black to light. At the sight of herself in the mirror, she gasped, her pulse jacking up to double time. What the hell?

She was in her bathroom upstairs now, out of her work slacks and blouse and wearing an old pair of Noel's boxers and a ratty gray Huskers T-shirt: her usual pajamas.

Whatever had happened, it wasn't like waking up, not exactly, because her eyes hadn't been closed. She stared at her startled reflection.

Not here, and now here.

Her hands shook, and she held them in front of her, palms up. Her fingers were greasy. The plastic bottle of Olay, which she'd put on her face every night since her early twenties (except nights she was too drunk to wash her face), sat cap off on the counter, and a swipe of white lotion was still visible on her face. What the hell had happened?

She looked around the bathroom for other clues. The hand towel was damp, so she'd washed her face. She felt the bristles on her toothbrush: wet.

Jesus Christ, what?

She turned toward the bedroom as Noel appeared in the doorway, and she was so startled she screamed, doubling over, a fist to her mouth.

"Shit!" She collapsed with her hands on her knees, her heart hammering in her chest. "You scared the shit out of me."

"I can see that." She looked at his face; he was trying not to laugh. Her startle response was a long-running joke. No matter that she knew he was home, or even on the same floor, or even likely to come talk to her, if he said her name and she hadn't heard him walk into the room, she yelped. Their favorite was the time she didn't realize he was in the bathroom downstairs, opened it to find him peeing, and *she* screamed.

"Jesus," she said, trying to laugh at herself as she stood up. "I didn't realize you were home."

Noel's expression changed from one of amusement to bafflement. "What do you mean?"

A thread of dread unspooled in her stomach. It was that feeling she used to have on a somewhat regular basis. Back when she was drinking, someone would tell her something she'd done or said the night before but no memory would surface, and she would have to laugh it off like she knew what they were talking about. But that hadn't happened for seven months, and as much as she missed the drinking itself, since then, her life had been easier, calmer, like a tight muscle finally unclenched.

She used her favorite rhetorical move when teaching: answer a question with a question. "What do you mean what do I mean?"

"I got home a half an hour ago. We talked in the kitchen?"

"Oh, right," she said instinctively, a smile wavering.

He stared at her for a long beat. "You okay?"

She rolled her eyes at herself. "Yeah. Sorry. I'm a little out of it tonight." She turned back to the mirror and washed her hands for lack of anything better to do. "I met with Tammy today about tenure," she said as she dried her hands on the damp towel. She felt a flash of panic like she used to feel: What if she'd already told him downstairs? It used to irritate Noel, all the conversations he had to replay for her the next morning, as she fumbled along like she'd only momentarily forgotten.

"What'd she have to say?" Noel asked. Tammy was her chair and head of the Sociology Department's promotion and tenure committee. Maris felt her shoulders relax that Noel had taken the bait to change the subject. But wait, she reminded herself: she had nothing to hide.

"That I should have been writing recognizable academic articles the past five years."

"Oh, Mare," he said sympathetically as she climbed into bed. "And the vote?"

"Twelve-four." She picked up her novel from the nightstand and set it on her lap, hands shaking. Every night when she came to bed, she brought up her phone, a glass of water, and her current novel, and there they all were on the stand, dutifully waiting for her. She had no recollection she'd done such a thing. It was so eerily like a night of drinking, for a moment she wondered, *Did I drink? Did I?* But no. There was no booze in the house. She was sure she was sober. She rolled her tongue around her mouth and tasted only mint.

Noel emerged from the closet, his scrubs replaced with sweats. "You're taking it better than I would have expected," he said, and lay down next to her on top of the covers, an arm tucked behind his head so she could see his armpit hair sneaking out of the sleeve of his gray T-shirt. She rolled toward him and rested her head in the welcoming crevice. "You sure you're okay?" he asked.

"I just need a good night's sleep." She worked a demanding job, was hounded by trolls online for her articles on rape culture and masculinity, was raising a teenager, and was in her forties. Of course she needed a good night's sleep. Had it really been as bad as she thought, or had her mind just been distracted? Sometimes when a migraine hit, she could lose hours of the day to the pain, but she didn't have a migraine now. Did she? Her head certainly hurt as adrenaline leaked slowly from her body, her fight-or-flight response activated.

Noel was quiet for a moment, and it reminded her of the first few months after she quit: if she worked late in her office or had to stop at the library on the way home, she could feel his eyes on her when she came in the door, watching her silently, speculating. The way she hung her coat on the hook, set her purse on the bench. At those times, she'd kept her head erect as if there were a book on top of her skull as she walked—right foot, left foot—into the kitchen, knowing she was being not only observed but tested. It was difficult to speak at your regular speed with your normal enunciation when you knew someone was listening for an error.

But this was different, she reminded herself. She hadn't mispronounced a word; she'd forgotten a chunk of the night sober.

Noel ran a hand over his hair. "Long day for me too," he conceded as he stood up, and she let out a breath of relief. "It's hard going from the night shift to day."

"We both probably need a good night's sleep."

He came over to her side of the bed, leaned over, and kissed her. Had he sniffed her breath first? As he closed the bedroom door behind him, Maris rolled over, her heart still racing. Did he believe her? she wondered.

Plus, the real question: Just what the hell had happened?

CHAPTER TWO

Maris awoke Wednesday morning, her first thought the blackout and her mind a hive of theories: stress-related disassociation, early-onset dementia, her migraines escalating, dormant alcohol use back to bite her in the ass. She was relieved when Noel stayed in bed so she'd have time to obsess, and as she brushed her teeth, she swore she would call her GP and get a battery of tests. She'd start taking B12 and solving sudoku.

She spit in the sink, then crossed the hall to Cody's room and knocked loudly three times, signaling it was time to get up. Code was in middle school now—that liminal space between childhood and adulthood. She still slept with Blanket Puppy, her favorite toy from the toddler days, but rolled her eyes at the bedtime her mother enforced. Both actions pleased Maris, not that her daughter would want to know that.

Maris was on her second cup of coffee when Cody made it downstairs, a too-orange lipstick on her mouth and a wobbly attempt at eyeliner, all makeup she and Scott had approved over the summer. As a champion of women's rights, Maris knew makeup could be used for female empowerment and as an expression of identity, and she hoped that was how Cody saw it, not as the trappings of the patriarchy. But who was Maris herself to judge, squeezed as she was into a pair of Spanx under her pencil skirt and suffering in heels that pinched both large toes.

Cody was dressed in jeans and a cardigan to follow the school's dress code, but a minute ago Maris had seen the picture her daughter posted to Instagram in just the jeans and a tank top. Over the last few months, the pictures on her feed had evolved from silly and goofy to curated, thoughtful, self-conscious. This picture had been taken in her bedroom, obviously on a timer, her mouth set to duck lips. The jeans weren't especially tight or the tank top especially revealing, but something about the studied, sexualized pose gave Maris pause. Despite her unease, she "liked" it on the app. She didn't want Cody to feel any more self-conscious than she already did. She was the only one in her friend group who still didn't have her period and had been devastated to enter eighth grade a "period virgin."

In the garage, Cody gave Maris the double whammy of prayer hands and puppy-dog eyes as she begged her mother for a ride to school so she wouldn't have to ride her bike. Maris agreed, even though she knew it would put her on campus twenty minutes later than she'd planned, the parking lot already full.

As Maris hoofed it from the overflow lot in those toe-pinching shoes, she ran through the class plans in her head, making a mental note to track down statistics for job prospects in the field and graduate school acceptance rates for her advanced sociology class.

She unlocked her office door and pushed it forward with her shoulder, weighted down with her purse, her lunch, and a bag full of books. There were three new dead flies on the windowsill—how did they get in every day in every season?—and she swept them into the garbage with a napkin, then booted up her computer, tugged off her shoes with a sigh, and got to work.

There was no time that morning for Maris to call her doctor, just fleeting moments she stole to worry about the blackout: sitting in the bathroom stall staring at the underwear she should have replaced six months ago or waiting for a student from her Intro to Sociology class who wanted to plan out the next two years of classes. During a long curriculum meeting regarding assessment, she struggled to follow what people were saying about accreditation with no time to let her mind wander.

There never seemed to be enough time for anything. Just yesterday her department chair, Tammy, had knocked her knuckle on Maris's door three times and held up her phone. "Do you have time for a quick faculty pic? We're updating the department website." Maris barely had time to smile, never mind apply lipstick, before Tammy had lifted the camera for six quick clicks. She'd had bags under her eyes by that time of the day, a smudge of cottage cheese from lunch on her light-colored blouse.

As the hours wore on and Maris finalized the assignment schedule for Sociology and Social Media and answered student emails and checked off tasks on her to-do list for the day, she wondered if she'd overreacted last night. She stole some time to pore over websites on brain circuitry and alcohol effects, searching article after article with keywords like *blackout*, *alcohol and long-term effects*, and *memory loss in your forties*, but the research began to feel removed, a problem that plagued someone else. She googled specific questions like *How does alcohol affect you after you quit?* but nothing in her research seemed to indicate such delayed effects, and she convinced herself it was nothing.

Surely it hadn't been as weird as she'd originally thought. She recalled all the times she'd been driving home from work, the same route she took most weekdays since she started the job, and how often she'd forget making certain turns or stops, yet she arrived home in one piece, her memory wiped. It had been like that, right?

As she lost herself in student journals of self-reported social media usage, she put the blackout out of her mind. It was a familiar pattern of denial, like sinking into an old comfy couch. It was just like her drinking days and all the times she'd wake up, vowing never to drink again. Vowing she'd call her doctor and tell him there was a chance she drank too much, and tell him the real number of glasses a night, not just two or three. But what was it her dad used to say? "The sun comes up, the sun goes down, and here you are." He said it in reference to the early-morning hangover when you were positive you'd never want to drink again, yet come afternoon there'd be a beer in your hand. As a kid, she heard him say it to his buddies, and after her first hangover in high school, he'd laughed as he said it to her, handing her a beer midafternoon, swearing by the hair of the dog.

Last night had just been a culmination of bad news, stress, and too little sleep. How many times had she woken in the night over the years with a sudden pain or shortness of breath, convinced she was dying, only to keep going? She'd cut back on caffeine; she'd do more yoga; she'd download yet another meditation app on her phone. Maybe she'd go back to her therapist, the only good one she'd ever had. She'd long joked that the way to pick a therapist was to find one who wore shoes you liked. If you could clear that hurdle, nothing was insurmountable. This was a completely normal reaction to exhaustion, right?

Her day nearly complete, Maris scrolled to the department website to see if Tammy had updated the page with her awful picture, and was relieved she hadn't yet. Maris was faced with the shiny, optimistic photo from when she was first hired, wearing earrings that matched her blouse. She fingered her naked lobes. She hadn't worn earrings in months.

◆ ◆ ◆

Over the next week, she worked on her formal rebuttal to the department tenure vote. This document, which she had only a week to compile, was her chance to address the lackluster numbers with further reasoning why she deserved her promotion. She outlined the shares and citations on each of her articles, listed her guest spots on TV shows and podcasts that demonstrated her public reach, and wrote draft after draft of a scholarship statement detailing how her experience and expertise in her area made her uniquely qualified to speak on her subjects. It was embarrassing to have to write such a thing—*here is why I am worthy*—when nationally she was recognized for her contributions tenfold to any of her colleagues.

This had been the rub since she'd joined the department five years ago. They'd hired her because they saw her area of public sociology as the wave of the future—a blend of cultural commentary and gender studies that she published in popular online magazines where she reached huge audiences, but that also left her colleagues scratching their heads. They wrote long scholarly articles with pages of foot-notes—*real* scholarship—while she "banged out" (as one colleague put it) shorter think pieces overnight when a news cycle blew in a direction she felt qualified to cover. *Bustle*? Vox? *Dissent*? How were those scholarly publications?

But her articles on the local Dylan Charter rape case had earned her a following of nearly eighty thousand on Twitter. She lived in the same Dayton, Ohio, suburb as he did and therefore had an insider's take, although she resided on the East side of Main and he on the West. The East side was what people referred to as Ghetto Oak Park, which in itself was in poor taste. Their crime rate in their "ghetto" was infinitesimal compared to the national average, and what crime there was consisted of the white-collar variety. Though she had been relatively new to Oak Park when Dylan Charter raped his victim a year and a half ago, she'd known instantly she would write about the case as a resident. She didn't have the deep generational roots of those whose ancestors had settled the state, but she well recognized the effects of the intergen-erational wealth and white privilege Dylan came from. He had deep pockets on both sides of his family and had been raised by the example that money, access, and the right lawyers on retainer could solve any problem. Dylan had been the poster boy of a "good kid": a strong student, a hometown sports figure on a basketball scholarship at Ohio State, parents who looked like extras from *The Stepford Wives*. They were the perfect people to hold up as an example of a supposed American ideal that was crumbling under its own exclusionary and toxic weight.

Dylan had been released from prison earlier that week, his joke of a sentence reduced from six months to four even though he'd been caught red-handed raping a woman in an alley behind a bar in the Oregon District. Maris's article in *Slate* about sentence reductions for white men versus men of color—"The Best Get Out of Jail Free Card? Be Born White"—had been shared more than one hundred thousand times.

As she concentrated on the rebuttal, the urgency of the blackout faded like a train whistle in the distance, like the ones that punctuated her childhood, the tracks behind her house.

She thought less and less about calling her doctor, and more and more how it must have been a fluke, a blip, nothing to be concerned about. She was just burned out from work, she decided, and added "burnout" to her list of things to research. Plus, she didn't want Noel and Cody asking why she was going to the doctor, assuming *they* would assume the worst: not that she was dying, but that she was drinking again. She could imagine Dr. Denkhart palpating her lymph nodes and sending her on her way, another hysterical woman wasting his time.

It was Friday, two and a half weeks since the blackout, when the first pictures of Dylan after his release surfaced on Twitter. They appeared to be taken by a nosy neighbor in front of the Charters' house. Dylan's hair was short from prison, and he was wearing shower shoes and an old Oak Park High School sweatshirt that would surely send the school board into a panic about their brand. His face was blurry as he dragged the garbage can behind him up the long, winding drive, and it was unclear if he appeared blurry because of the photo quality or exhaustion. Maris thought he looked hungover.

She wondered how she could use the pictures to shape an argument for an article. She'd written about his shortened sentence as a white criminal, but what about all the amenities and privileges that awaited him based on his class: a place to stay, food to eat, the ability to stay home in shower shoes during normal working hours because his family had most likely secured a job for him already.

She was shocked, frankly, that he took in his own trash can and wondered if perhaps it had been a photo op of some kind.

To what gain? What did this photo say?

And as she pondered all the possibilities, jotting notes as she went, her last shred of concern about the blackout vanished, evaporating like the last drop of wine in an empty glass.

CHAPTER THREE

Maris loaded her workbag at the end of a satisfyingly productive Tuesday. In her first class, two female students had complimented her on her blouse, and in the second, she'd made a stats joke so funny the students had erupted in laughter. The university might look at end-of-term student evaluations to determine if she was a successful professor (despite studies that proved female professors routinely scored lower than men), but she knew when her teaching was making a difference. She could see it in her students' relaxed and engaged faces, hear it in the laughs that said they were a team. She only wished she could remember the joke so she could add it in the rotation.

She'd also managed to clean out her email and, most miraculously, with a stretch of no interruptions, completed a rough draft of an op-ed about Dylan's smooth reentry into civilian life postprison. She thought it might be a fit for the *Washington Post*, an outlet she'd been trying to place with for a while.

Since the first pictures in front of his house had surfaced, Dylan had been spotted at Savory's buying premade sushi and a Mountain Dew, a baseball cap pulled low on his forehead, and at Marion's pizza having lunch with a buddy. By contrast, his victim, Jane Doe, had been interviewed as a voice-altered shadow on CNN saying she was too afraid to leave her house.

Maris clicked off the light on her desk and turned off her computer. Office hours had just ended, and she was hoping to sneak in a Starbucks run to surprise Cody with a pumpkin spice latte when she picked her up from school.

She reached below her desk to put her shoes back on, and when she sat up, a woman stood in her doorway. She wore a black sweatshirt and jeans, black eye makeup ringing her emo-goth eyes, and a thick foundation that looked drugstore cheap. Even from the doorway, Maris could tell her skin was smooth under the terrible makeup and wondered why the girl was hiding so deliberately. Her hair was covered in a slouchy beanie, the kind hipsters wore even in the heat of summer.

"Dr. Heilman?" she asked. "Can I come in?"

Maris tugged on her second heel. "Office hours just ended, and I'm sorry, but I'm heading to a meeting off campus." She felt a trickle of guilt putting off a student just for basic-bitch PSL reasons, but one of the blessings of academia was a flexible schedule. God knows she'd more than make up the hours late into the night trying to catch up on student papers and class prep after spending the afternoon on the *WaPo* op-ed.

"It won't take long," the woman said, and walked in, shutting the door behind her and leaning against it.

Maris felt her heart rate tick up a notch but smiled at the woman. "Please leave that open," she said, but the woman took a seat as if she hadn't heard her. Maris was always paranoid about behind-a-closed-door situations with students, and found it best to cut that off at the pass.

Maris glanced at her watch. "Really, I'm expected somewhere, but I'd be happy to make an appointment for ne—"

"I read your articles," the woman blurted out. "The ones about Dylan Charter."

"Ah." This had happened a few times since she'd begun writing about the case, and she let the door remain closed, realizing the woman might be more willing to talk if there were privacy.

With Dylan local, it was inevitable some of his classmates would end up at Glenn State. Her articles centered around rape culture in America, and many were on Dylan in particular: "How Is Rape Up for Debate?"; "Why Americans Blame the Victim, Not the Rapist"; and perhaps her most controversial, "Dylan Charter Needs to Be Held Accountable Full Stop." She'd been on ABC and MSNBC to give her professional take on rape culture and had gained some minor celebrity during Dylan's trial, and then she made another round on media when his ridiculously short sentence was further reduced.

A few times she'd arrived at campus to graffiti on her office door—the unimaginative *bitch* and even *ugly cunt* scratched into the wood or Sharpie-d in crude block letters—but the women who showed up always wanted to talk. They'd known Dylan in high school and couldn't believe someone like him was capable of what he'd done. Sure, he'd been a jerk in the halls sometimes, but he was so popular. So cute he could have had anyone. Rape? Really? But they'd also tell stories of him at parties: drinking too much, being an asshole, getting in scrapes with guys from his basketball team who would work it out by Monday and be back to pals.

"I just wanted to say how awesome I thought it was," the girl went on, "that you went after him that way. Saying all that shit about him and how his neighbors are part of the problem, and that he should be recognized as the monster he is."

Maris had argued throughout the case that it was wealth and privilege that allowed a man like Dylan Charter to thrive, and that a city like Oak Park was a breeding ground for such conditions. "The (White) Boy Next Door," her first article on the case, pointed out that Dylan Charter's actions were in line with the values of a perfect midwestern town like Oak Park, where, for the affluent, rules were more like suggestions and "no" meant "not yet." She asserted that towns like this existed all over America, raising these special (overwhelmingly white) snowflakes to assume they were the exception and not the rule, exempt from taking responsibility for their actions. It was something she'd seen as far back as her own high school days, when boys cornered girls at parties and coerced them into doing things they didn't want to do. The same boys who the next morning parted their hair and sat next to their moms at church service.

"That's not exactly—"

The woman waved a hand. "I'm paraphrasing, I know."

Maris folded her hands and, below her desk, tugged her shoes off with her feet. "What can I do for you?"

"I know your stance on his sentence," the woman said. Maris opened her mouth, but the woman went on. "I read your article in *Dissent*, about how white guys get way shorter sentences, blah blah, and now you're working on an article about how easy his life is after prison? Isn't that right?" Maris felt another spike of concern wondering how the woman knew that, but like all sociologists with a side hustle, she put her entire professional life up on Twitter, hoping she'd make the leap from pitching articles to outlets contacting her.

"I found it completely unfair," Maris said. "But that's the criminal justice system for you." Changing it seemed like a Sisyphean task given the stacked Supreme Court, but Maris kept doing her part, pushing the boulder up the hill, hoping her voice would make a difference.

"Yeah, but." The woman slumped in her chair and shook her head. "Doesn't it royally piss you off? That guy's had his life handed to him on a fucking platter." Maris blanched at her profanity. It wasn't the word itself, but she was surprised to hear the woman say it with such vitriol. Her startle reflex shot up again, and Maris pulled her collar away from her neck. The uncirculated air was stifling, and she stood suddenly, barefoot, and opened the door. A rush of cool air sucked into the room, but rather than be greeted with the sounds of a bustling hallway, there was eerie silence: her colleagues mostly gone for the day, late afternoon classes still in session.

"I mean," the woman continued as Maris sat back behind her desk, "he's a known rapist loose in the same streets as your daughter."

Maris narrowed her eyes at the mention of Cody, her mama-bear instincts kicking in: *leave her out of this*. "What is this about? How do you know about my daughter?" she asked, but that, too, wasn't hard to find out.

Maris had been attacked by trolls since she'd garnered any kind of following, but in the beginning, trolls notwithstanding, the attention had been a rush. People were interested in what she had to say; people contacted her for sound bites for their own articles. But a few months into her academic celebrity (a misnomer if ever there was one), she received a rape threat against Cody. Code was twelve at the time, not that there could be an age such a thing might be appropriate. After that she stopped any reference to her husband or child, so this woman must have done a deep dive. It still shocked her how young children were sexualized these days. These, too, were the effects of toxic masculinity and rape culture and something she'd had a front-row seat to all her adult life as a drinker. In college, before she had Scott to protect her, she'd had plenty of hazy nights and scrapes to discover in the morning, and perhaps more than her share of waking in unrecognizable rooms, but she'd never been raped.

Or at least she didn't think she had. But sometimes she'd wake in the night, short of breath and sweating, and wonder if there had been more. Alcohol research had told her blackout memories didn't store in the brain, but what about muscle memory? Sometimes she wondered what secrets were in the very cells of her being, and what they had endured. It was no surprise, really, that rape culture became the focus of her research agenda.

"Four months," the girl said, ignoring Maris's questions. Maris blanched that she'd thought of her as a girl when she had to be over eighteen, but there was something young about her, something vulnerable, even if she was college age. "I can't believe that's all he served when he screwed up that girl for life."

Maris could tell the woman's hair wasn't naturally black, as if she were in hiding. Her eyebrows were an almost white blonde above the dark rings of eyeliner. She was certain she hadn't had the woman in a class before, and something dawned on Maris.

Was it possible this was Jane Doe?

There was little information out there about Dylan's victim; surprisingly, she'd managed to keep herself anonymous, referred to as only Jane Doe in the media. Maris had long wondered if she'd been reading Maris's articles, if they helped her to feel she had someone on her side. She'd wondered if, even hoped that, the woman might reach out and ask Maris to tell her story.

"Are you . . . Jane?" she asked, and the girl snorted.

"I am *not* Dylan Charter's victim."

"I'm sorry, I . . . I don't understand why you're here. *Are* you a student at Glenn State?"

"Oh please," the woman said with a look, like, *What a ridiculous question.*

"I want to help you," Maris said, "but I don't know what you're asking of me." She couldn't shake the thought the girl was asking for something specific as the first pulse of a migraine started behind her eye. She'd started getting the headaches in her late thirties, and they almost always aligned with her period. Sure enough, she could feel the bloat of blood in her stomach, the cramp in her lower back.

The woman leaned in closer, and Maris could smell the thick makeup, the scent of drugstores and Play-Doh, and that quickly Maris felt her stomach flip, a curdle of vomit climbing up her throat. She smelled like middle school and vulnerability, like practicing adulthood. Like Cody.

There was a flurry of shuffling feet and voices in the hallway; classes were letting out.

"If you could change things and make them fair, would you?" the strange woman asked.

"What do you mean?"

"You said yourself it's not fair," she reasoned. "I mean, he ruined that girl's life. Wouldn't you want to do something about it? Hold him accountable *full stop*," she said, referencing the title of Maris's own article.

Settled behind the safety of her desk, Maris grabbed on to semantics. "I don't know if *ruined* is the right word," she said. "I think what happened becomes part of who she is, but it doesn't have to define her. *Change* her, yes, but define her, no." Two of her articles had been around the problematic labels of *victim* and *survivor* for the women, yet no one wanted to say *rapist*.

The woman locked eyes with her and then snorted, unsatisfied with the answer. She stood suddenly and retreated to the hallway. When she turned around, the beanie on her head tilted to the left. Was there a wig under there? Nothing seemed quite right, and Maris gripped her phone like a can of mace, her migraine now coming full force. She thought of the mysterious blackout. Could it be related to the migraine? Was something wrong with her brain?

The woman shuffled through her purse, and Maris held her breath—a gun?—but the woman took out her car keys and a stick of Juicy Fruit. She unwrapped the silver foil and folded the gum against her tongue. "Four months," she said, shaking her head. "It's almost worse than no punishment at all."

CHAPTER FOUR

After the woman in her office, Maris was already forty minutes late to pick up Cody from school, even without the stop at Starbucks. On the way she'd taken her Imitrex medication in hopes it would knock out her migraine while she was driving, doing her best to convince herself it was nothing out of the ordinary. It was a godsend the day she'd realized the meds worked just as well on hangovers as migraines. For a few years she'd been using the full prescription allotted by insurance, down to an empty bottle each month, but now she had a seven-month backlog of pills. Sober, she usually got only one or two migraines a month, but the ones she got were doozies.

She squealed into the parking lot to find her daughter sitting criss-cross against the brick building, her head bent over her phone.

"I'm sorry I'm late," Maris said, her car still in motion. "A student stopped by my office."

"It's fine," Cody said, but she didn't make eye contact as she climbed into the passenger seat, her backpack on her lap.

"I really am," Maris said again, and Cody nodded, unconvinced. "Why were you waiting outside?"

"They're waxing the floors," she said, and looked pointedly at her mother. "Probably for career day," she added, although it was still a week away. Was she so convinced her mother would forget?

"I got it," Maris pushed back gently. "It's because of that great career I'm late, by the way. Emergencies come up." Was the girl an emergency, or was that Maris exaggerating once again to excuse poor behavior? It was hard for her to tell, but that seemed to settle Cody somewhat. "Let me make it up to you," she added, and that got her daughter's attention.

She proposed dinner out, but Cody only shrugged, even though most nights she begged to eat out. Maris wasn't above bribing. Growing up, her own parents had never apologized for anything, much less tried to make things up, and Maris had sworn she wouldn't be that way. She worried at times she was buying her daughter's affection, or that her daughter's affection was for sale, but really, it was more that life was so hard they constantly deserved treats. Dinners out when she was too tired to cook. A five-dollar coffee to get her through the day. Online purse shopping between classes, convinced she was one crossbody bag away from a better life. No wonder Noel was on the night shift and she was hustling seventy hours a week to publish articles that paid peanuts. She had a sense that if she were to just slow down and be conscious about it all, they could get out of debt, but the lead-up to better decisions was exhausting. Wasn't it enough she was now sober?

At home, she tiptoed into the master bedroom with a cup of coffee, the room womblike thanks to the blackout curtains and white-noise machine. She sat at Noel's hip and put her hand on his shoulder. They'd been married three years, but still the sight of his naked chest gave her a thrill. He had the lanky but muscular body of a man in his forties who hit the gym a few times a week but got most of his exercise through regular life, one of those people with energy to burn.

She gave him a gentle shake, and he turned toward her, a smile starting on his mouth before he'd opened his eyes.

"DiSalvo's," she whispered, her breath hot on his ear. It was their favorite Italian restaurant. His eyebrows shot up, and an eye peeked open.

"I defrosted some pork chops," he said, and she grimaced. She didn't want to cook or to feel guilty while Noel did it. She wanted to sit across from her family and have people bring her food.

"I have a migraine," she told him as an excuse. It was receding now thanks to her meds—the pain still there but felt at a distance. "Plus I had a student stop by after office hours that gave off a weird vibe." She told him about the woman and her unsettling energy as he sat up and took the coffee, listening intently.

"Do you think she was dangerous?"

Away from the situation, the claustrophobia of her office, Maris shook her head no. What harm could that young woman have done? She shooed away the thought, dismissing the spike of fear about the closed door, the girl's hand reaching into her bag. "Troubled, more than dangerous, I'd say. Fragile."

He took a sip of coffee and set it on the nightstand, pushing aside the covers. "If you want DiSalvo's, I'm in," he said, and kissed her neck on his way to the shower. Once he started the water, he poked his head back in. "Cody coming?" She nodded. "Good. I want to hear more about her DNA project."

Maris nodded, but she had no idea what he was talking about. What project? Sometimes she thought Noel, the guy who'd been on the scene for four years, was the best parent Cody had. She devoted most of her waking hours to her career, and Scott was eight hundred miles away.

Noel was the one who kept track of the calendar, paid attention to her schoolwork, and seemed to have an easy way with Code. Part of it was his status as a stepparent—there was a different kind of pressure—but also, he was just good with kids. She often wondered why he hadn't become a pediatrician. When she and Noel got together, they talked briefly about having a baby but, given their careers and her "advanced maternal age" of thirty-eight, decided against it. She still hadn't gotten around to starting a 529 for Cody and was banking, quite literally, on her attending Glenn State, but she couldn't think about that now, her tenure up in the air.

No wonder she thought she deserved a dinner out.

Twenty minutes later, Maris stood in the foyer with her phone, checking Twitter DMs one last time as she waited for Noel and Cody. The ones from female avatars were usually women or girls reaching out to thank her for the articles on Dylan or to tell her about their own sexual trauma. Others wanted to engage in conversation, wondering if she'd read this or that on a subject. These messages alone were exhausting to keep up with (and to some extent, she'd given up), but the lion's share of DMs were from trolls.

The absolute vitriol men spewed through the internet was breathtaking. Death threats, rape threats, comments on how ugly and unfuckable she was, lists of reasons she should kill herself. These came in daily, and she'd learned to block and delete anything with an American flag avatar or some version of Don't Tread on Me. Twitter had come with a learning curve, but she knew she needed it to keep gaining followers, to keep hawking her articles and views.

She opened a DM from a

—

—

—

her finger on the screen as she watched a pit bull rescue video on Dodo. Cody started down the stairs in black tights and a short denim skirt.

Maris blinked as awareness rushed back. She pressed "Pause," only fourteen seconds into the video. Her heart rate shot up as she clicked over to DMs to see the one she'd been about to open was now open, a request for a link to an article from a high school girl.

She checked her phone's home screen. She'd been blacked out less than a minute, two at the most.

It took Maris a second to readjust back to the world: she and her family were getting ready to leave for dinner. "Code?"

Cody paused on the last step. "Yeah?"

It didn't seem like Cody had noticed anything out of the ordinary. Maybe it had been just a little pocket of darkness in an otherwise fine day. Maybe this was normal, she told herself, although her hands were shaking. Maybe a new version of her migraines. Maybe, even, this was what had happened the other night when she thought she'd lost an hour or more. Rather than validating the oddness of the first blackout, Maris convinced herself she'd exaggerated, that the blackout she'd had before had probably lasted no more than a few seconds, like a movie where you zone out over the boring parts.

Maris's mind circled as if sucked toward a drain, but this was just stress, she knew it. Everything was fine. "Did you forget your pants?" Maris asked, looking at Cody's short skirt. She was determined to proceed with the evening, with her happy family eating a dinner they could pretend to afford.

"Hardy har," Cody said, but she pulled the open flap of her flannel shirt over her tank top.

"You look cute," Maris amended, knowing how much it hurt to be teased about your appearance. Maris remembered how self-conscious she felt about everything when she was that age, how sure she was that people were making fun of her at every turn. Even walking down her own street in her small town, she'd be convinced people were looking out their windows, laughing at her hand-me-down clothes, shaking their heads at her cheap haircut or her too-skinny legs, or some other body part she hadn't even thought to hate yet. The only time she truly relaxed was in her own room with the curtains drawn and the door closed. She'd roll down her pajama bottoms and look at her stomach, filling it with as much air as she could and then watching it deflate. She'd pick her nose. She'd chew gum with her mouth open.

Yet at the same time, as she'd grown older, male attention was something she and her friends were proud of, even when it crossed lines. The man who locked the frat room door behind him. The one who held your wrists and grinned as panic lit up your back. The man who chased you up the dorm stairs like it was a game while you were trying in earnest to get away. She and her girlfriends would swap these stories over syrup-drenched hash browns and bacon on Sunday mornings in the cafeteria, and while they'd hint at the fear, the real pulse-throbbing fear, it was under the guise of flattery. It had taken Maris two decades and raising a daughter to realize that it wasn't flattery, and it wasn't their fault. Aware as she was of the destructive role of rape culture, it had taken her a long time to get over the internalized blame. Could that be an article?

Noel bounded down the stairs with wet hair and grabbed the car keys from the hook by the door. "We ready?" he asked, defusing any tension in the room, but Maris still felt uncertain.

Had that blackout really just happened? She knew how quickly her mind could wander, and it had only been a minute; it was nothing like the near hour of the first time. Maris caught herself, realizing this logic meant that in order to invalidate the blackout that had just happened, she needed to validate the one before. Fear clogged her throat. What the hell was happening to her?

Maris mentally shook herself: *Concentrate on your family.*

Outside, she grounded herself by focusing on three things: the red car across the street, the hump-butt of Noel's Prius, and their neighbor Eula Moore weeding her front flower beds. With each image, she felt her hands begin to steady.

Eula heard the car door open, turned, and waved. In Oak Park, the lots ranged from manageable yards to sloping acres of grass in front of mansions. Eula's lawn was comparable to the others on their street, but still a lot for an older woman to maintain on her own. She'd lost her husband less than a year ago to a stroke, and Maris was impressed she had kept on so efficiently. Carl had been sweet, another academic at Glenn State, only in engineering. He'd been the one to invite Noel and Maris to their annual cookout when they moved next door. The one to mow their grass when they got dangerously close to a city citation for its length, even though he'd been in his seventies.

Maris waved back and quickly climbed in the car. Since Carl's death, she hadn't spent as much time with Eula—a spunky old lady with a mouth full of surprises—as she had when they first moved in, but for now she concentrated on steadying her breath. She'd try to stop by Eula's in the next week or so, maybe over the weekend when she had more time.

As Noel pulled his seatbelt across his lap, he looked at her closely. "You okay?" he asked. Was that concern in his voice, or something else?

"Just hungry," she said, knowing that hid a variety of sins.

"Then we'd better get going," he said, and put the car in reverse.

CHAPTER FIVE

Settled at their table with waters for all three, Maris perused the menu, although she ordered the same thing every time: eggplant rollatini. She wanted her head bent in contemplation as if deciding what to eat, while actually thinking, *What the fuck?* Had there been a second blackout different from the first, and if so, what did that mean? Cody had seemed unfazed coming down the stairs—was that normal teenage self-absorption, or were the blackouts that undetectable? She tried to think like a researcher gathering data, only this wasn't some abstract experiment. It was her life.

The waiter came over and took their orders, gathering the menus as he left, and Maris reminded herself to stay present. This was one of their favorite restaurants in Dayton, family owned and run for at least two generations. It was relatively small, but there were mirrors on three of the walls, giving the space a busy—almost chaotic, yet festive—feel. Everywhere you looked there was movement—forks raised to mouths in triplet, wineglasses clinking from every angle. The smell of spicy arrabbiata sauce hung in the air along with the thick scent of garlic, and Maris's mouth began to water as she thought about the crusty garlic bread they always placed on the table.

The waiter returned with the bread and set a glass of white wine in front of Maris. Her eyes shot from the wine to Noel to Cody. "I didn't order this," she said adamantly to the waiter, who smiled in return.

"It's from the gentleman at the bar."

She peered through the wide doorway to the barroom, where a lone man hunched over with his back toward her. She looked in the mirror and saw his face repeating in reflections, a grin as he raised his own glass of red. Her stomach soured. It was Hollis Grant.

She originally met him at the Moores' cookout, when Eula introduced them over a plate of deviled eggs, letting them know they both worked at Glenn State. Hollis was a scientist who dabbled in engineering, which was how he and Carl became good friends. When Maris told him her area was sociology, he crossed his arms and looked at her, amused as if she'd said she taught home ec. Hollis seemed like the benign kind of sexist, old and somehow forgivable, until he told her that he'd led a committee years ago investigating women's productivity in tenure-track positions, claiming child-rearing inevitably got in the way. "Women want all the perks of a paycheck while their children are little without actually doing as much work, and once their children are raised, it's nearly impossible to get them caught up, much less invested in doing all that's required in the academy." He said it matter-of-factly while shoveling a deviled egg in his mouth, leaving a smear of yellow and paprika on his upper lip.

He continued, stating as if fact, that women didn't really have the bandwidth for the kind of intellectual rigor demanded at the university level, basing this on his research. She looked him up later, and indeed he had caused quite a stir back in the eighties with his theories on gender and neural capacities, disproven of course, but protected under the tenets of academic freedom and tenure.

"But you're in sociology," he added at the picnic. "That seems harmless enough."

"Why is that guy sending you wine?" Noel asked, suspicion in his voice. She knew him well enough to know it was about the wine, not the guy.

She smiled shakily. "I guess I'll go find out."

She set her napkin on the table and picked up the wine, swerving her hips through the tight space between tables as Hollis watched her in the mirror. Even holding the glass in her hand made her shake. *Do not drink it, do not drink it, do not drink it,* she repeated in her mind.

Hollis had come back into her life after she started publishing on Dylan. She knew writing about a local boy might piss off some of her Oak Park neighbors, but she hadn't anticipated a colleague like Hollis Grant would make it so personal.

He'd ranted to the faculty LISTSERV and the *Oak Park Gazette* editorial section, and he eventually published a *New York Times* op-ed discussing his older research on women's neural capacities, using her work as an example of logical fallacies and why women struggle in academia. She was shocked that a well-regarded newspaper would even run such a thing, but she knew all too well how much publications depended on clicks. Hollis wrote that taking her work as scholarship was an insult to higher ed, and that her publications were "little more than the free-rolling thoughts of a woman with too much time on her hands and a bone to pick with men." The op-ed ran well before she quit drinking, and Maris read it hungover on the couch as her dehydrated brain pulsed in her skull. In the moment she thought he was right: she clearly was a failure. It was the first time her name had appeared in the *New York Times*.

"Dr. Grant?" she asked, irritated she had said his name as a question as if she had no authority.

"Dr. Heilman." Was it her imagination, or had he said *Dr.* with a smirk?

"The waiter said you sent this over." She held up the wine and then set it on the bar, careful as she reached not to spill a drop. She knew if it landed on her hand, she'd stick her finger in her mouth so fast she wouldn't be able to stop herself.

"Yes. I heard your tenure vote came in. Twelve-four."

She blanched. They both knew a solid case should make it through with a unanimous vote, but how had he found out? The votes were meant to be confidential, although she recognized they rarely were. One loose-lipped committee member, and the word was out.

"Not exactly a landslide, now, is it?"

"It's still a majority vote," she pointed out.

"True," he admitted. "But when your own department has votes against you." He tsked and smiled a fat-cat smile.

She felt like he was playing with her, but why? "I know you're not a fan of my work—" she began, but he cut her off.

"It's important to support junior faculty at the university," he said, surprising her. "It's the reason I volunteered for the university's promotion and tenure committee this year."

The words settled on her, and she realized what he meant. He would be voting directly on her case. She made a note to check university policy to see if she could argue to have him removed, given that he'd attacked her publicly. There had to be something about a conflict of interest, and lord knew it was documented.

Back when he published the op-ed, she had responded in the comments. Every writer online knew the first rule was don't engage the trolls, but because he was a colleague, and because she was hungover and lacking impulse control, she'd done it. She assured him of her qualifications as a PhD and assistant professor and cited other academic careers in her area that had been built on similar publications. But all it had done was activate more trolls, an army of trolls, who sided with Grant and said her whiny response proved she was a woman ruled by emotions and unfit for her job. A dozen or so of the people who attacked her through the comments then found her on Twitter and blasted her there, three or four of them hunting down her university email and sending her horrible links to snuff films and rape depictions. It had been a quick and dirty lesson about how to use her profile and social media, and she'd never made the same mistake again. She tried to remember if there had been positive responses too. Certainly there had to be, but those voices were all too often drowned out.

Now in the restaurant, the small room felt even smaller, the mirrors closing in. "You volunteered?" She looked up and saw Noel and Cody watching her, although they were sitting behind her. She locked eyes with her husband, whose brow furrowed. He set his napkin on the table and pushed back his chair. "Why?" she asked Hollis.

"I want to see junior faculty get what they deserve."

Noel approached and put a hand on her lower back, and she pressed her body gently to his side, the hand holding her up. "Hello," he said, no agenda to his voice.

"Do you remember Dr. Grant?" she asked. "We've seen him a few times at the Moores' cookouts." In the shorthand of relationships, she knew that would be enough for Noel to recall who he really was—the awful man who had attacked her.

Noel knew Hollis's vitriol against Maris eventually led him to pull Tammy Lerner in, asking what she was doing as chair to uphold the academic mission of the university. Tammy was worthless, citing chapter and verse of the academic freedom definition but never actually defending Maris or her work. "He has a right to his opinion," Tammy told her. "You should be flattered he's paying attention to your work."

"Sure," Noel said neutrally, and he and Hollis clasped hands and shook. Hollis hadn't extended her the same courtesy.

"Everything okay?" he asked Maris, but Hollis answered.

"I was just congratulating your wife on her vote and telling her I was looking forward to watching her case progress."

Noel's face narrowed. "She's a shoo-in," he said. "Best in her department."

"I don't drink," she blurted out, pointing at the wine he'd sent.

"Ah," Hollis said, and scooted her glass closer to his own. "I must have forgotten."

In the mirror, she saw the waiter return to their table, three plates stacked up his arm. He grabbed the spaghetti crooked in his elbow and set it in front of Cody. Maris had wanted to spend an evening with her family and forget about work and her sinking tenure case, but here she was with the one colleague she hated as her daughter sat at the table sprinkling Parmesan cheese all by herself.

"We should get back," she said to Noel, pointing toward Cody. They said pleasant enough goodbyes and returned. "Sorry about that," she said to Cody as she and Noel settled in, napkins returned to their laps.

"Is that Dr. Grant?" Cody asked, surprising Maris.

"How do you know him?" she asked. Cody would have surely met him at the cookouts, but not many kids remembered random adults they saw once a year.

"He's the guy who wrote the op-ed, right?" It was no secret that Cody read her mom's work, but Maris hadn't realized she'd paid that much attention. She wrote about adult topics, obviously, but it was a world Cody lived in and was hurtling more and more to the center of the older she got.

Maris nodded. "You read that?"

"I was googling your stuff the other day and found it. Getting ready for career day since I have to introduce you."

Maris glanced at Noel with a look of love in her eyes that said: *This kid.* He squeezed her hand. She knew Cody was impressed that her mom had a lot of followers on Twitter and that she had a career that mattered to her, but she hadn't realized Cody might actually be proud to introduce her on career day. The thought brought a lump to her throat.

"Seems kind of like a jerk," Cody said as she spun a twirl of spaghetti on her fork and put the efficient pasta ball in her mouth.

"He is," Maris agreed and grinned at Cody. "And I think he's taken up enough of our night."

Cody nodded and twirled more pasta, holding it in place with her garlic bread. Noel picked up his fork and cut off a bite of chicken piccata, the meat so tender no knife was needed. Somehow, despite Hollis sending over his spiteful glass of wine, they'd ended up with the family dinner she'd wanted.

◆ ◆ ◆

Getting ready for bed that night, at the double sink next to Maris, Noel said, "That was weird," and elaborated that he meant Hollis Grant sending over the drink. "He's been such a shit about your work."

"It was passive-aggressive, or maybe just aggressive-aggressive," she said, and explained how he had volunteered for the committee. Slathering Olay on her face as Noel brushed his teeth, she was reminded of the first blackout. She had come to with the lotion on her hands, feeling powerless and alone. Even with the shorter blackout, tonight by contrast had been wonderful. Cody complimentary about her work, Noel and herself aligned against Hollis. Maybe she didn't have to keep every struggle to herself.

"Have you ever had, like, a little blackout?" she asked him.

He wiped a towel across his mouth. "Like what?"

"Just, a moment where you kind of space out and come to, and you realize some time has passed?" He looked at her quizzically, and she backpedaled. "Like you're reading a book and realize you've read a chapter but don't really remember it? Or you're driving home and suddenly you're there?" It wasn't quite what she meant, but his face relaxed.

"Sure. It's automatic. I can't tell you how many times that happens, even in the ER. I'll be filling out paperwork on autopilot, and next thing I know, it's done."

"Kind of," Maris agreed. "But when you think about it, you can't remember anything that you filled in? Like you look and you don't recognize the patient's name or their case? Anything?"

"Did something happen?" Noel asked, and Maris knew this was her moment to tell the truth, but maybe she had just overreacted. Maybe it had all been just like the paperwork at the hospital. Plus, it had been such a nice night.

She grimaced. "No, just aging I guess." He swatted her butt with his towel.

"Better your mind than that ass," he joked, and she laughed as he pulled her to the bed.

It was only later, her mind finally relaxing as she eased toward sleep, that she thought again about the quick blip as she'd been watching the rescue-dog video on her phone. *Had* there been another blackout? If so, it was much shorter than the first.

But was that a good sign or a bad one?

CHAPTER SIX

The next morning, Maris's alarm went off at five thirty. She slid out of bed and put on the running shorts and long-sleeved T-shirt she'd laid out in the bathroom the night before, then tiptoed downstairs in stocking feet. On the porch, she laced her tennies, stretched, and took in the bracing cool air of fall before setting off down the block.

She'd hoped when she first started running that it would be a way to empty her mind, but her mind ended up the opposite: a whirl of activity. And emptying her mind had been just a side hope; she'd really started running in undergrad in the hopes of shedding a few pounds.

Almost everyone she knew had added a little chunk those first few years; they *all* drank like crazy back then. Fishbowls at Duffy's on Tuesdays, margaritas in the backyard kiddie pool, game day at the Watering Hole, cases of Old Mil at house parties. These were the parties she'd always wanted to join when she was a little kid, watching her dad and his buddies drink beer and shots as they watched the Huskers on Saturday afternoons, everyone seeming to have a good time.

When Maris and Scott had married at the end of senior year, she had a sense they were playing house—they still drank like teenagers whose parents were out of town, but now they had a matching set of fancy dishes. They'd grown up in similar households—with crosses on the walls and dads who liked to drink and moms who were killjoys—and they took all the things that made that life fun and jettisoned the rest. No crucifixion scenes or party poopers for them. And while they might have drunk like their fathers, Maris and Scott were rigid about succeeding. Maris's father had bounced from job to job, but Scott was in his second year of law school by this point, and she had an enviable entry-level job at the *Lincoln Journal Star*. Sure, they might not have had any savings yet, but they were still in their midtwenties and that was to be expected. They thought it was funny that next to the fancy dishes they used thirty-two-ounce plastic glasses from U-Stop. Plus, by then she ran four times a week, keeping her body tight with no visible signs of weakness.

Turning off Peach Orchard Street, she wondered if she should have thrown on a vest, but figured she'd be warm enough after a few more blocks. She loved running in fall. The crisp air, the bite in the lungs just a little bit punishing.

Maris had quit drinking while pregnant, and when Cody arrived—raw red and screaming, and the most heart-thumping perfect thing they'd ever seen—Maris stayed sober. But Scott's drinking increased, and she slowly started identifying with her mother, the unfun one, not her father. Why didn't *Scott* take off work to bring Cody in for her first-year shots, or empty the dishwasher, or at the least pick up his empties from the living room? Why should these be Maris's understood responsibilities? Did he think she *wanted* to be this angry about the dishwasher? In his second year at the law firm and hungover most mornings, Scott helped little with the baby, and the gulf between them widened, until eventually he showed up drunk to Cody's plastic-piano recital at her toddler music class at the Y, and Maris rented a two-bedroom apartment on N Street.

She was a newish mother fresh off a divorce when she started the PhD program. Scott had embraced sobriety with AA after the recital, and once she moved out, it was Maris's turn to cut loose. She told herself she was back in school and things were bound to get crazy. She and her grad student friends spent afternoons drinking kamikazes at Cliff's, talking about the works of Gilda Ochoa and Audre Lorde. They had ironic theme parties, like ones where you had to wear a toga, or the one she cohosted called the Sexy Whiskey Party, where everyone dressed sexy and drank whiskey. For many it seemed like the last rebellious phase before adulthood really kicked in with families and tenure-track jobs, but for her it felt like coming home. She was able to divide her life in two—days as a mother, nights as an intellectual—and only when she moved to Dayton for her assistant professor job at Glenn State did those two roles have to coexist.

After Maris moved to Ohio, Cody lived with her during the school year and spent two months of the summer with her dad. She was eight by then. Old enough to be left in a bath alone while Maris went down-stairs to refill her wine, yet young enough she didn't quite understand what her mom was doing. Those first two years in Dayton—before they moved in with Noel and when Maris was on her own with Cody—were the only two of her adult life when she wasn't disciplined enough to run twenty miles a week, too tired from her new life as a professor and a full-time single mom.

She turned left on Schantz toward Carillon Historical Park, the fall air full in her face now, tears stinging from the corners of her eyes. Carillon wasn't so much a park as a historical district showcasing Dayton's inventions and technologies throughout history. A bike path circled one edge of the park, followed a stretch of the Miami River, and within a mile, turned away from civilization and into the country. For Maris, that, too, felt like home.

She increased her speed, hoping to outrun her own thoughts, to concentrate only on the steady rhythm of her breath, the pulse at her throat, the pain that had started in her knees when she turned forty. She rounded the curve past the river, where she could smell the wet mud of the shore. Six ducks smoothed across the water's surface. Her breath was strong and steady, feet in a comfortable rhythm

—

—

—

left foot down and her right stuttered, and it was as if she was catching herself in a fall but no fall was coming. She slowed and stumbled to a stop. Her heart rate was accelerated; her face pounded with blood. She leaned over and put her head between her knees as she pressed two fingers to her throat and calculated her pulse: 156, her normal running range. She looked at her fingers, shaking and swollen with red knuckles from the cold.

What in the actual hell was happening to her?

Her watch proved she had followed her normal five-mile route. The last thing she remembered was the curve around the river. That would have been—she did the math—about twenty-five minutes ago.

She held back a scream. Was she going crazy? Other than coming to, it seemed she had just been going on with her life.

With the first blackout, she'd nearly convinced herself it was what Noel had talked about—that blip where you lose track of time, and next thing you know you've finished the paperwork, or grabbed all the stuff you need at the grocery store, or driven all the way home. But this third time had her winding herself into a panic. Could it be her drinking had taken this long to crumble her mind?

She walked around the neighborhood until she had quit shaking and was pushing it to get home in time to get Cody up for school, get herself ready for class, pack lunches, and do everything else she had to before it was time to leave for Horace Valley at 7:50. She had a graduate committee meeting first thing on campus, then a meeting with a student between classes about an honor's thesis, and finally faculty senate, where she always worked to keep her face as blank as possible, anxiety rising at how little she understood about the structure of higher education. She still needed to take a roast out of the freezer for dinner and work on her op-ed, and later, after she picked Cody up after school, she had to stop at Savory's for a fresh baguette. How was it she could so clearly see the day laid out in front of her but have no memory of the last half hour?

Cody met her on the porch as she rounded the corner to home. She was still dressed in pajama pants but with a full face of makeup. "Where were you?" she asked as if it wasn't obvious her mom had been on a run. "Did you wash my jeans?" she continued. "I don't have any clean pants."

So Maris wasn't quite on top of *everything*, but when was she? Another thing that had slipped her mind. It was just after seven in the morning, and she already felt defeated. "Just wear yesterday's," she told her daughter.

Cody folded her arms against her chest. "I have for the last three days."

"I have more important things to do than laundry," Maris snapped, and instantly regretted it as Cody blanched. "I'm sorry," she said. "Go ahead and order some from Macy's, and I'll pick them up on my way home." No wonder they were constantly broke, but how was she supposed to get ahead of it when the next expense, the next emergency, was the only thing in front of her face? She'd been telling herself that once she got tenure the pressures would ease up, but the thought made her heart sink. And now she had these other problems, but she wouldn't think of those now. One good thing about drinking: it had taught her compartmentalization.

"Can I get some tops too?"

Maris sighed. "*A* top. One."

She added Macy's to the mental to-do list. As well as looking into who else was on the university promotion and tenure committee, and whether or not Tammy had a chance to read her rebuttal. Career day was only two days away, and she'd make it up to Cody then. She'd remind her how proud she was of her working mom.

She took the roast out of the freezer to defrost in the sink. One thing checked off and three added. It never seemed to end.

CHAPTER SEVEN

That afternoon, Maris was on her way to Horace Valley to pick up Cody when she got a text from Janice Lambert, Code's best friend's mom. Her stomach soured to see her name. Janice was the computer science teacher at HV who also handled some counseling services thanks to a bachelor's in social work, and in addition had been the one to witness Maris's last night of drinking in February. Given the close friendship between their girls, they'd seen each other many times since that night, but contact always left Maris uneasy, worried Janice would bring it up.

Cody in my office not after school care, the text read, followed by a second: I'll let her tell you why.

Maris's first thought was that Cody had gotten into some kind of trouble, but that wasn't likely. She was a brainy kid who spent her solo time creating Percy Jackson memes and learning old lady crafts like cross-stitch, but as Maris had noticed, Cody was changing, growing up, splashing her life on social media. Maybe ironic cross-stitch wasn't cutting it anymore.

While Cody faced some of the same social pressures at Horace, it was a school overrun by geeks and kids driven by scholastics. By contrast, all the schools in Oak Park shut down for a week in February for an official break known as Ski Week.

In the school, Maris rounded left at the cafeteria, the smell of corn dogs ever present in the air, and headed toward Janice's small office.

Cody was sitting by herself in a worn plastic chair just inside the doorway, a book open on her lap.

"Hey," Maris said, slumping in the empty seat next to her daughter. "So what's the big news? Did you set a fire in the science lab?"

Cody glanced at her mom and back at the book. "I got my period," she said quietly.

Maris's eyes widened, and she grasped Cody's arm. "No more period virgin!"

Cody grimaced. "I haven't made the official announcement to the school yet, so maybe keep it down?"

Maris held her hands up in apology. "I'm sorry, Code." She knocked her shoulder against her daughter's. "But it is exciting."

Cody shrugged again.

When school had started and Cody still hadn't gotten her period, they'd come up with a text code so she could let Maris know: three red balloons. Red for blood, with the added ominous nod to Pennywise the Clown, and by association, Carrie (Cody had started reading Stephen King in the last year). She and Cody had been preparing for this since her first health class film in fourth grade. They'd bought the supplies, Maris had shown her daughter how to attach the pad to her underwear, they'd talked about a game plan—go to the school nurse; if you're at a friend's house, you can talk to her mom—and packed the supplies in a smaller bag within her backpack.

"Why didn't you text me?" she asked, but she knew the reason.

"I figured you were busy at work."

So much for her attempts to shield Cody from her work drama; it was just so hard when she wanted to succeed so badly. All through graduate school, she'd struggled with feelings of inadequacy, having come from two high school–educated parents in a small town. She'd spent hours catching up on theory her classmates seemed to inherently understand, sneaking in study sessions between sewing Halloween costumes for Cody or baking cookies for her first-grade class. Tenure was the one unassailable fact of success, and everyone in her cohort, as well as her professors, regarded it as the holy grail. She felt a spike of fury that the sacrifices she'd made might have been for nothing, her hopes of tenure slipping away.

"You know you come first," she said to her daughter, and when Cody turned toward her, Maris was shocked to see tears in her eyes. Cody had never been a public crier.

"I know your work is important, but it just seems like you're not really there lately."

Maris blanched, thinking of the blackouts, but Cody was right. Even discounting those, she hadn't been as present as she needed to be for her daughter. Since they'd come up with the plan for the three red balloons, Maris had been planning her reply: a pin (to pop the balloon), a chocolate bar, three flower emojis to indicate Cody had bloomed into a woman, and an eye roll so Cody wouldn't worry she was making *too* big of a deal of it. She had to wonder: If she'd gotten the text, would she have answered it right away? What if she'd been teaching—or worse, in a blackout? "I'm sorry if I've been distracted, really. You can be mad at me."

"Thanks for the permission," Cody said, but she tucked the bookmark back in *'Salem's Lot* and dropped it in her backpack. Cody refused to read e-books because she loved the "new-page smell," and she'd been making her own bookmarks for years, laminating covers of old paperbacks and hole-punching the tops to insert a yarn tail. Since Cody had started preschool, her teachers had all praised her for being her own person and beating her own drum. All along it had struck Maris as sad that these teachers would be so surprised to see a girl just be herself.

Cody pulled out her cell phone, her thumbs a flurry. Can we act like nbd

Maris nodded and texted back, absolutely. She scrolled right on the emojis and found the pin, clicked it into the message, then swiped left, scanning the food until she found the chocolate bar.

"I get it," Cody said. "Thanks."

"You craving anything special for dinner?" Maris asked, but before Cody could answer, Janice breezed in, waving a Hershey bar.

"Pretty sure you don't have a peanut allergy, but better safe than sorry." Cody mumbled a thanks and held the candy in her lap. "Maris. Good to see you," Janice added.

"You too." She was sure to use her normal voice—not one quiet with shame, or the loud voice she used to fake authority in the classroom.

"So big day here," Janice said, and for a heartbeat, Maris thought Janice was talking about her fight with Cody, that everyone knew she'd failed her. *Focus, Maris,* she thought to herself. "Cody said you've talked about all the specifics and supplies?"

"Of course."

"Then that should about cover it." She snapped her fingers—"Oh, wait!"—and pulled a pamphlet out of her bottom drawer and handed it to Cody. Maris read the cover over Cody's shoulder: *Hello, Aunt Flo.* "I know you probably know all this, but it never hurts to have another source. Isn't that what they're always telling you in Language Arts?"

Cody smiled at that one, and Maris was glad to see her daughter wasn't all the way replaced by a self-conscious teen. "Thanks," Cody said, and stood up. "I need to get one more thing from my locker."

"All right then," Maris said. "I'll wait for you up front." She didn't want to get stuck alone with Janice, but even so, as she was leaving, Janice touched Maris's arm.

"And you? How are you doing?" Maris said something inane about how kids grow up so fast, but Janice was having none of the dodge. "I heard you quit," she said. "Good on you." She wondered if Cody had volunteered this information, or if Janice had asked.

Either way, nothing made Maris want to drink more than someone else's condescension. "Just a break," she said breezily. She knew if she were to act defensive—I wasn't drinking *that* much—it would only lead to more conversation, maybe even a terrible pamphlet. Plus, if anyone wasn't going to believe she didn't have a problem, it was Janice, who'd witnessed it firsthand.

Since February, she'd begun to realize the enormous gulf between not putting your child in danger and keeping her safe. She was forced each day now to confront just how poorly she'd behaved, and the kicker: no wine to dull that sharp, ragged edge. She had thought when she quit drinking that she'd feel a rush of adrenaline—or, at the least, peace—but in the sober light of day, it just highlighted everything she'd done wrong.

Still. She had made it work. For months now she'd held a death grip on her sobriety. She'd done the one thing required of her: not drink. Since she'd quit, she rarely went a few days without bursting into tears, white-knuckling it through to bedtime. A few times, the desire for a glass of wine was so strong she had to lean over and put her head between her knees. She cried in her car, and in the bathroom, and in the backyard, and at Lowe's, and in her office with a fan on so no one could hear.

Why didn't she feel better? Why, if sobriety was so great, did her life now seem to be falling apart? Cody was angry at her, her job was shaky at best, Noel felt more like a time-share roommate than a husband, and there was the growing sense that the blackouts were more than just a blip.

"I'm glad I got a chance to speak with you before career day," Janice said.

For a second, Maris felt a jolt of irritation: Was Janice going to remind her of the date too? Did no one believe she would remember to attend? "I'm glad to participate," Maris said. "It's circled in red on my calendar."

"It's great that we have some careers focused outside of STEM for the kids, and I hope you know what a fan I've been of your work." It was true that Janice had followed her work closely, as had most people around Oak Park since the Dylan Charter case was local. "And as the counselor, I talk to these kids about pretty touchy subjects. Domestic abuse, rape, STDs." Maris nodded, unsure where she was going. "I'm just hoping for your presentation, you can steer clear of mentioning the Charter case too directly."

Maris furrowed her brows. "I'll certainly keep it age appropriate." Even though she'd let Cody read everything she'd written about the case, she wouldn't make that decision for other parents.

"I'm not worried about that," Janice said, and wrung her hands. "Some children at the school might be sensitive about this particular case."

"I don't understand."

"It's confidential," Janice said as Cody walked toward them carrying a clay model of a DNA strand in a shoebox. Maris hadn't even known about the project. How out of touch was she with her kid's life? She promised herself she'd ask about it on the way home. "But can you respect my wishes?"

"I'm not sure—"

"Please?"

Maris nodded, not quite sure what she had agreed to or why. She could talk about her job without the case—that was easy enough—but why didn't Janice want her to mention it?

In the car, Cody pulled out 'Salem's Lot and kept reading, nibbling on the edge of her laminated bookmark, and Maris let her read in peace. They were all the way home when she realized she hadn't asked anything else about Cody's period—how she found out, who she told, if there was a stain on her jeans—much less the DNA model.

Cody climbed out of the car, stuffing the shoebox in the garbage at the curb before she slammed the door on her way into the house.

CHAPTER EIGHT

It was nighttime, the witching hour.

As I turned at the drugstore on the corner of High Street, a car screeched past with some drunk asshole hanging half out the passenger window, an open beer can in his hand.

I flipped him off and he howled, laughing into the night. Fucking men.

While the suburbs had turned on their porch lights and locked their doors, perfect families tucked in for the night, the streets near the college were alive with a hazardous energy. Frat boys snaked into the street like live wires ready to strike. Men emerged from the shadows in masks. Three blonde girls wobbled their way down the street in unmanageable shoes, all of their arms crossed against the cold in their tiny Ohio State cheer uniforms. One moved in an up and down stride, a heel already broken. I wondered if she'd left that perfectly good weapon in the street.

"Hey," the broken-shoe girl said to me.

I said "Hey" back, smiling because I hadn't aroused any suspicion. I was just another college girl on her way to a Slutty Blank Party.

When I was little, I loved October and everything Halloween. Both my parents worked full-time, so my costumes came premade from Walmart. We'd stop by late on the thirty-first, most of the racks empty, the few costumes left hanging in disarray. One year I was a generic pirate, a lame, off-brand wizard the next. Even then I was a tomboy and just glad to not be going as a princess, a girl whose only goal was to grow up and get a man.

Now that I was all grown up, I still didn't want a man. I wanted revenge.

But tonight I was playing the part. I checked the directions on my phone and saw the blue line climb three blocks north and one east to the frat house, my blue circle inching closer to the destination. The frat was throwing a Halloween party a few weeks early, but everyone knew the bros referred to it as a Slutty Blank Party, guffawing that girls could make any outfit slutty if they put in a little effort. Nurse, teacher, maid. Before Dylan Charter's arrest, the house used to hang a bedsheet out the top floor window, *Slutty Blank* spray-painted across the front. It was supposed to read as *Slutty _____*, but they thought this was funnier; girls were the blanks. Now that party name was just whispered.

I was wearing a headband with ears attached, eyeliner whiskers across my cheeks, a black tank and a too-short skirt, goose pimples dotting my legs and arms. I knew it didn't really matter—slutty funeral director would have worked just as well—because when it came to men, they could look at any outfit and think it was an invitation. Even jeans and a cardigan.

I took a quick peek at Dylan's social media to see if he'd posted he was at the party yet, but all sites were silent. He didn't post as much as I'd assumed he would, but why bother when every other day he was trending on Twitter with publicity he didn't want. The thought made me smile. He hadn't even posted he'd be coming, but one of his bros had tagged him on Insta and asked if he'd show, and he'd responded with the devil-horn emoji. I was pretty sure that meant *yes* in bro language, and so I had driven to Columbus for the party, my shitty car shaking on the interstate when I hit sixty-five. Dylan had been kicked out of OSU and his basketball scholarship was rescinded after the criminal charge, but once a brother, always a brother.

He was like every other rich, white boy in the world who'd been canceled and still ended up on top.

The three-story house loomed in front of me, the pounding bass punctuated by the occasional scream of laughter. I reached my cold hand in my tank and yanked my boobs higher, smoothed my skirt to midthigh, and put on a vacuous smile. I didn't know anyone at the party, but there was no way they wouldn't let me in. I was a young, pretty girl out on her own, paying five bucks for all-you-can-drink. I was what they hoped for when they threw a party like this. I'd read the articles about the "red zone" for college freshmen and those first few months at school when they were adjusting to life on their own. Men took advantage that they were still the naive girls they'd been in high school, inexperienced with alcohol, and slipped things into drinks.

Men were the predators; they were the prey.

I laughed, thinking I should have come dressed as a hunter in camo pants and face paint, although dressed as I was, that wasn't far off. I was a slutty hunter camouflaged in the wild, a smoky eye and red lips my face paint.

The guy at the door—frat douche, double collar popped, but maybe it was a costume?—cupped a hand at his mouth and yelled at me. "What's so funny?"

Your dick, I wanted to say, but I widened my empty smile instead. "I think I might be lost?"

He smiled appreciatively at my outfit. "I don't think so," he said. "We're having a costume party, and unless you dress like a cat every day, you're in the right place."

"Meow," the guy behind him purred, then snorted with laughter. So original.

Frat Douche elbowed his buddy. "Sorry about him," he said, turning back to me. "He's already a little drunk."

"That's okay," I said, because I was agreeable! And smiling! "Maybe I'll just go in and see if my friends are here? We were supposed to meet up after studying." I rolled my eyes. "First year, and it's killing me."

"Yeah, of course," he said. "Get yourself a drink. It's the weekend. You deserve to have some fun." So nice of him to be concerned with what I deserved.

I held out my five-dollar bill, and he folded it into the pile of bills in his hand. "You have any trouble in there getting a drink, let me know. I'm Jeremy."

"Thanks, Jeremy." I knew this approach all too well: the helpful guy, the good guy, but wait until he got you alone.

I followed the thundering noise to the stairs, my heels catching on the green shag carpet as I descended. In the dark basement the stench of stale beer and bodies clung to the air, wrapped in the heat those bodies generated. It was so humid it felt like it might rain, and I strained my eyes to see around the mass of people, the wall of sound that was Megan Thee Stallion's "Hot Girl Summer."

With every step, my shoes stuck to the cement, and I had to stop and steady myself to keep from tripping. The heels were low by heel standards, but I was used to Chucks. I thought about the girls I'd seen earlier in the night, how their legs shook like a new foal's in their five-inch spikes. I hoped I looked the same, knowing it would seem to anyone paying attention like I'd been pregaming.

A girl in a belly dancing outfit leaned her back against the bar as two men grabbed her legs from the ground, hoisted them in the air, and rested them on their shoulders, a butt cheek against each chest. A slick of adrenaline shot through me as they pushed her bottom half higher and her shoulders and head fell behind the bar, hidden. Her exposed stomach was cavernous around her ribs, and a third man licked the bare skin, then shook salt into her belly button. As soon as he took the shot and licked her salted stomach again, her face shot up, laughing, her hair in disarray.

As the crowd was distracted by Slutty Belly Dancer, I grabbed the nozzle on the keg and poured a beer; an amateur mistake was taking the one handed to you. I grimaced at the bitter taste. How did people like this, much less drink enough to get drunk?

I made a few more laps through the sticky, dense basement, checked in the bathroom as another handful of songs played, and then: there he was.

With a jolt I recognized his sandy-brown hair, now short from prison. The broad shoulders from shooting hoops. He held a red Solo cup in his hand and was one of the few guys not in a costume, although an argument could be made for Rapist in Natural Habitat. He threw his head back to laugh at something another guy said, and I wondered what girl they were talking about.

I'd read every article the esteemed Dr. Maris Heilman had written on Dylan Charter, including the one analyzing his father's character statement about how tough the trial had been on poor Dylan. He was no longer able to enjoy his favorite foods. He was no longer able to live a normal life. It was more bullshit from the Charters, because here Dylan stood, beer in hand, ogling a sea of young girls like they were laid out on a buffet.

I edged next to him, nearly full beer in my hand, and as he went to take a sip from his own cup, elbow out, I knocked into his arm and spilled most of my cup down my tank top. The shock of cold made me gasp, but mission accomplished: the already tight shirt now glistened, the smell of beer even more pungent.

"Oh, shit, sorry," he said, whipping around. He locked eyes with me and smiled, then quickly scanned the overheated party. He leaned toward me. "Let me get you a napkin," he shouted, his breath hot and wet in my ear.

"The kitchen maybe?" I yelled back.

"Right." He put a hand on my lower back to steer me toward the stairs, and the snake of pure revulsion that slithered through me made him stop.

I forced myself to laugh and pointed at my beer-soaked chest. "Cold."

The noise barely lessened as we climbed the stairs. In the kitchen, he slammed cupboards open and closed, finally locating paper towels on the third try. Of course he wouldn't know where anything in the kitchen was, this man who'd been waited on his whole life. The basement thudded below us like a living thing.

He tore off a paper towel and held it out.

I introduced myself as I patted my shirt, although I didn't give him my real name, any more than these were my normal clothes, my life as a cat.

He hesitated before saying his first name, and stopped before his last.

I lowered my voice. "I know who you are."

Dylan blanched and looked abashed, but I knew it was another act.

"I think it's shit what happened to you," I continued, and Dylan paused from tearing sheets off the roll. "I mean. It takes two to tango, right?" My stomach flopped at the words, but already he was nodding along.

"I appreciate you saying that."

"I bet this has been a stressful year," I added, thinking certainly he'd know I was laying it on too thick, but he kept on nodding, glad someone saw he deserved some sympathy. "It's good you still have your friends here to hang out with."

"The guys have been great," he admitted.

"What've you been up to since you got home?" I asked, but I knew the answer. Even though he didn't post on his own social media pages, he commented on his bros', anxious to reestablish his old friendships, to let them know one little rape charge wouldn't keep Dylan Charter down.

"Working at my dad's firm," he said. "Just a holdover job until I finish my degree and get into law school."

He was so confident it would happen—his setback of getting kicked out of college little more than a speed bump in his life's plans. He was just the kind of guy who would become a lawyer—one who would let more men like him go free. Most likely he'd end up on the Supreme Court.

"Maybe you can show me your briefs," I said, and slapped a hand over my dirty little mouth like I hadn't planned the line ahead of time. As if I hadn't driven all the way to Columbus just to flirt with him while he downed beer after beer, my camera at the ready. By tomorrow, Twitter would *really* have something to talk about.

A sly grin escaped the side of his mouth. "Good one." He held out his hands for the soggy towels.

"Thanks." I dropped the wad into his outstretched palms. "I suppose I should get back downstairs," I said. "Let you get back to your guys?" I turned, the trap set.

"Wait." I paused, one foot pointed toward the stairs, and looked over my spaghetti-strapped shoulder. "Let me at least get you another beer," he said.

And the trap clicked shut.

PART TWO

CHAPTER NINE

Maris put the final touches on her PowerPoint Friday afternoon, her career day presentation an hour away. She reminded herself that what impressed middle schoolers wasn't academic articles but likes on Twitter as she finalized the last slide and took a slug of her cold coffee, setting the mug in the empty sink. Finally, an audience that would appreciate her.

She'd been looking forward to this day as much as Cody. Standing in front of a classroom was what she did best, and she knew she'd gain a fast rapport with the students, maybe even get a few laughs. She admitted, she'd even thought about Cody in the audience, her desk chair grouped at a table of six in the open-learning style of Horace Valley. Maris imagined she'd grin proudly at her mother's accomplishments, maybe clap extra loud at the end. Afterward, she might even think about hugging her mother, although she'd never do it in front of everyone at the school. Even Maris's daydreaming couldn't take it that far.

She loaded her workbag and threw it over her shoulder, stopping to run her fingers through her hair in the foyer mirror before

—

—

—

woke up, an oxygen mask strapped over her nose and mouth and a woman's face hovering a foot above her. Maris blinked rapidly as her heart galloped into another gear. Her arms shot out—one hand grabbing a metal railing, the other slamming against a wall. A painful zing ran up as she hit her funny bone. *Where the fuck am I?*

The woman turned to another person crouched beside her. "She's awake." They were both in navy EMT uniforms, and Maris could feel bumps on the road beneath her, the uneasy feeling of moving while lying down. She was in an ambulance.

She clawed the mask away from her mouth and gasped. "What happened?"

The EMT's eyes were kind and focused as they flicked up to lock with Maris's. "Car wreck," she explained, and repositioned Maris's oxygen.

It had been one of Maris's worst fears as long as she could remember— that she would get in an accident when she was drunk—and it had almost come true last February. Her father had two DUIs and had wrecked his truck and broken his leg with the second one, calling it lucky that no one was injured but himself.

Panic gripped Maris again, and she grabbed for the EMT's hand. "Was anyone hurt?"

"Besides you?" the woman asked. Maris nodded. "Nope. And other than some scrapes and bruises, my educated guess is you got off easy."

The brakes squealed, and the ambulance stopped rocking. She recognized Noel's hospital out the tiny back window. As the doors opened to a blast of cold and she was hoisted into the air, her bed set on the ground, she tried to remember if he was working today. What day was it?

It felt like every bone had been scraped with glass. She was covered in scratches and bruises, and could tell from the deep pain that her side would be purple by the next day. They passed a mirrored wall, and she saw a deep scratch on her face, wincing as she brought a shaky hand to the bruise on her forehead. She ran through her memories like a rat through a maze trying to grab on to something in the last hour, but there was nothing there. My god, *had* she been drinking? Was that possible? Maybe she was in denial even from herself. She clenched her jaw, pain radiating from the cut. No. She was in a car wreck, and she wasn't drunk; accidents happened to everyone.

The woman backed her stretcher in next to a bed and lowered the gate on the side, helping Maris gingerly from the trolley to the mattress. She hoped to god Noel hadn't picked up an extra shift, although she had to remind herself: she had nothing to hide. The woman squeezed her hand. "Is there someone we should call?"

Maris shook her head no, wincing at the bruise on her face. Even though she had nothing to hide, she wasn't ready to explain this to Noel. She could say she hadn't been drinking, but that didn't mean he'd believe her. When had they lost so much trust in each other?

Jesus. She could have died. She could have left Cody without a mother, and with that she remembered: career day. With a wave of nausea, she imagined Cody at the front of her classroom with her intro-duction note cards, all the good parents lined around the room.

Certainly almost dying was a good excuse to miss it, but she hadn't wanted a good enough excuse. What she'd wanted was to be there for Cody.

Tears dripped from the edges of her eyes onto the pillow until finally Maris drifted in and out of sleep—she assumed if she had a concussion someone would have stopped her—and eventually a woman came in wearing scrubs and a white jacket, her phone and a Kit Kat visible through the jacket pockets. "Maris?" she said. "Do you remem-ber me?"

Maris closed her eyes, and willed a memory—something, anything—that had happened between loading her workbag and waking up in the ambulance. She shook her head no, tears coursing down her face.

"We met a few years ago at one of Eula's cookouts? I'm Karen Patel, one of Noel's colleagues."

Maris opened her eyes with a flutter of relief, the smell of rubber still deep in her nose from the oxygen mask. She was worried they'd met during the blackout and she'd forgotten, but this was just run-of-the-mill forgetfulness. "Oh yes. Karen, hi." She'd been the one to tell Noel Miami Regional was hiring for an ER doctor. "Nice to see you again."

"You too, although I certainly wish under different circumstances." Karen put a hand on Maris's shoulder. "I called Noel. He's on his way."

For one scrabbling moment Maris thought about asking her to call him back and say everything was fine, but as much as she wanted to just ignore her problems, she wouldn't be able to hide the fact her car was likely destroyed, or that her face and body would be bruised and sore for weeks.

Karen lowered her voice, barely audible over the beeps of the machines in Maris's room. What did they have her all hooked up to, and why? "Do you remember what happened?" Karen asked, and Maris shook her head. She couldn't really tell her that the last thing she remembered was packing her bag.

"That's not that unusual," Karen admitted. "A lot of patients forget things right before or after a traumatic event." Maybe that was it, Maris thought, but she knew better. "The EMTs picked you up on Patterson where you hit a light post on the opposite side. It's a miracle no oncoming traffic was involved. That's a pretty busy street."

Maris thought of all the times she'd driven down that road with Cody in the passenger seat on their way to school or home, their stolen ten minutes to check in on their days. Now Cody had gotten her period and hadn't even let her know, and she'd missed the one school event she promised to be at.

"But you don't remember anything odd happening before the crash? Any pain or seizing up?"

Maris shook her head. "Why?"

Karen flipped through Maris's chart. "Based on your oxygen levels and some of your reflexes, it seems something . . . unusual might have happened. We ran some tests, and it appears your autonomic functions shut down, no matter how temporarily. Breathing, heart rate, blood pressure."

Maris's eyes flared open. "Do you mean I died?"

"No, not that," Karen said, shaking her head. "Because it appears other functions were still active. Just not the autonomic systems. It's like something shut down your brain stem and then turned it back on. Like a computer reset." Maris gave her a skeptical look, and Karen grimaced. "I know. It sounds crazy, but trust me, every day the human body still finds ways to surprise us."

Maris paused, trying to sound casual as her breath hitched in her throat, sure, suddenly, this was all related to her drinking. "Could it have anything to do with memories forming?" All those years—decades, really—where alcohol had inhibited the formation of memories. It had somehow finally come home to roost. Another wave of nausea ripped through her as she imagined termites eating a house: even if she had stopped, they were still there, still chewing.

Karen cocked her head. "What do you mean?"

Maris backtracked. Surely if Karen thought it was alcohol related, she'd say something. "Because I don't remember what happened before the accident?"

Karen was nodding before Maris had even finished. "Like I said, that's common. Nothing to be concerned about." She patted Maris's hand. "That doesn't have anything to do with it."

But of course Karen would think that. She didn't know the whole truth.

Noel swooped in thirty minutes later, his messenger bag thrown behind his hip as he leaned down to hug her gently, his face sincere but tense. "How are you feeling?" he asked, but that wasn't her biggest concern.

"How was career day? Is Cody pissed?" Maris tried to scoot up but couldn't given the ache in her side. Even her hair felt bruised. She pushed the button to raise the hospital bed upright, but they never sat up far enough.

His eyes scanned back and forth as he looked into hers, assessing her pupil dilation and other doctor-y tricks. "I'm sure she'll understand."

"So she doesn't know yet?"

"I was on my way home from Horace when I got the call."

Maris put a hand to her tender head. "So she thought I just forgot or blew it off?"

Noel reached for her chart, avoiding her eyes. "That's what it looked like at the time." He scanned the metal clipboard in his hand, flipped the page, then placed it back at the foot of her bed.

She sat up straighter. "Is that what you thought too?"

"Well. Cody told me you made a big deal about putting a reminder on the fridge like you were going to forget."

She remembered the night of the first blackout, how she'd written it down and snapped the note under the fridge magnet. "I wanted her to see it was important to me!"

"Well to her it looked like something you had to remind yourself to do, like a chore or some task you were dreading."

Maris rested her head against the uncomfortable pillow. "That's not at all what I meant." For a second she thought about telling him everything, but she wasn't sure where to start. There wasn't just today. There were the blackouts prior; the night back in February; the white-knuckling every day to not drink. And what about that missing time between when she was packing her bag and the car accident? Was it possible she had stopped for a drink?

Karen breezed in, smiling at them both. "Quite a scare," she said to Noel, "but accidents happen. All things considered, she got off lucky. A few broken ribs, a few scrapes." She smiled. "But all in all, no worse for wear."

Noel smoothed a hand down Maris's face, and, despite their friction, she pushed her cheek into his palm, his hand scented with aloe from the constant sanitizing at the hospital. It was one of her favorite smells.

"You're so lucky it wasn't worse," he said. Did he mean it as a warning?

Maris grimaced as she tried to sit up farther. "I don't feel very lucky."

"Probably not, but wait until you see the car. One of the EMTs took pics." He pulled his phone from his pocket and thumbed through three pictures of her unrecognizable Rogue. The front was folded in like an accordion, glass glistening on the street. How had she survived that?

Noel said he had a little hospital business to take care of, and left her to pull her clothes out of the plastic drawstring bag, her heels at the bottom, her teal-and-pink-striped earrings tucked in the toe. They were the ones she'd worn in her original faculty picture, the one full of so much promise. She slipped off the gown, grunting as she fit her arm through the blouse's sleeve, her side throbbing from the broken ribs.

After a $150 copay and a prescription for Percocet (that she was certain Noel had side-eyed), she was discharged from the hospital and climbed gingerly into his Prius to head home.

Cody was lounging in the living room when they arrived. Noel escorted Maris to the couch, a hand supporting the tender skin at her elbow. Cody flinched when she saw her mother. "Noel texted you were in an accident. What happened?"

Maris backed her butt toward the cushion, bent her bruised knees, and hoped for the best. "Women drivers, am I right." She glanced at Cody's tight mouth—she was having none of her mother's humor—and wanted to shout, *It's not my fault!* But was she ever willing to admit it was? Maris vacillated constantly between not accepting responsibility for anything and thinking everything that happened in the world was because of her personal shortcomings. And while she still wasn't always able to stop this hyperbolic thinking, at least she was aware of it. Wasn't that the first step?

"Are you okay?" Cody asked begrudgingly. "What happened?"

Maris told her what she knew—driving down Patterson, no one else hurt, car totaled. "I'm so sorry about missing today, Code. I had a PowerPoint and everything."

Cody shrugged. "It's fine. Noel was there, and Dad videoed in. He even gave my teacher free legal advice about dealing with her landlord."

Maris was glad they had been there, but felt the sting of the stepdad and the parent eight hundred miles away being more reliable than the one right here. "I'm so sorry," she added again.

"Your mom really wanted to be there," Noel reiterated to Cody. Maris appreciated his efforts and that they presented as a united front, even though he'd been somewhat cold in the hospital. "We're just lucky she's okay."

"I'm glad you're fine," Cody said, then mumbled something about homework and headed upstairs. Maris felt like she'd been slapped—did Cody not care?—but it wasn't that. She knew her daughter well enough to know when she didn't fully believe something. It was the same look she had on her face when she was seven and a classmate hired a magician for their birthday party. A grown man in a cape pulled a plastic coin from behind her ear, and her face said, *I know funny business when I see it.* It was another reason it didn't make sense to tell full truths. People were going to believe what they wanted anyway, but it pained her to think Cody thought she was lying. *Not this time,* she wanted to yell, but it sounded far from convincing, even to her.

That night, as Noel tucked her into bed, he leaned over to kiss her good night and let his mouth linger. He pulled back and looked into her eyes, finally setting his hip on the mattress edge. He put a hand on her stomach and rubbed a slow, small circle below her broken ribs. "I have a confession."

She clenched her body so hard Noel must have felt it through her thin T-shirt, the one he had bought at a Derailers concert and she had immediately claimed for herself. She wanted to put a hand on his mouth and tell him, *No, don't tell me! We can still get back on track!*

"I ordered your tox report in the hospital."

She scrunched her brows and remembered Noel at the end of her hospital bed with her chart in his hand, how he had left her to dress alone. She thought he'd looked at her chart because he was concerned about her, but it was to see if they'd ordered one already. Another wall between them. She shook her head, tears burning her eyes. "I can't believe you didn't trust me."

He looked at her, exasperated. "I know I should have just asked you, but can you really not believe it, Maris? Really? You're forgetting conversations, missing stuff in your life. You're secretive and distracted." He took a deep breath. "I was so mad at you at Cody's school, I thought the worst."

She hated to ask but had to know. "And did Cody too?"

He nodded. "You were first in the lineup, and when the teacher asked Cody if you were there, she had to say no. She asked before each damn presenter: Is she here yet? Is she here? Until Cody couldn't even answer but just shook her head to keep from crying." Cody, her tough-nut girl who didn't cry in public. She felt sick and wished for just a second that the accident had been worse.

Her self-pity morphed into anger as she wiped her own tears away. "I haven't been drinking, but I guess I know now what my word means to you." It would be so easy to tell him how tempted she'd been to drink, but what was reason in the face of righteous indignation? Fact was, she hadn't, and it had taken every ounce of her willpower and courage, so screw him for thinking she had. "When will you get the results?"

"Not for a few weeks."

"So until then, you just won't believe me?"

"Mare, let's talk—" he started, and she rolled over, wincing at her ribs as she did. She was 98 percent sure what the results would be, but that wasn't the point: if it took a tox test for him to believe her, they'd already failed.

CHAPTER TEN

After a fitful night's sleep, Maris rolled over and winced as she reached for her phone. There was a voice mail notification from Karen Patel. When she and Noel had met Karen a few years ago at Eula's cookout and she'd mentioned a job opportunity for Noel in the ER, she'd given Maris her cell. She'd made a joke about how the wives always ran the details, but Maris recognized it for what it was: neutralizing of a threat. Even though Karen had been at the cookout with her own wife, she didn't want Maris worrying she was hitting on her husband. She remembered how much she'd liked Karen for that.

She sneaked into the bathroom and hit "Play" on the message. "Maris, hi, I'm just checking in to see how you're doing after the accident." She knew it was standard protocol for the ER to call the day after a visit, but usually it was a nurse practitioner or nonmedical staff.

"I was wondering if you could give me a call back as soon as possible. Something . . . odd happened yesterday on rounds, and I wanted to run it by you and perhaps hear more about your lead-up to the accident." Maris felt an electric jolt of panic shoot down her back. "You mentioned something about memories forming when you were in yesterday, and I wanted to hear more about that. Anyway." She left her contact information and said goodbye, and as soon as the message was finished, Maris threw her phone clattering into the sink as if it were a snake about to bite her.

What did Karen want to know, and why? What odd thing had happened? And what in the hell did it have to do with her?

◆　◆　◆

For the rest of the weekend, Maris's memories stayed intact. Noel called off work to stay home with her and Cody, and as she lounged on the sofa dipping saltines in a melted peanut butter–chocolate chip sauce (a poor-girl's candy bar from her childhood), she could remember dip by dip, cracker by cracker, how many she'd eaten. Standing in front of the bathroom mirror with a foamy toothbrush in her mouth, her body bright with pain from the accident, she could trace back every moment from the kitchen—throwing her tenth LaCroix can of the day in the recycling; stopping to pick up her library book from the end table and setting it on her nightstand for bed; turning on the hot tap to wash her face, the water heating as she brushed her teeth. Had she knocked something in her head back in place with the accident?

But still, she wanted to be prepared in case it happened again, the threat of another blackout imminent. She knew, logically, that she should call Karen back, perhaps request an MRI, but who knew where that might lead. At least the blackouts and secrecy were the devils she knew. Frightening as the incidents were, there was also something familiar about them, the ghosts of drinking past. She thought of all the times she'd tried to focus on these moments when she was drinking—the nights when she took her mental pulse after four drinks, five drinks, six drinks, and yet somehow, that moment when she could no longer remember, always seemed to happen one more drink in. That was the problem: when you no longer tried to remember, you stopped recording memories. But what if she recorded what happened instead of the memories? Instead of trying to remember the blackouts from the inside, she could try to capture them from the outside.

She grimaced as she folded her legs on the couch and set her laptop in the crook of her crossed legs, a newly discovered bruise asserting itself on her thigh. Online, she scanned indoor security cameras, figuring if she could record herself during a blackout, it would give her a clue what was going on. She flipped through the websites, marveling at the money people would pay to try to protect themselves, the sheer volume of fear that could be marketed upon. People were buying cameras to protect against home invasion, to prevent babies dying from SIDS, to monitor their teenagers. It was amazing how much fear there was out in the world. Cameras started around $300, which wasn't ridiculous, but where could she put them in the house that no one would notice?

The midrange camera she was looking at with audio was the size of a beer can, and she thought she could tuck it on the bookshelf in the living room, just background noise to the side of the fireplace. She wanted to record the whole house but knew that increased the chances of Noel or Cody seeing the cameras. The living room was the space she spent the most time awake in, her laptop snug on her lap, Cody at the other end of the couch when she used to spend more time with her mother. She hated the idea of anyone, even herself, recording Noel and Cody without their consent, but how could she explain that it wasn't that she didn't trust them but that she didn't trust herself?

She pulled out the credit card she kept deep in her wallet, a leftover from her single days postdivorce before she and Noel opened a joint account. She remembered walking to the bank with him carrying their new licenses with their new address, their social security cards worn almost to the feel of fabric. When she'd married Noel, she didn't think anything could ever go wrong between them, yet when the credit card came two years ago with a new expiration date, she tucked it in her wallet and didn't tell him. There were too many memories of her mother from her childhood, too many reminders of a woman with few options. Maris had vowed when she turned sixteen and started her first job at the Dairy Barn that she'd never be financially dependent on a man. She entered the card number on the website and hit "Purchase."

All day Saturday, she was just shy of enough time alone to call Karen back, or that's what she told herself. She'd spent too many years avoiding anyone who might tell her to cut out the drinking. Had too many formative years of Nebraska stoicism where you only went to the doctor if you lost a limb. She remembered one time her father had dropped a cinder block on his foot. Three of his toes turned black, swollen fat with fluid, and still he refused to go. When she asked him if it had hurt, he'd said, "Didn't tickle."

Only now did it occur to her he'd probably been drunk when it happened.

◆ ◆ ◆

Sunday morning, Eula stopped by, a nine-by-thirteen Pyrex in her hands. "Lasagna," she said, holding the dish out. Eula was dressed in sweatpants and a Glenn State T-shirt from a decade-old blood drive, her short white hair spiked in the back like a spry elf's. Other than gardening and Sunday mornings, Maris rarely saw Eula out of real-person clothes—she mainly wore linen shirts and pants, or jeans and wool sweaters—and was impressed the woman kept up appearances when she didn't have anywhere to go. Maybe Eula felt the same as Maris when she faced a class: she didn't want others to think she was incompetent, so she gave them little reason to think so appearance-wise. "Noel told me about your accident," she said as Maris reached for the dish, the extra weight tugging at her tender side.

"A little fender bender," she said, downplaying it. Who else had Noel been telling?

"Noel made it sound a bit worse than that," Eula chided, and followed Maris into the kitchen, where Maris set the dish in the fridge and then held up the kettle to ask Eula if she wanted some tea.

Eula nodded and sat down at the breakfast bar. "It seems the universe has it in for you." Maris looked at her quizzically. "Your tenure vote."

Maris held the stove knob to light. "How did you hear about that?"

"Noel again." Why was Noel talking so much to Eula? "He actually wanted to know what I could tell him about Hollis." Was he digging up information for her, or was this another way of checking up on her word? Maris felt a wave of exhaustion. When had she started doubting everything the man she loved did? The easy, righteous answer was: when he started doubting *her*.

Eula flipped through the basket of tea bags Maris set in front of her. "Did you know my husband is the reason Hollis came to Glenn State? He had tenure at Cincinnati U and gave it up to study with Carl. We'll blame him for your troubles."

"Were they in the same area?" She would have sworn Carl had been an engineer.

"No, but Hollis had read some of Carl's articles and thought there might be room to collaborate." She plucked an Earl Grey from the bunch and tore open the small package.

"And did they?"

Eula thought about it for a moment as Maris retrieved their mugs. "They did, for many years, but in the end they weren't well suited philosophically. Carl was a lot more open-minded than Hollis." She smiled at Maris. "He was excited when you moved in next door—a person in the social sciences."

"I remember," Maris said. At that first cookout, he'd cornered her for what felt like an hour to talk about the advantages of mixing the arts with STEM, positing that if the two disciplines were to make a baby, what would pop out would be her field. She told him she'd taken a few engineering classes as an undergrad and he'd lit up, and as the new colleague and neighbor she had little recourse but to smile and nod. Too many academics couldn't understand why their areas of research weren't interesting to others, especially other academics. "Carl seemed like a sweetheart." She thought of the few times he'd mowed their lawn when she and Noel couldn't squeeze it in their schedules, saying since retirement he had nothing but time on his hands. It was such a kindness to come home and see the shorn grass, the fresh yard. "I'm sure you miss him."

Eula shrugged. "It gets easier each month, but I admit, it's hard. I hadn't imagined we wouldn't be together. I thought it would be like the king died, then the queen died of grief. Connected somehow. Some people might say we were lucky to grow old together, but I thought we'd have another decade or two. Everyone thinks old people are old except for old people." Maris knew what she meant. When she was twenty, she thought forty-two sounded like you had a foot in the grave, but despite the math she still wouldn't call herself middle-aged.

The kettle whistled, and Maris plucked it from the burner.

"Did I ever tell you I was home when Carl died?" Eula asked. Maris shook her head. She knew he'd had a stroke and was taken to Noel's hospital, but hadn't heard this detail. "I was in the kitchen with him," Eula said, pointing toward Maris's own kitchen counter. "Toasting a bagel. He made a strange gargling noise, and then he went down like he had no bones. Like one of those plastic puppets you push at the bottom that just collapses. It happened so quickly, my first thought was, what is Carl doing on the floor?" She shook her head and steeped her tea bag. "We'd fought the night before, and then boom, he died the next day."

"Eula." Maris grimaced. "How awful for you."

Eula laughed, a strangled noise. "I'm pretty sure it was worse for Carl. Our fight didn't last, and luckily we'd smoothed it all out by morning. We'd been married thirty-five years and didn't see a lot of use in fighting anymore."

Every now and again Maris was reminded why she went into sociology in the first place. It wasn't just to write about terrible things and men like Dylan Charter. It was because she loved people and their stories. "How'd you two meet?" Maris asked.

"I was his graduate assistant," Eula said, and Maris raised her eyebrows.

"Really?"

"Scandalous, I know," Eula said, adding honey to her tea. "But it was the early eighties. No one said boo about a professor dating a grad student. It was a perk, like library privileges." Maris knew times hadn't changed as much as Eula might think.

"Of course, he was married when we met," Eula went on. "But his wife was an absolute dolt. He could never talk to her about his work."

Maris asked Eula why she'd quit graduate school after her MA and didn't continue to the PhD. While she taught the occasional intro class at the community college, she'd basically left the academy behind.

"We didn't have room for two professors in the family, and Carl was the one with the name in the field. Besides, I wasn't somebody anyone would have taken seriously back then. Everyone assumed I had just slept with him to get As." She grinned at Maris. "I did sleep with him, and I did get As, but they were wrong about the causation. Plus, I'm not sure Carl could have handled having a colleague as a wife."

Maris smiled. "Too much competition?"

"Definitely," Eula said matter-of-factly. "Instead, he took a lot of the accolades for work that was rightfully ours."

"I'm sorry you didn't get the career you deserved," Maris said, and was surprised when tears welled in Eula's eyes.

"We decided early on we would focus on his career and not mine," she said. "We also decided against having children—we raise ideas, Carl used to say—but now I'm all alone and I miss him."

Maris squeezed Eula's hand. It was less common for a married woman of Eula's generation to not have children, and Maris had wondered if that was a decision they'd made or one that had been made for them, but it was always too personal of a question to ask.

Back when Maris and Noel were first together, their talk of a baby had felt like a purely hypothetical future, something they lobbed back and forth like the villa in Italy they would never be able to afford. She'd wondered at times if he'd been serious, if he really wished they'd tried, but she'd already had Cody and was through the worst years, which she'd survived by the skin of her teeth.

Eula slapped her knee. "Well. Hollis to my marriage. I guess we covered the gambit today."

Maris poured Eula's still-steaming tea into a traveler and handed it to her. Maris pictured Hollis Grant at the cookouts, always talking to Carl or another male colleague, wearing a button-down shirt so wrinkled it looked like it had never met a hanger. "Did Hollis ever marry?"

"Not that I know of," Eula said. "At least he wasn't married here. But he didn't talk a lot about his life in Cincinnati. I got the sense maybe something had happened there with a woman, something he didn't want to talk about."

That piqued Maris's interest. "But you don't know for sure?"

Eula shook her head. "It was a long time ago." She smiled at Maris. "I could talk to him if you'd like. About your tenure?"

"Oh, that's okay." She didn't think Hollis would react well if he knew she was asking about him, but she filed the piece of information about Cincinnati away. Had there been a scandal of some sort? Maris thought about Hollis and his rants against academic women in general and her in particular, and how determined he seemed to stop her tenure, versus Carl out there in ninety-degree heat, mowing her lawn. "I'm surprised Carl would work so closely with him. Hollis seems like a bit of a jerk."

"You got that right," Eula agreed. "But Carl saw the good in people. He thought everyone wanted to use advancements in science and knowledge for good."

"But Hollis didn't?"

"No," Eula said. "Hollis didn't."

CHAPTER ELEVEN

Maris didn't teach on Monday, so she canceled an undergrad committee meeting and stayed home, figuring another day to recover would do her good. It was hard to believe she was six weeks into the semester. Her Intro to Sociology students were finalizing their thesis statements for their diversity and inclusion research papers, while her Social Media students were presenting next week on social constructions. She'd logged a lot of office hours and emails helping them hone their topics and was excited to see what they came up with. It had been almost a month since the first blackout—four in all, but nothing had happened since the accident Friday.

Noel had taken Cody to school that morning, then came home and climbed back in bed, and that afternoon Maris decided she'd walk to the public library to finish the *WaPo* op-ed, now accepted, that was due on Wednesday. It was a nice distraction walking outside, the pain once she got moving at a minimum. Karen had told her she shouldn't run for six to eight weeks with her broken ribs, and it felt like Maris's world was getting smaller, more claustrophobic.

Many of the houses on her route were decorated with oversize skeletons and tombstones, polyblend spiderwebs spun across the porches. This side of Oak Park wasn't so rich the residents had crews come in and put up the decorations. It was the wives who woke an hour early before work, still squeezing in their run. Last year after the holiday, Maris had spent thirty minutes trying to unwind the sticky spiderwebs before finally cursing and cutting them down with scissors, vowing to stop at Target later to buy more at half off for next year. Had she? She couldn't remember. Given the blackouts and the accident, she hadn't decorated this year, even though in years past, the three of them had gone to Lowe's to pick out one new lawn ornament, the bigger and scarier the better. She thought of the huge spider gathering dust in the basement that last year they'd perched on the roof. Cody hadn't even mentioned it this year. Noel either. Although in all fairness, neither had she.

Just through the library's entry, Maris breathed in the scent of old books, long-gone burritos, and fresh-ground coffee from the attached coffeehouse. For as long as she could remember, libraries had been her church, a place of solace. Work had always been a respite for her, even during the worst of Scott's drinking days, the grueling grind of grad school, the job market and all its insecurities.

The downtown library branch even felt like a church, with large windows on three sides, the sun streaming in like a benediction.

Since her talk with Eula the day before, she'd been thinking about Hollis in Cincinnati and Eula's suspicion that something had happened with a woman. She wondered if it might be a sexual assault case or some other scandal, and laughed to think of all the gaskets Hollis would blow if Maris were to write about *him*.

Settled in on the second floor, she texted Noel and told him she was going to catch up on work and would be home in an hour or two, and would he mind getting Cody from school?

No prob. Picked up extra shift tonight. Be home by 5 so we can eat together?

She sent him a kissy-face emoji and two red hearts followed by another kissy-face emoji even though she was disappointed he was going to be out that night. It was what they agreed—grab what shifts he could—but she'd hoped they'd have a family night at home, not one shoving down a few bites before he was out the door. The weekend had felt in a strange way like a vacation, and she was able to recognize what a bad sign it was that having to recover from a car wreck was as close as she got to a vacation.

Evenings like tonight when she got home from work and Noel was due at the hospital, they did their best to squeeze in a few minutes together, but he was already mentally halfway out the door, and she was exhausted from her day and looking for some downtime. They'd long given up on hanging out together on Saturdays when she had errands to run with Cody, or research to do on campus, or he had something with the house—a busted garbage disposal, or a shorting doorbell—that needed his attention. Sunday afternoons had become their standing dates, although even that hadn't happened for a while thanks to a medical conference he'd attended in San Diego and a water heater they needed to replace. The water heater debacle was technically a Sunday together, but six crabby hours in Home Depot and the basement hardly seemed to count.

She shook her head to clear it. The fastest way to get home was to get to work, and she turned to the task at hand. She figured the best place to start was on straight-up Google, searching for Hollis Grant and Cincinnati. From there she'd pivot to Cincinnati University's website, and then their own library's archives, and maybe even take a romp through microfiche if things got spicy.

She grabbed a large coffee from the café, put her phone in airplane mode so she wouldn't get distracted by Twitter or Candy Crush, and set to work.

◆ ◆ ◆

When she finally looked up, she'd found out both less and more than she'd hoped. She started with an updated CV on the Glenn State website and read through his long list of published articles. Many had been coauthored with Carl Moore. She scrolled farther down to his articles from the nineties, and she was surprised to also find two that included Eula's name. "Neural Capacities and RFID Circuitry" and "Cellular Transmissions through Neural Oscillations." Maris hadn't realized Eula had stayed so active in the field after receiving her degree, and she made a note to ask her neighbor, along with a list of questions about Hollis's particular research.

She still didn't know if Hollis Grant had ever been married, but she knew from the public university's very public records that he'd last been assigned classes in spring of 1993, yet still received his salary through fall. Maybe he'd been on sabbatical? But no, she found that roster as well in CU's archives, and his name wasn't listed. It was possible that his classes were taught by adjuncts and bankrolled by a grant, but that wouldn't explain why in late November 1993 he received a considerable check from the university, and was no longer listed as faculty come spring.

She went back to Google and looked up Hollis's granting organizations, but there didn't seem to be much information there. She moved to microfiche and the 1993 *Cincinnati Enquirer*, concentrating on local news, op-eds (faculty loved to write these, herself included), and business. There were plenty of articles about Cincinnati University, most of which rabbit-holed her over to sports and their football team, but she was cruising through the obits when she finally spotted Hollis Grant's name.

The obituary was for Diane Garland, a woman in her twenties who had died in the hospital following a stroke. Maris assumed the obit had been upgraded to the local news section given the oddity of the woman's age for death by stroke, and they'd interviewed her family and colleagues for the article to discuss the sudden and tragic loss. Garland had been one of only two women in the neuroscience master's program, along with Bethany Novak. She had been a college athlete and teetotaler (*See,*

Maris thought to herself, *even nondrinkers meet untimely ends!*), and in graduate school she was particularly interested in the separation of neural oscillations. Her graduate adviser: Hollis Grant.

Maris followed that lead, and found numerous articles about Diane's undergrad swimming career at Notre Dame—her coaches had thought she might have a chance at the Olympics—but she'd ended up forgoing sports for education and the opportunity to study with Hollis at CU. It was obvious from the articles that her departure had left her coaches scratching their heads. "For a family is one thing," one of them had said. "But for graduate school?" After moving to Ohio, it seemed Garland followed that path until her untimely death.

Maris turned her attention to Bethany Novak, and a half hour in found out she still lived in Cincinnati, was married to a man named Anthony, went by Beth, and was now a supervisor at the Ohio Bureau of Motor Vehicles. How was it that a woman who had clawed her way into a graduate program in neuroscience given the boys' club of the nineties was now working at the BMV? Maris felt that tickle in her gut that told her she was onto something, and opened her laptop and clicked on her email. She copied and pasted Beth's email address from the oh.gov website, identified herself as a sociology professor at Glenn State, and asked if Beth might have a chance to chat about her association with Diane Garland and Hollis Grant. She debated adding more context, but what could she say? She didn't know what the context was. It was an old trick she'd learned from her journalism days: put just enough that they tell you the rest.

Done, she scooted away from the library computer and reached for her phone tucked in her bag. She turned it over: 6:14. *Shit. Shit shit shit.* She turned off airplane mode, and as she feared, the texts from Noel dinged through.

Pizza ok? 🍕 3:58 p.m.

Ordering so here at 5. ⏰ 4:23 p.m.

Are you blowing me off lol? 4:57 p.m.

Let me know you're okay? 5:13 p.m.

Leftovers in fridge. 5:28 p.m.

Maris ran her hands over her face. She'd screwed up again. It was only one dinner—not that big a deal—but these little deals had been adding up. Not only were there the blackouts but everyone in the house was under their own individual strain. Noel was always short on sleep; Maris was stressed about her tenure case; Cody was inching ever further into the teen years. And each of them had taken it out on the others. Maris and Noel were only three years into their marriage. How had things turned bad so quickly?

When she and Noel started dating, they called it second adolescence, only better than the first because they had high limits on their credit cards. In those early months when Cody was at a friend's or in Nebraska with her dad, Maris and Noel would lounge in bed until their stomachs growled. He would disappear into the kitchen and fix them something inexplicably delicious from odds and ends in the fridge: scrambled eggs with cubed pancetta, linguine with Parmesan, huevos rancheros.

Many of those late-night and early-morning meals were bleary, both of them either drunk or hungover. She would be more so, but they both attributed that to her sex and size—she was a petite woman; of course she couldn't drink as much as he did!—but she knew it was the gulps she took in the kitchen, the times she'd lift his glass instead of hers. One time, she was rooting through his cupboard and found a bottle of gin, took a swig, and put it back. She stood there with the cupboard door open, gobsmacked that her reaction had been to sneak a chug. But much like she pushed that bottle of gin behind a jar of pasta sauce, so went the thought of what that could mean, tucked underneath the success of her career, the giddiness of new love, the fact that drinking was just for fun.

She remembered how, in the beginning, Noel still had a flip phone. It had touched her heart to think of him having to tap the "8" button three times to get to the *V* just to type "very funny" in reply to something she said, rather than just "funny" when it was easier. Later he admitted he used "very" instead of "that's" because he couldn't use an apostrophe on the flip phone keyboard, as if she wasn't already stupid-deep in love.

But after the wedding, when they were living together, things looked different. Those blurry mornings became a thing of the past, at least the ones they had together. Too many mornings she woke with a pounding in her head, and a pounding in the closet as Noel slammed the dresser drawers. He'd come out with his jaw clenched and arms crossed as he stood next to the bed, and she would pray for the vomit to stay in her stomach. If she was honest, which she rarely was with herself, it was one of the reasons she encouraged him to take the night shift, to escape his judgment in the morning. By the time he got home, sometimes not until nine when he finished his paperwork and stopped at the gym, she would have applied her makeup and sucked down enough coffee to pass as a competent adult.

Then February happened, and she quit for good. She never told him about that night, only that the migraines had gotten too bad, she was sick of fighting those few extra pounds, she wondered if her sleep might improve. She hadn't been able to face telling him she had a real problem, and when Noel just nodded along, she assumed he couldn't face it either. She left a tire mark on the yard for god's sake, and he never mentioned it, just sprinkled handfuls of seed come spring.

She wondered, too, if maybe he was just too relieved to question it. He never gave her an ultimatum about her drinking, and she knew that in the early days he liked it when she drank. Her usually closed-off communication style opened up. She was always quick-witted, but more honest when she drank. Plus there was the drunk sex, which, if they hit it during the right window—after inhibitions but before sloppy—was fantastic.

But it had a cost, too: the days when she had to lie down in her campus office to get through the day; the few times they fought and Noel had to remind her of the terrible things she said; the one time at an anniversary party when she rudely made fun of another doctor's wife, thinking her voice was quieter than it was, and then apologized by insulting her further ("I didn't mean she shouldn't wear that dress because she's so fat, but because of her *hair*.").

Eventually, Noel stopped opening wine with dinner, or suggesting a quick drink at the Treasure Club, or bringing home growlers from new breweries, and Maris just drank by herself. And then February happened, and she realized he didn't necessarily want to know *why* she had quit as much as he just wanted her to stay sober. She swore after her divorce from Scott that she'd be more communicative if she ever married again, but it went against the image she grew up with: her parents had lived mostly separate lives. Her father always pickled with alcohol, her mother always drowning in her anger. Her dad at the bar on Saturday night, and her mom in the Lutheran church on Sunday.

There was the niggling question behind the drinking as well: maybe things hadn't been as great as she thought. Noel had told her early on one of the things he loved about her was her self-sufficiency. He loved that she made her own money (even though she was still paying off her crippling student debt), had a strong relationship with Cody's dad (it was easy to get along with someone eight hundred miles away), and was raising a smart, funny kid (no qualifiers there).

She bypassed talking to Noel about her struggles, assuming he just hadn't noticed his wife went from buying wine by the case to chewing gum any time she was awake. From lying awake most nights plagued by dehydration and a roiling heartbeat, to a solid five or six hours of sleep. Although half those nights, he was at the hospital while she slept. It seemed he was always at the hospital. While she made dinner and put the trash on the curb, while she scooped the walks in the winter. Even that time last February when she defrosted the bathroom pipes with a hair dryer during a blizzard after googling how to deal with another old-house problem. He loved that she was so self-sufficient, so what would happen if he realized she didn't have it all under control, not even close? She never doubted her love for him, but sometimes it felt like love wasn't enough. Sometimes she thought she'd trade the notion of love for the solidity of someone who was *there*.

And the irony, of course, was that today she hadn't been there for him.

She texted Noel a lame excuse about getting caught up in work and left the library with a sloshing bucket of guilt in her stomach. Was there any way drinking had been as hard and awful as not drinking, or had she just traded one problem for a worse one? When her thoughts turned in that direction, she'd relive flashes of that night in February, the look on Cody's face, and remember: nothing could be worse than that.

CHAPTER TWELVE

On the brisk walk home from the library, ribs aching, Maris silenced another call from Karen and listened back once she received the voice mail notification. "It's Karen again. Listen, Maris, I really need you to call me back. I had some similar cases after yours the day of your accident, and I'd like to talk to you about what happened beforehand. You mentioned something about memory, correct?"

Maris clicked out of the app, her pulse already at double time. Similar cases? What could that have to do with her? She wondered for a second if Karen meant other car accidents, but that didn't make any sense. Had Karen made the connection between Maris losing memories and the autonomic functions, and was she saying it had happened to other ER patients as well? It seemed ridiculous, unfathomable, and she filed it in the ever-fattening folder of things she'd deal with later.

By the time she arrived home, Noel was gone and Cody was in her room.

"Code?" Maris asked, knocking on her bedroom door. "You want to watch TV or something?" She knew she'd screwed up dinner with Noel but hoped Cody didn't mind too much, happy at least that she got pizza.

There was a long pause. "No thanks."

Maris both understood that Cody might be miffed, and was irritated she was. "Can you at least open the door and say hi?"

She remembered how rude she used to be to her parents at this age, always pushing the limit of what sass she could get away with. She knew it was developmentally on track for Cody to be pulling away, but at the same time, it aggravated her. Her parents had sucked, but she was trying. She had a career for god's sake, not a job, and wasn't that something Cody admired about her? With a jolt Maris realized that maybe her childhood had been her parents trying too.

There was a shuffling noise, and a moment later, Cody opened the door, never taking her hand off the knob, ready to shut it again.

"I'm sorry I missed dinner. I just have so much with work, plus I'm recovering from the accident," Maris justified, a sick feeling in her stomach, worried what her daughter was thinking. She couldn't help thinking, too, about that troubling voice mail from Karen.

Cody locked eyes with her mother. *What is she looking for?* Maris wondered.

"It just seems like before," Cody said. Maris knew "before" meant before February, back when she was still drinking. She had wanted for years to believe that her daughter didn't really realize when she'd had too much to drink. How many conversations had she lost over the years, or how many memories? She pinched the back of her hand, to feel the shame as a physical thing.

She leaned toward her daughter, and could almost taste her own adrenal sweat. Vinegary, like wine. "I'm not, Cody, I swear. Not a drop."

"It's fine," Cody said, and shut her door.

Fine wasn't the same as *I believe you.*

◆ ◆ ◆

Tuesday morning, Maris saw Cody off to school on her bike, placed her workbag and purse gingerly on her shoulder, grabbed her lunch, opened the driver's side door of Noel's Prius, slowly maneuvered into the driver's seat with a hand over her ribs, hovered her finger over the

"Start" button, and froze. She had been so concerned about recovering, it hadn't even occurred to her how dangerous it would be for her to drive with the possibility of a blackout.

Her breath came in shallow gasps as her hands started to shake. She grasped the steering wheel in hopes her hands would steady, sure that the force of them would rock the whole car.

Her eyes darted around the garage for three objects to catalog, the one calming tip she'd learned before abandoning yet another meditation app. She concentrated on the Ping-Pong ball hanging on a string from the ceiling, resting against the windshield. Her grandparents had hung one when she was a kid—a way to assure they wouldn't smash into the freezer or the lawn furniture—and it wasn't until many years later that Maris had realized they needed it because of how often her grandfather drove home drunk from the American Legion.

She hadn't blacked out since the accident, but all she could imagine was her mind going blank, her body shutting down, and coming to in a ball of fire with a corpse in front of her car, along with the terrible feeling she was paying the price for sins long ago, that the bill had finally come due.

She knew she had to call Karen, but first she had to figure out what to do about work.

In her five years at Glenn State, she'd only missed classes two times (could a real drunk say that?)—when her grandmother died, and when she herself came down with shingles—but there was no way she could make it to campus today. Even if she took a Lyft, the thought of standing in front of her students, her body once again collapsing, wasn't a risk she was willing to take. She'd worn a skirt today. What if, when she was going down, the skirt flipped up and showed her Spanx? As long as she'd been teaching, she'd been paranoid a gunman would come into her class, but rather than shooting her, he would make her strip down to her cotton bra and old-lady underwear, understanding somehow that this would be more awful for a woman. How was it women were made to feel that living was worse than death? Her terror filled the stuffy car, the smell from her armpits like an unwashed tongue. No. She could not go in today.

She dug like a raccoon in her purse and grabbed her phone. She opened Safari and the Glenn State website, where she looked up Tammy, her chair, in the directory. Tammy's page loaded, and there was a picture of her that must have been taken in the early aughts, her clothing already out of date and from the nineties. She wore a blocky blazer, her bangs secured to the side with two miniclips. Something about the out-of-date picture tugged at Maris's brain as she clicked on the number to call.

The Bluetooth connected to the car, radiating the impossibly loud ringing through speakers on all sides. When Tammy answered, Maris cleared her throat and told her chair in a shaky voice about the accident and how it had had more long-term effects than she had originally suspected. She was going to need some time off from her classes.

"How long are you thinking?" Tammy asked.

She tried to pick a number that would give her time to get her bearings, but not so much HR would have to be heavily involved. "Two weeks? Three?"

Tammy made a lot of noise sucking in a breath; she loved having you believe she was doing you a favor. Never mind that Maris had accrued months of sick time and had a contract that allowed for family medical leave. "You realize, I'm sure, that I can't just grant you a leave without some paperwork. There needs to be some kind of proof there's a problem." Maris assured her she'd take care of whatever she needed to and have the documents turned in on time.

"Since it's a relatively short time, I'll contact Jerry and see if he can cover your classes while he's on sabbatical. I know he and Martha aren't traveling right now."

Jerry Scanlon was in his early sixties but was the only other member in her department with a Twitter presence: 234 followers. She admired the work he was doing on the inherent racism and sexism in hiring practices (he was one of the votes for her tenure case, she was sure), but it was a fascinating topic he somehow made dull. Her students would be bored out of their minds, but what choice did she have? "Tell him I'd really appreciate it," she said.

"I will. And, Maris?" Tammy added. "I hope this won't further affect your tenure case."

CHAPTER THIRTEEN

Maris knew that if she wasn't going to work, she needed to figure out what was causing the blackouts—and fast. No more denial. No more hoping the course would correct itself. Her first task: text Karen.

She asked her if she'd be able to talk that afternoon before four, when she was supposed to get Cody from school. There was still the question of what she'd tell Noel about not teaching today, or how she'd pick up Cody if she couldn't drive, but those were problems for future Maris.

Almost immediately, the three rotating dots appeared on her phone. Yes. Absolutely. At hospital today but say when and I'll find the time.

Maris texted back 1:00 and headed over to talk to Eula about Hollis. She was hoping she might be able to tell her more about their research together, or that another tidbit might slip about his life in Cincinnati. If nothing else, she needed a way to pass the time before meeting Karen, the hours stretching before her. Maris wasn't a patient person at the best of times; it was one of the traits that made her such a successful drinker.

She rang the bell, and Eula pushed open the screen door a moment later with her elbow, rubber gloves on her hands. "Maris! So lovely to see you." She held it open and stepped out of the way. "How are you feeling?"

Maris told her everything was fine, ignoring the constant stitch in her side when she breathed in, the bruising still evident on her face.

"I don't want to take a lot of your time," Maris said, stepping into the foyer. "You look like you're in the middle of something."

"I'm making worm tea from worm castings," Eula explained as Maris followed her into the kitchen. "It's great for tomato plants." She placed a strainer over a five-gallon bucket and poured a smaller bucket of muddy water over the top, what looked like dirt catching in the strainer. She'd always had an impressive garden. Even this year, after Carl had died so unexpectedly last December, Eula had planted all her regular vegetables and flowers in the spring. Maris was impressed Eula had the energy to follow through, Maris's own spindly garden consisting of two dead planters in the backyard.

Maris peered in the dark and dank-smelling bucket. "I hope you don't drink it."

Eula laughed. "Not that kind of tea. So what can I do for you?"

"Actually, I was hoping I could talk to you a bit more about Hollis and the work he published with you and Carl."

Eula raised her eyebrows: *How'd you know about that?* "How much do you already understand? Neuroscience isn't exactly a hobby for most."

Maris had interviewed people across dozens of occupations over her time as a journalist and sociologist and was good at finding the digestible bits of research that explained a body of work to get herself up to speed. At the library, she'd read enough of Hollis's abstracts to understand that the bulk of his work was in the separation of neural oscillations, or the breaking down of thousands of neurons into smaller groupings to understand what specific pathways were responsible for.

She seesawed her hand back and forth. "I understand enough," Maris assured her, and gave an overview of what she knew. His work divided sensory, motor, and intersensory neurons by the millions in hopes of differentiating which neuron specifically identified the feel of a hot stove, or gave you the ability to move your hand from the burner, or the neurons communicating these messages all through the body so the hot burner would result in the moved hand. He was a leader in his field at assigning roles to neural clusters, and from there was attempting to differentiate into smaller and smaller batches the work of individual neurons.

Eula raised her eyebrows. "Impressive," she said as she held a plastic bottle under the strained water to fill it, screwed the sprayer on top, and rinsed it in the sink. "So what specifically are you interested in?"

"Was it his work or yours that brought Hollis to town?"

Eula admitted it was probably her more than Carl, but there was overlap across all three. "We shared some interests across neuroscience and engineering," Eula said, holding another bottle in the water. "I worked with Hollis back when he first moved here in the nineties, but didn't care for the way he treated me. Eventually I left my research behind and let Carl continue their partnership."

"What specifically was the overlap in your work?"

"Do you know what an RFID is?" Maris shook her head no. "It stands for radio-frequency identification. You probably know RFIDs as the microchips people put in their pets so they can identify them if they run away, but they're used for all kinds of things. There's one in your faculty parking pass so the gate's arm goes up when you pull into the lot. They're in the books you check out of the library nowadays that replaced the barcodes you used to scan."

"Sure," Maris said, and passed Eula another empty bottle. She knew from the many interviews she'd done that the best way to get information was to just let someone lumber along until they unwittingly said something you were looking for. She didn't know what RFIDs had to do with anything, but had faith Eula would connect this to Hollis's work.

"So with RFIDs you have three parts," Eula continued. "The microchip, the receiver, and the responder. The chip sends signals, or waves, to the receiver, which transfers them to the responder so they can send back what to do: identify Fido, raise the arm gate, check out the book. Carl's area was receivers, specifically parabolic dishes." Eula swept a hand in a valley like she was dusting the inside of a bowl. "They're the satellite dishes you used to see on people's roofs when cable TV first started, but they're used for all kinds of things: to collect solar energy, to boost Wi-Fi. These dishes are made to focus energy and receive signals, and they have to be incredibly precise. Not angel-on-the-head-of-a-pin precise, but looking-at-a-strand-of-the-angel's-hair precise."

"So you don't want to mess it up," Maris echoed.

"Yes, but that not-messing-up was what Carl worked on for decades. His entire career was built around perfecting these dishes to meet the most minuscule and precise of wavelengths from the greatest distance and with the smallest dish. It might not sound like the most exciting area of engineering, but it affects everything from the Hubble Space Telescope to that faculty parking pass, and his work revolutionized the field."

Maris cleared her throat; maybe she was on the wrong scent after all. "But how did that tie in to Hollis's work on neural oscillations other than they're both very, very precise?"

"Yes, well," Eula began. "I was the tie between them." After a long pause, Eula continued talking. "While I certainly respect the work Carl did, I was less of a meat-and-potatoes engineer than he was. I wasn't so much interested in perfecting a process already discovered, but in the theoretical side of biomedical engineering—what might be possible in connection to the human body. As I mentioned, for an RFID you need three pieces." She held up a finger. "An antenna or dish for receiving and transmitting the signal." A second finger went up. "A responder or server that the signal can land on." And the third finger. "And a circuit that stores and processes the information."

"The chip," Maris said, and Eula nodded. What little Maris did know about RFIDs, which she hadn't known the name of until today, was that there were already privacy concerns around the chips. She'd been in a Facebook moms' group that had conspiracies about what was being recorded, but when they turned out to be a bunch of anti-vaxxers,

Maris had quit the group. Still, she'd wondered sometimes as she was pulling into the parking lot, what other information was on those chips beyond "this car can park here." Her home address? Her phone number?

"Yes, the chip. But remember, it's not the chip itself that's important, but the circuit. Something that stores and processes information. Can you think what else that could be?" She looked expectantly at Maris.

"I—I don't know," Maris said.

"Think," Eula said. "It's clear you understand this better than most. What's the best information processor you know?"

Her first thought was a supercomputer, but the realization slowly dawned how this might connect to Hollis's work.

"Neural oscillations. The brain."

"Exactly. Carl thought it was ridiculous, but god bless him, he wasn't someone to see the possibilities. That was me, and it was another one of the reasons I never pursued an academic career. My theories were too revolutionary. Even those few articles I published with Hollis ended up panned by other scholars."

"So if someone wanted to test your theories about neural oscillations as the circuit in RFIDs, how would they go about it?"

"They'd start by breaking every ethical law there is." Eula laughed. "There's no way a review board would sign off on research like that. You'd basically be mucking through someone's brain trying to figure out what the connections did."

"And that's possible?"

"No one's tested my theories," Eula reiterated as she winked at Maris. "But for the record, that doesn't mean I wasn't right."

CHAPTER FOURTEEN

After Eula's, Maris grabbed a granola bar for lunch then killed time at the library, anxious for her meeting with Karen. It was odd going to the hospital in the middle of the day. She was used to the late-night rush when she would bring Noel dinner in the ER after they were first married—chicken salad from Savory's, or a greasy bag from Five Guys—and there would be the constant chaos of shouting, monitors, and running feet. She'd loved seeing him in his element, focused and calm, just the presence she'd always needed. Once they had a slap and tickle in the chapel of all places, but nothing past second base. Those had been the early days, before she told him she had too much work to do and would stay home and get drunk. Sometimes it surprised Maris they'd been together so few years given the distance they'd allowed to grow between them.

Maris tipped her Lyft driver on the app and stepped inside. The air in the hospital had that repurposed smell, overly sanitized and covering up something that smelled much worse. On the fourth floor, she found a bleary Karen in her office, a cup of coffee in her hand. The office was surprisingly small given her clout as a doctor. When Maris was little, she would have guessed doctors had spacious mahogany desks and a view, but in reality, Karen had an overstuffed space with two chairs, a desk, and an old green floral couch that looked like it had seen a lot of naps between rounds. There was a cross-stitched pillow of Michelle Obama flattened at one end. Maris felt a pang; Cody would love that pillow.

Karen sat at the metal desk, a pile of files teetering at the edge with a shorter stack in front of her. Maris knocked a knuckle against the doorframe, and Karen looked up, a grim smile on her face. "Thanks for coming," she said. She had that rumpled doctor look Maris knew all too well from Noel and his own long shifts.

She assured Karen it was no problem and sat down on the couch, moving Michelle Obama into her lap.

"So," Karen said as she got up and closed her office door, making the small room even more confining, then took her seat again. "Before I begin, I'm going to ask that you not share any of this with Noel."

Maris started. She wasn't sure what Karen was going to tell her about whatever odd thing had happened in the ER the day of her accident, but she hadn't expected it to be something she would have to hide from Noel. If anything, she had hoped Karen would provide answers she could actually share. "Why not?"

Karen took a long drink of her coffee, and Maris could tell by the way she gulped it down it had gone cold. "What I'm going to tell you isn't exactly a HIPAA violation because I'm not going to give you any names, but let's just say I'm skating up against it." *What in the hell?* "And in case you're wondering," Karen continued, "I haven't told Julie anything about this either." Julie was her wife. "I haven't told anyone, actually, because I wanted to talk to you first, since you're the other one I know."

"The one what?" Maris asked.

Karen leaned across her desk and lowered her voice, and Maris was suddenly very glad the door was shut. "After I treated you last Friday, three more women came in with similar issues. Their autonomic functions had shut down—breathing, heart rate, all of it—and they collapsed. And none of them could remember what had happened right before."

"But you said that was normal," Maris reminded her, and Karen shook her head, pausing as another doctor was paged over the speaker system.

"They didn't all have accidents, so there was no preceding event that would have affected their memories. One was quite young—early twenties—and she luckily was lying in bed when it happened, but was freaked out enough given her health and age that she came in. One collapsed in the kitchen, but she also works at the hospital and so had enough sense to come in."

"And the other? The third?"

"She ended up two doors down from you in the ER. She fell at work and sprained her ankle going down, so her employer insisted she come in and have it looked at."

"And none of them could remember anything before it happened?" It had to be a coincidence. Surely they couldn't have experienced the same blackouts Maris did.

Karen shook her head no. "And the woman who works here? I know her, so I asked her a bit more about what's going on, and she said she's been having memory issues for some time now. Since September, actually." Maris tried not to blanch; September was when her troubles started as well. "She said she's been having these memory lapses. Sometimes she'll lose a minute, and sometimes she'll lose an hour or so." Maris took a deep breath in, a deep breath out. "At first she thought it might be related to aging—she's in her early sixties—but these weren't issues with regular memory retrieval. And she wasn't just losing random details, but *chunks*." Karen took another sip of her coffee, lining her naked mouth up with the old lipstick print. "Four women in the ER with autonomic function shutdown," Karen continued, tapping the file folder in front of her. "There's no way it could be a coincidence." Maris thought of the gut tickle she'd get when she was onto something in an article, that special feeling that things were connected or important. Karen obviously got it too. Another announcement came over the loudspeaker, and Karen paused, then leaned back in her desk chair. "So can you tell me what's going on?"

Maris considered bolting right then. She had worked for years to build walls around her vulnerability, so the thought of telling someone the crazy and unexplainable things that had been going on made her skin feel wobbly. In a way it would have been easier if Karen were a stranger, like all those times she'd told secrets at bars back in her twenties, no repercussions because the person didn't know her. But Karen was a doctor, and unlike Noel, not one she was married to. If she wanted some answers, she had to give at least a little.

Maris took a big breath and did her best to capture the experiences she'd been having: blank spots in her memory, like a film strip that had been sliced and put back together, and the smaller blips that seemed to happen more frequently. "For the most part, there doesn't seem to be much difference between the awake me and the blacked-out one, until last week when my whole body seemed to shut down, not just the memory, and I had the car accident." She remembered the stripe of panic that shot through her body as she gasped awake in the ambulance.

Karen nodded, as if that's what she had suspected.

Maris let out a shuddering breath, salt piercing her eyes. "I thought I'd done some long-term damage with alcohol. Mind you, my drinking wasn't that bad. I could make it to classes, take care of my family"—she wouldn't think about February—"and I haven't had a drink in eight months, but then when this started, I felt like it was my due. Like I finally had to pay for all those years of drinking."

"I'm sure that was terrifying," Karen said, and the sympathy in her voice made Maris burst into tears.

Maris's body nearly collapsed in on itself with relief—her head in the pillow, a slump to her shoulders, her butt nearly sliding off the sofa. She hadn't realized the stress, the absolute weight, of carrying around her own secret alone for over a month. But still, who was to say she could trust Karen?

She shook her head and tried to compose herself. "How do I know you haven't just made up these other cases and said they mimicked my own?"

Karen's eyebrows crumpled in confusion. "Why would I do that?"

"Okay, then tell me their names." If Maris could talk to the sources, she could confirm the truth on her own.

Karen glanced at the file on her desk and then quickly back up. "You know I can't do that, Maris. You're married to a doctor. It's a HIPAA violation."

"But how am I—"

"You're going to have to trust me."

Another page came over the speaker system, this one for Dr. Patel needed in Emergency. "I'm sorry, but I have to go," Karen said. "I'm supposed to be on rounds."

"Just first names," Maris begged as Karen crossed the small office to put on the white coat she'd hung on the hook on the door back. As her hand caught on the sleeve and she took it off to readjust, Maris grabbed the top file and shoved it in her bag, her heart racing.

Karen adjusted her collar and turned around. "I'm sorry," she said. "I can't violate their privacy that way," she reiterated, and Maris nodded and said she understood.

"I'll let you know as I figure more out," Karen said, and tucked a Kit Kat in her jacket pocket. "And I know you understand this, Maris, but this is serious. I'm not sure what's going on, but I don't think it's natural."

Maris's hands itched over her purse and the stolen file as she followed Karen out and they said their goodbyes, promising to stay in touch with new information. As soon as Karen entered the stairwell, Maris bolted to the bathroom, slamming the door to the second stall and scrabbling in her bag for the file.

She flipped through the first two patients and stopped cold as she read the third name: Janice Lambert.

Chapter Fifteen

Maris jumped out of the Lyft and ran to the double doors of Horace Valley, her broken ribs throbbing. The usual secretary was there in her high-waisted jeans with a smile that faded as she buzzed Maris in and saw the distressed look on her face.

"I'm here to see Janice," she said, and scurried past. She'd texted Janice from the hospital bathroom and told her she needed to talk ASAP. I know about what's happening, she'd written, despite all of Karen's warnings about confidentiality.

Come to school. Can talk between classes, Janice wrote back.

It was a few minutes before the bell when Maris reached Janice's office, her heart racing to catch up to her stuttering mind. Behind the shock of what she'd learned was the staggering relief that maybe she hadn't brought this on herself. If someone as pious as *Janice* could get blackouts, they couldn't be related to her drinking.

The classroom doors opened one after the other as kids filed into the hallway, a line forming at the drinking fountain. She glanced around, hoping to see Cody, or maybe hoping not to: she didn't know how she would explain why she was here. Janice rounded the corner with a stack of files and a textbook on computer programming, a boot cast on her leg and a pinched look on her face. Her eyes landed on Maris, and Maris remembered that Karen had said the other woman had sprained her ankle in the fall.

Janice unlocked her office and bumped the door open with her hip, dropping the files on her desk before collapsing in her chair. "So what do you think you know about?"

"The blackouts," Maris said, holding her bruised side, and watched the color drain from Janice's face. She moved the hand to her chest. "I'm having them too." She explained what had happened—when they started, the frequency—culminating in her trip to the ER. "Turns out we were neighbors," she said. "You were two doors down." Janice collapsed her head on her desk and took a deep breath. "Can you tell me what's happened?"

After a long moment, Janice sat up. She relayed her own version, with the first incident taking place in August, earlier than Maris's. She went to her GP after the second one, but all tests were inconclusive. "Honestly? I was too scared to look into it any further. Each time I convinced myself it was a fluke, until this past one." The words and logic sounded so familiar, Maris flinched. How many women had talked themselves out of trusting their own bodies?

Janice sat up straighter, wincing as she knocked her boot against the desk. "Is this related to our girls?"

"I don't think so," Maris said, and pulled the stolen file from her purse. She'd had time to think about this on the ride over—the heart-pounding worst-case scenario of this being tied to her daughter, and she didn't think so. "There are others," she said, and looked at their histories. "One is in her twenties, and the other is near retirement, so they wouldn't have kids the same age as ours."

"Where'd you get that?" Janice asked, and she admitted to stealing it from the hospital. "So you stole confidential information?" she asked, and Maris almost laughed at the absurdity.

"Something is *happening* to us. Don't you understand? Something that seems deliberate. I don't think a stolen file is our biggest concern right now." Maris felt like someone had told her the earth was flat, then strapped her in and sent her flying over the edge. What did this all mean? She tried to silence her hysteria. "And our daughters are friends, but it's not like we get coffee or go for mani-pedis together."

"And you're sure it's not about the girls?" Janice said.

Maris thought about it. "The best I can say is I hope not."

"Assuming something is really going on—"

"Assuming?" Maris's mouth hung open. "Janice, it's happening to *you*. You're having the blackouts."

"I'm sure there's some kind of explanation—"

There was nothing like someone else's denial to wake you up to your own, Maris thought. "There *is* an explanation," Maris agreed, "and we're going to find out what it is." She rolodexed through who she had in their corner. Karen would surely be upset she'd stolen the file, but she could deal with her down the road. Eula obviously had more than a passing understanding of how the brain worked and could be a resource.

Noel? She would tell him everything when she got home, she promised herself.

She asked Janice what she'd been doing since the first blackout to gather information, but beyond the one appointment with her GP, nothing.

Maris wanted to ask when that had ever helped solve a problem but almost laughed at her own hypocrisy. "Can you think of anyone who might want to target you for something? Any enemies?" As she said the word, her mind flashed instantly to Hollis Grant—the man who was set on blocking her tenure. He was a scientist as well, with a specialty in neural capacities; that couldn't be a coincidence. Certainly she felt he was out to get her, but she had assumed it was just that he didn't like her work, or thought she was silly, or saw her as a stand-in for all the women who let him down. She hadn't really believed he wanted to *hurt* her.

Janice started to say something, then stopped and shook her head no.

"Are you sure?" Maris pushed.

"Yes," Janice said, her voice resolute. Maris wasn't willing yet to share Hollis's name—she wanted to investigate herself—and realized Janice might feel the same. Who was she thinking of right now?

The bell sounded for the next class, and Maris stood to leave.

"Thank you," Janice said. "I can't tell you how unhinged I've felt since this started. I keep waiting for the other shoe to drop. Only it's not a shoe, it's my life."

Maris put a hand over Janice's and squeezed. "Trust me. I understand."

Janice picked up her textbook and water bottle as the warning bell rang and hobbled into the hall.

Maris said her goodbye and turned, running head-on into Cody.

CHAPTER SIXTEEN

Pain flashed through Maris's side as she steadied her hands on her daughter's shoulders to keep from falling. Cody held her algebra binder and book tight to her chest. "What are you doing here?" she asked.

Janice responded, "Semester projects" just as Maris said, "Parent-teacher conference."

"I'll leave this for you," Janice said, and smiled wanly at Maris as she scurried with her boot cast to class.

The halls had a final long blast of noise as students dashed to their rooms, dropped their books, and scooted chairs closer to their friends. Doors slammed up and down the hallway, and Maris and Cody were alone.

Cody looked suspiciously at her mom. "What's going on?" she asked, and *oh boy* could that mean a lot of different things.

"What do you mean?"

"What's going on with you?" She ticked her research off on her fingers just like Maris did when providing evidence. "You show up at school. You don't show up at school. You were in an accident. You're forgetting conversations. You're distracted all the time. Plus"—she held up the other hand, squeezing her books against her chest with her forearm as she held up the sixth finger—"you and Noel seem weird."

Maris blinked; she hadn't realized it had been that obvious, but of course her attentive, smart kid would have picked up on everything.

Was she talking since the blackouts, or further back than that? Had she noticed how little as a family they seemed to laugh anymore, or the anger Noel held before she quit drinking? Or what about the anger Maris herself held after she quit and the growing distance between them?

"Cody, I—" But what could she say? It wasn't like she could tell her daughter about the blackouts, or that it was happening to her best friend's mom as well. What could be more terrifying than knowing your mother's life was in danger? She tried instead to concentrate on the issue at hand. "This is some tension between me and Noel, Code. It's not about you."

Cody guffawed from her diaphragm, her face contouring with anger, and the sound echoed through the cavernous hallway. "It's not *about* me? It affects me. It has *always* affected me."

Maris felt a sick lurch. "What do you mean?"

Cody squeezed herself tighter, her head bowed. It was like she was getting smaller, younger, in front of Maris's eyes. "It's because of your drinking, isn't it?" she whispered.

Maris shook her head, aware of her bruised face. "No. It's not. I haven't had a drink in months." Even the admission of her abstinence made her feel sick, because with the abstinence came the admission of the problem.

Cody shook her head, tears now pooling in her eyes. She looked like she had that night back in February, when Maris had shown up drunk at the Lamberts' apartment, car keys in her hand. "I don't believe you," Cody said.

The reaction tore out Maris's heart—she'd never wanted to see her daughter look like that again—but at the same time, it sent a flame of anger up her spine. For years she'd been able to sidestep the truth with half-truths that covered her drinking, and now that she told the *actual* truth, she was like the drunk who cried wolf. "I don't know how to convince you. Do you want to smell my breath? Look in the recycling?

Check the credit card statement?" These were not things to yell at her child!

"What I want," Cody said, her voice rising again, "is to be able to believe my mom!" They had never been a screaming family. Cody had her share of tantrums as a small child, and she'd watched Noel and her mother fight, but Maris could count on one hand the number of times she and Noel had raised their voices with each other in anger, and couldn't think of a time Cody had since she'd outgrown that mode of communication. Cody swiped at the tears on her face. Her daughter wasn't a crier, she thought instantly, but who said people had to stay the same? Who said they couldn't grow?

"I want to go stay with Dad for a while," Cody said, her voice quieter.

Maris blanched. "He was a bigger drinker than me!"

"Was," Cody said, "and that was years ago." She was right. Maris was running on memories of a Scott that didn't exist anymore. She'd looked at him as a rock-bottom case, not recognizing he'd spent the last decade of his life growing into a new person. Scott had been adamant about being honest with Cody and his membership in AA since she was nine and started asking why he didn't have wine with every meal like Mom.

"But I believe him when he says he's not drinking. He doesn't forget all the shit going on in my life, or try to fake his way through a conversation over dinner, or try to drive me home from my friend's house while drunk."

Maris felt like she'd been slapped as every fear she had of Cody's resentment of her hit home.

That Saturday in February, the one that finally pushed her to stop drinking, had been like hundreds before when nothing bad happened. She'd spent that afternoon attempting to work, her attention divided between an article, helping Noel install a ceiling fan in their bedroom, tracking down cardboard and glue sticks for Cody's school project—"Mom, can I also have a snack?"—and flipping laundry into the dryer, the sheets overdue for a wash.

It was like so many Saturdays: her waiting out the clock for Noel to head to work and Cody to Lynette's for the night so she could get some actual work done. Yet as soon as they'd left, twelve hours alone stretching in front of her, Maris had poured a glass of wine to drink while staring into the fridge, deciding what to eat for dinner. She had so much work to do, but didn't she also deserve a little downtime? Weren't people always talking about self-care? She had topped off her glass while the oven preheated, swearing she'd get to work while she ate, but then there was another glass with her first slice of frozen pizza. And a glass with her second, and then just a glass and a glass and a glass.

By eight thirty that night, Maris was drunk. And when her phone rang and she looked down to see Janice Lambert's name, she knew she had to pick up. What if something had happened to Cody? She took extra care with her voice, making sure not to slur, although what resulted was a thick, cotton-mouthed drawl that gave away how hard she was trying.

Janice told her Lynette had thrown up and it was clear the sleepover was canceled. Could she come pick Cody up? Maris scrambled for another option, visualizing the slow-moving cogs of her brain. Could Cody sleep on the couch and wait until morning? But she heard the suspicion in Janice's voice about why Maris was asking.

She slipped off her flannel pants, bumping a shoulder against the wall as she did, and pulled on a pair of jeans. In the bathroom she slicked her hair and wiped off the mascara that had smeared under her eyes. She squirted Visine and gargled mouthwash. She convinced herself this was what a sober person looked like, never mind the slack mouth, the heavy lids, the utter lack of personality in her face. In her car, she tilted her chin down and listened to the blood thrumming through her body. *Sober, sober, sober,* she thought in rhythm. How many times had she ridden in the back seat of her parents' car with her dad in the driver's seat, one eye squinted shut, the radio blaring? She and her friends from small towns used to swap these stories back in college—all their parents had behaved that way—and her memories had garnered the rosy glow of nostalgia, but had that always been the case? As a child had she laughed watching her father's head tilt toward the window on his thick neck, or had fear zipped through her body? Her mother hadn't been a big drinker; why hadn't *she* driven?

◆ ◆ ◆

In hindsight, this would be one of the moments Maris would play over and over on the shame screen in her mind. If she'd made a different choice, given a better excuse, or even just said, *I shouldn't be driving*. At that point, had she really done anything wrong? Alcohol wasn't illegal. She even could have sent a Lyft, but Cody was only thirteen and hadn't ridden in one alone. It seemed like bad parenting to have her climb in a strange car at night by herself for the first time, even with Janice there to suss out the driver. How had she not weighed that as the lesser of two evils?

But that night in February, rather than think about all that, or even about Cody, the thought that screamed in her mind was: I can't let Janice think I have a drinking problem. One of her greatest shames would be that she was more concerned about looking like a terrible mother than being one.

Her daughter was right. Maris was a terrible parent, her father the reliable one. At different points, Maris had thought about calling Scott to talk about her drinking, thinking he'd be a sympathetic ear due to his own problems, but what if he wasn't? What if, after climbing out of that hole himself, he saw her in there and kicked in the dirt? She'd been the one to ask for the divorce. The one to move across the country with his daughter when he was early in recovery. Maybe his answer would be, "Screw you. And by the way, I'm taking back our kid."

But what choice do I have now? she thought, standing there in the hallway. Cody was correct that her mother hadn't been there for her lately, just not for the reasons she thought. Maybe she would be better off in Nebraska, out of harm's way.

"We can talk to him," Maris said calmly, and Cody took a stumbling step back in full fury now.

"You don't even want me here!" she cried, her mouth convulsing with anger and hurt.

"Cody, that's not true, it's not—"

"Everything okay here?" the teacher in the closest classroom, Ms. Neises, asked, sticking her head out into the hallway.

Maris said it was fine, and Ms. Neises looked pointedly at Cody.

"I'm late for class," Cody muttered to her mother, and darted down the hall.

Maris heard the slam of her daughter's door.

She took four deep breaths—in and out—and tried to figure out what to do. Should she contact Scott? Talk to Cody?

What if she really was losing her mind? And yet hadn't she been giving it away for free for years? Sip by sip, cell by cell. Like a gun in her mouth with the most delicious trigger.

CHAPTER SEVENTEEN

On the way home, in the back of her Lyft, the old grooves lit up, the ones that told Maris to get the wine. She felt the need for a drink slide through every vein in her body, pulsing just under the skin. One of the seductive traits of drinking was how it allowed you to hold your problems at bay. All emotions, really. Fear, terror, helplessness. With enough wine, she wouldn't have to feel anything—including her bruised face and battered body. She'd feel nothing but the cold glass in her hand, the vinegar wash in her throat. That dull throb of delicious heat and blankness spreading through her body.

Noel's car was still in the driveway when she got home, and there was a Best Buy package the size of a shoebox waiting on the stoop. Maris was thankful the doorbell hadn't woken her husband up so she'd have to explain. This was still the evidence-gathering stage. She didn't want to present her case until she had her ducks in a row, until she could lay it out in front of him and say, *See? How dare you doubt me*. She'd install the camera, talk to Eula again, do more research on the brain, look into the other women, and *then* talk to Noel. She felt the soothing balm of a to-do list forming in her head, a plan taking place.

She shoved the camera box and receipt deep in the garbage outside, then read through the directions and peered around the living room. Could she put it on the bookshelf around the fireplace? On the mantel? Above the door? How often did Noel really notice the decor in their house? Or Cody for that matter? Like most people, they had their necks cranked down looking at their phones, and as long as it wasn't in the view of the TV, she told herself, they'd be fine.

She inserted the batteries in the back and pressed the button until it flashed green, then hauled the step stool out from behind the kitchen door and set it in front of the tallest bookshelf, pausing for just a second before climbing. What if she blacked out right now? she wondered, but she had to take the risk. Her ribs throbbed as she climbed the two steps, a hand against her side to hold the bones in place, then set the camera on the top shelf next to a porcelain bird and a black iron bookend.

She downloaded the app on her phone and opened the live video. The camera was shooting toward the crown molding, so she reached up, wincing, and adjusted the lens, keeping an eye on the app until she saw the couch in plain view. She scooted the camera farther to the right. Off the stool, she walked to the other side of the room, and turned around as quickly as she could given her injuries. Would she notice it if she didn't know to look? The camera seemed somewhat innocuous, and she thought she'd get away with it, but what if she didn't? What would be her excuse if Noel caught her? Maris shook her head. One lie at a time.

After installing the camera, she heard Noel stirring upstairs. She quickly packed her bag for the library and scrawled a note and stuck it to the fridge. Maris didn't want to admit it, but she wanted to be gone when Noel woke up, her mind swimming with thoughts she wasn't able to share with him yet. A glance at her watch told her Cody would be home soon, and then she remembered with a sickening feeling she was supposed to pick her daughter up from school. She texted Cody and asked if she could get a ride with a friend, and Cody texted a curt K back. She didn't know how to tell Cody she wanted nothing more in the world than for her to stay, but it would be safer if she went to Nebraska. How could she say those words without saying the impossible ones?

Karen texted while Maris was en route. **Did you take it???** the first said. **I could be fired!!!** And the third: **CALL ME.** She felt a spike of guilt as she deleted the message, but her world felt like it was on shifting sand, ready to sink. She needed the solid comfort of answers no matter the cost.

Settled at her favorite table on the second floor of the library, the one surrounded on three sides by windows and natural light, she opened her laptop and started her deep dive on the other two women in the folder: Shelby Steele and Beverly Halberg. The others in this strange sisterhood who knew the absolute terror with which Maris had been living.

Shelby had graduated from Glenn State two years ago. The university website said she'd been a mathematics major, so no connection to Maris directly, but she wondered if she'd had her in an Intro to Sociology course. She combed her brain for the name, but after a while, all students blended together—the Shelbys with the Kaitlyns with the Erikas. She made a note, though: a student at her own university had to be more than coincidence.

Beverly Halberg was on Miami Regional's website: the director of the Women's Center. She had a friendly grandma face and wore a statement necklace, and she looked as generic to a different demographic as Shelby's name sounded. It was possible she'd met Bev at a hospital function or party—maybe the very one where she'd insulted another wife's hair and weight—but didn't remember it.

Noel texted and asked how her first class back went. Anxiety like a bird in her chest, she started thinking how her life had been so much less complicated when she drank. There were blackouts, sure, but wasn't she in control of them? Wasn't she the one to determine when they'd occurred? Now there was an unknown entity, a threat, in charge of what she was allowed to know about her own life.

She typed and deleted a few different options to Noel: I requested a medical leave . . . Too scared to drive . . . I think we need to talk. She went so far as to close out of the text altogether and pull up his contact in the phone app, but as with everything, what could she say? How do you start to tell the truth? Eventually, she switched back to the message app and typed Great!, and like that, she had another secret from her husband. She knew the secrets were building, brick by brick, like a wall between them, but it seemed easier to let another pile on top. She was the one who dealt directly with the medical insurance over email. He never had to know about the leave.

She dug a little further into the two women, but found little other than a few articles Beverly had written on women's health care and recognition from the Dayton Women's Association highlighting her career. There was surprisingly little social media for Shelby—a deactivated Facebook account and an inactive Twitter—but she found a six-year-old high school graduation announcement for a school about an hour away.

On a hunch, she looked for connections between the women and Hollis Grant. Two things were clear: he didn't like her, and he understood the brain. And while logically she couldn't see a direct connection between A and B, her research method had always been to leave no stone unturned.

Shelby had taken a class with Hollis before switching her major from premed to mathematics, and there was a benefit for Ohio Sciences and Humanities in 2011 that had honored both Beverly Halberg's work in the Women's Center and Hollis's work in neural oscillation separation, but both of those connections seemed flimsy at best. Still, they were something.

Digging through the Glenn State website looking for club information or connections to Shelby, she found Tammy's outdated photo on their department page and, ever vain, clicked on her own name to see how the picture Tammy had taken a month or so ago had turned out. She was surprised to see it was the same pic that had been up since her first week on campus five years ago—the eager smile, a professional blouse with a jean jacket, those teal-and-pink-striped earrings so students could tell she'd be fun. She'd been so young then, she thought now. So full of professorial promise.

Maris slowly became conscious someone was watching her, partly attuned to the embarrassment of looking herself up online.

Two teenage girls were walking toward the YA section, both wearing the same kind of high-tops Cody wore. There was an elderly man in a wingback chair to the left fighting off a nap. And to her right, the young woman from office hours with thick makeup and black hair stared back at her.

Maris jolted as their eyes locked, surprised when the woman didn't look away. *Was* she a former student? For a crazy second she thought it might be Shelby Steele, the student she was looking up, but Shelby had brunette hair and healthy skin, while this woman was pale and gaunt.

"Are you following me?" Maris asked.

"Yes," the woman said, and slid into the seat across from her. "And I have a favor to ask."

CHAPTER EIGHTEEN

Maris scrambled to remember the details of what she'd talked about with the mysterious woman during her office hours. It had been about Dylan Charter, and the conversation had left her uneasy, although talking about her work was usually one of her favorite pastimes. She remembered the claustrophobic feel of her office as the woman had closed the door, the fight to get air in her throat. She had the same zap of unease now but willed herself to stay calm and not give away her surprise.

"What kind of favor?" Maris asked.

"I want you to write another article," she said. "Saying Dylan Charter raped another girl."

Maris did her best to keep her face from betraying her; she'd been wrong a moment ago when she'd thought she could contain her surprise. She had expected the woman might ask her to write another strongly worded article about Dylan's early release, but not *this*. "Why?"

"Because he's a rapist and deserves to be in jail," she said simply. "Four months for ruining that woman's life? It's a joke. You said yourself it wasn't fair. And there's no way she was the only one, so it's not like you'd be accusing him of something he didn't do, or won't do again."

"I can't just write whatever I want and expect people to believe me," Maris said incredulously. "I have my reputation to think about. Plus there are fact-checkers, legal issues. The police would be involved. There would need to be a victim to corroborate the story."

The woman waved her hand like that was no big deal. "You wouldn't need to name names, just put the idea out there. Raise the question of whether he'd done it more than once."

Maris switched tactics. "Why would I do that?"

"Because he's a monster?"

"There are plenty of monsters out there." Even as she said it, she knew the woman understood that. She looked young enough to be in her late teens, but had the hollow look of a woman whose life had been ruined by someone else. "And why is this so important to you?"

The woman picked at her cuticles until her thumb bled. It was a habit Cody had developed since she started middle school and the social pressures kicked in. She remembered now that the woman had brought up Cody in her office. She'd pointed out that her daughter was loose on the same streets as a rapist, and that saying so had felt like a threat disguised as a warning. It reminded her of when she was single and men would offer to walk her home from the bar, saying, *You never know what kind of dangers are out there, but you'll be safe with me.*

"Do you know him?" Maris asked. "Dylan Charter?" The tight feeling in her chest was returning, only this time it didn't feel like claustrophobia but cooking alive. The blinding sun streamed in the library's large windows like a heat wave. She moved her arm out of the band of light as if it might burn her.

"It's what he deserves," the woman said. "As bad as you've said he is, he's worse."

"It's not that easy to accuse someone of a false crime. You need evidence, and—"

"It *won't* be a false crime," the woman insisted. "I mean, look at him!"

"I—" Maris started, then stopped. Fact was, she agreed with the woman. She'd been outraged when he was sentenced to only six months for a rape that had happened with witnesses, and she'd been incensed all over again when he was released after four, but what could she do? The legal system, with all its flaws, was the system they had. She'd gone on CNN and MSNBC to discuss the case and its outcome, hoping to raise discussion for future cases, but what was done was done.

"Four *months*?" the woman said, and the librarian at the help desk looked in their direction. She raised her eyebrows at Maris, a regular at the library, and Maris gave her a subtle shake of her head: *I'm fine.*

The woman leaned forward, and Maris instinctually pushed back, blinded temporarily by the sun. "What happened to full stop, huh?" the woman said, referencing again Maris's article, "Dylan Charter Needs to Be Held Accountable Full Stop." "What happened to accountability?"

Maybe this woman was right; maybe Maris had gotten too lax on her stances. She thought about the op-ed she'd drafted about Dylan's easy return to regular life, and wondered if she needed to reframe it. Not around how easy he had it, but around the women who were sick of that ease. But who would her source be? This woman hiding behind a wig with her bloody thumb? Maris couldn't risk the credibility. Also, as much as she hated to say it, she had to admit, "He served his time. What's done is done."

"What about what *he's* done?" the woman said, and pushed her chair away from the table, shaking her head in disgust, the black hair slipping too low on her forehead. Maris was sure it was a wig now, positive, but why? Who was this woman?

"You're not going to do shit, are you?" the woman asked.

"I can't. I'm sorry."

The woman narrowed her eyes. "Yeah, well, a lot of people are going to be sorry someday."

◆　◆　◆

Rattled, Maris left the library and walked briskly, her laptop slapping against her hip with each step, another bruise forming. She found Noel in the kitchen making coffee when she got home. He was dressed in scrubs, his handsome face speckled with five-o'clock shadow. She remembered what a relief it had been to come home that day after first meeting the woman on campus, how he had agreed how weird it was. She opened her mouth to tell him about it as he turned around, a dark look on his face. She did a quick rewind of her day and was sure she hadn't had a blackout, so why did he look so upset?

"What's going on, Mare?" he asked, and she wondered for just a second if he'd found the camera.

"What? Nothing, I—"

"Are you drinking?"

She almost laughed. To be accused when she hadn't been filled her with righteous indignation. "Why would you think that? I told you I haven't been. Eight months. You want to order another toxicology test?" She refused to think how many times she would have come close to failing just that test. It was always just a split-second bad decision away.

He slammed his coffee cup down on the granite countertop, and she was surprised to see he had as much emotion as she did just under the surface. "I want you to talk to me and tell me what's going on."

"What are you even talking about?" she said. "I just went to the library. I left you a note."

He snorted in disgust. "You snuck out of here when you heard me get up," he said, throwing up his hand. "I saw you scurry away out the window." He tucked his shoulders up and hunched down like some kind of troll.

"I just—" She replayed the bad moment she left but also the moment she came home, excited to share with him something genuine from her day. *The weird girl! Remember when we bonded over that!*

He rolled his eyes and took a step toward the living room, and she realized she hadn't denied it.

"Noel, wait," she said, and grabbed his arm, and god bless him, he did. He stood in the doorway to the kitchen with his broad shoulders and big heart and waited for her to explain away all that was going on, but where to start?

"Are you having an affair?" he asked. "Is that it?"

She winced at the thought. "Of course not."

"Of course not," he repeated. "Because that would be ridiculous. Maris, just tell me what's going on," he said imploringly, but what could she say?

"Noel, listen—" she started, and Noel barked out a bitter laugh.

"Listen to what? More lies? Jesus, Maris, you've been acting weird for weeks—longer than that, if I'm being honest—and now—" He paused. "Does this have something to do with the ER? Something about your accident?" She didn't say anything, her breath catching as she thought, *Maybe he will figure it out.* She felt a spark of hope, of cautious optimism. He was a doctor; maybe he'd figure it out.

"Yes," Maris admitted, and even in that small truth-telling she felt her pulse start to calm. Maybe this was salvageable. Maybe that was how you told the truth: one word at a time.

Noel rubbed a hand down his face from forehead to chin. "You haven't even asked about Cody," he said, and another layer of guilt weighed on Maris's shoulders. "She texted me and asked me to pick her up at school. I dropped her at Lynette's for the night even though it's a school night." Maris's eyes widened. Was she safe at the Lamberts'? About as safe as here, she figured. "I thought you could use a night to yourself," he continued. "A night to think some things through." She wasn't exactly sure what he meant by that, but before she could ask, he kept going. "Aren't you curious why Cody wanted me to pick her up? What she had to say?"

Maris felt her stomach tighten. "What?"

"That you want her to move back to Nebraska."

Maris almost laughed, it was so ridiculous. "That's not at all what I said." Was that really what Cody had heard, that she wanted her to move away? My god, she wanted nothing so badly in this world as to keep her daughter safe. The car accident, the connection to Janice. She felt like everything was about to collide in the dark, and she couldn't see how.

"Then what *did* you say?" Noel asked.

She explained the conversation, and how Cody had mentioned temporarily moving in with her father and Maris thought it might not be the worst thing in the world. *Temporarily.*

Noel shook his head. "It doesn't make any sense. That kid is your *life*. There's no way you'd just let her move away if you were acting like yourself." Noel threw up his empty hand. "If it's not the drinking, then what is it?"

Her head spun through the options: The blackouts? Her body shutting down? The camera in the living room? Her secrets had snowballed so quickly. It had been one thing to keep secrets when they seemed small unto themselves, and were just thoughts, not actions—*at this very moment I want to drink, and at this moment too*—but now? It was why she never skipped her runs: the snowball effect. Next thing she knew, she'd never leave the couch again.

"Fine," Noel said, and Maris realized too much time had ticked past, her window closed. "But I'm not going to wait for the truth forever."

Chapter Nineteen

I sat outside Dylan's house, my hands gripping the steering wheel, willing myself to get out. His large ranch was over two thousand square feet, and this was the *guesthouse*. His parents lived in the front house, a brick behemoth I'd looked up on Zillow: seven bedrooms and five baths, a staircase snaking up both the right and left sides of the foyer.

Dylan and I had been texting all week, little jokes and GIFs and selfies, until finally he asked if I wanted to come over for dinner. Dont go out much, he texted. You know.

Yeah, I thought. *I know.*

I'd been surprised the night of the frat party to discover Dylan hadn't had a drink since his release from prison. The Solo cup he'd carried was little more than a prop full of Coke, and no matter how much his frat bros tried to bro him up, he hadn't given in to the pressure to drink.

My plan had been to get him drunk, strip him naked, and write RAPIST on his chest in Sharpie. I was going to blast the pics on social media and see how *he* liked it, but when that didn't pan out, I moved to plan B: ask Maris Heilman for help. It was clear that was a no-go as well, but no worries. I'd spent a long time relying only on myself.

I'd been careful all week to keep the hook baited. When he texted, I was sure to let hours lapse before texting him back, letting him know I wasn't waiting around for him, although I was. I'd sent a selfie from a coffee shop, the tip of my finger in my mouth. I found dumb pictures of sandwiches on Instagram and told him they were what I'd eaten for lunch. I flirted, but not too much, keeping him guessing about what kind of girl I was—the cat from the party or a good girl.

I was hoping tonight on our "date" that I could convince him to drink in the safety of his own home, but if not, rather than getting new pictures, I'd find a way to sneak a look at his phone and find whatever incriminating evidence I could. There was no way, given Dylan's past behavior, that he didn't have damning pictures on his phone.

Dylan stuck his head out the front door and shuffled out in jeans and a T-shirt and shower shoes. Even his shuffle was carefree. "I thought that was you," he said, bending over as I rolled down the window. "What're you doing out here?"

"Lipstick," I said, and dug through the Coach handbag I'd found at the Oak Park Goodwill for thirty dollars. I'd dyed my hair a honey chestnut from its mousy brown and applied contoured makeup I learned from YouTube tutorials. I knew if I was going to get him to trust me, I had to look like I fit in: a rich little college girl. As I climbed out of the car, I grimaced at the fifteen-year-old Toyota I was driving and said, "So embarrassing. It's my aunt's car. Mine's in the shop."

"It's fine," he said, and smiled as he looked me up and down, disgust shooting through to my fingertips and toes. I'd dressed in boyfriend jeans and a light-pink cashmere sweater with a deep neckline, my makeup soft with a nude lip. Dylan had been the one to teach me my body was just a thing to be used for manipulation.

He walked behind me into the guesthouse as his parents' mansion loomed in the distance, gothic and old money.

In the kitchen, he asked what I wanted to drink, and I said a vodka soda as I looked around. At the frat party he said he wasn't drinking because of the drive back to Dayton, but here he was, safe at home. There was a laptop on the breakfast bar, his phone on the counter.

"My bad," he said. "I don't have any booze."

I worked to keep the irritation off my face. "None?"

He shook his head.

I leaned against the breakfast bar, a little pout in my voice. "So you don't drink *ever*?"

"Not anymore," he said. He pulled a Coke can from the fridge, popped the tab, and slid it across the counter to me. He apologized and said he wasn't much of a chef either as he pulled two frozen pizzas—one deluxe and one cheese in case I was a vegetarian—out of the freezer. "I never really learned to cook," he said, and I wondered if he'd grown up with a personal chef.

"Looks great," I said, and offered to preheat the oven like Betty Homemaker. I sneaked closer to the phone, which he grabbed to set the timer and then slid in his back pocket.

We went through the regular first-date bullshit about our pasts and futures as the pizzas cooked and as we ate our cardboard slices. I told him I was originally from Florida (lie) and was now shelving books at the library as a temp job (lie) but had graduated from U Miami before moving to Oak Park to be closer to my aunt (lie, lie, lie).

At one point I told him I was cold and asked if he had a sweatshirt I could borrow, and as he sauntered to the back bedroom, I slammed open the laptop, heart racing, but the screen remained black. I pressed frantically on the keyboard, but nothing happened. He'd let the battery run down even though the charging cord sat right next to it, and his carelessness sent a jolt of rage through me.

Back in the kitchen, he handed me an Ohio State hoodie that had the same fresh scent of laundry detergent as the clothes he wore. He looked different than he had the night of the party, away from his frat bros and the testosterone saturating the air. More relaxed. He sat back down, sliding his phone out of his back pocket, his wallpaper a picture of a golden retriever that I stared at until the screen went black.

He told me again that he'd been working the last few months at his dad's law firm, studying the different funding models in their family business, which his dad and uncles wanted him to take over one day. In addition to the law firm, they had their hands in a bunch of pots—real estate holdings, geo-mapping, bioengineering—with names from both branches of the family line featured in Carillon Historical Park. It was the kind of generational wealth that had bought Dylan's way out of jail and back into this sprawling guesthouse.

"Can I ask you something?" he asked as he folded and unfolded the paper napkin next to his phone.

"Of course." I kept my face engaged: *You're so interesting!* "You can ask me anything." I hated playing the simp, but nowhere near as much as I hated him for falling for it.

"Why are you here?" My heart raced in my chest as I tried to look confused. Had he recognized me? "I mean, I got letters from girls when I was in prison, too, and some wackos have stopped by the house. Is that what this is?"

I reached out my hand to set it on top of his, relieved he hadn't figured out who I was. Just touching him this much had me fighting the bile in my throat. "Listen," I said. "I'm here because I like you." I hated myself. "I know everyone makes mistakes."

He nodded slowly. "I didn't mean to hurt anyone."

I had to keep myself from raking my fake nails down his face. "I know."

He seemed relieved and changed the subject, asking if I wanted to watch something. While the last thing I wanted was to be on a couch next to him, I told him to pick something out while I went to the restroom. There, I frantically searched through the cupboards for some Tylenol PM or something else to crush up in his Coke. Toward the back was a Zolpidem prescription in his mother's name, and a quick search on my phone confirmed it was a sedative.

I stilled suddenly as I heard a muffled knock on the front door. It creaked open and Dylan said hello, and then there was the sound of two new voices. Who the hell? I slid the pills back in the cupboard, flushed the toilet, and steadied my breath in the mirror before exiting.

In the kitchen stood an older version of Dylan and an emaciated older blonde I guessed to be Dylan's mother. Shit.

"Eric Charter," the man said, holding out his hand, eyebrows raised. "I didn't realize Dylan had company." He winked at his son, and I dug my fingernails into my palms, leaving crescent moons. No one would have remembered me from the frat party—just another slutty blank— but now his folks could identify me. "We were just stopping by to see if he wanted to come up to the big house for a nightcap."

"Dad, I've got plans," Dylan said, and exchanged a meaningful look with me. He'd told me that his father hadn't been very supportive of the work he was doing to improve himself, and I guessed that included not drinking.

"You can come too," he said to me. "Be good for us to know what kind of company he's keeping."

"I should get going," I said, looking around for my purse, as if I didn't know exactly where it was. I knew a woman had to stay vigilant, plus it was the most expensive thing I owned. Dylan's phone sat on the kitchen counter, but there was no way I could nab it now.

"Here," Dylan said, and motioned to the door. "At least let me walk you out."

"Is that your car out there?" his father asked, and I nodded. "Surprised it made it up the drive. I thought for a second the help was here."

"Dad!" Dylan said, and Eric laughed.

"She knows I'm teasing." I knew no such thing, but I could definitely see where Dylan got his charm.

At my car, Dylan opened the door for me. "I'm sorry about them," he said. "He can be a jerk." My heart pounded in my chest as he leaned ever so slightly forward. "I'd rather hang out with you," he whispered, and I bolted into the driver's seat.

Dylan leaned down with one arm draped over the open car door and the other over the roof. "My dad's organizing this dumb dinner for my birthday next Saturday. Any chance you can come?" I nodded. I would have agreed to anything to get out of that claustrophobic moment, his chest looming above me, spots in my vision. "Sweet."

He took two steps back and shut the door. My hands shook as I turned the key, nausea roiling up my throat. He waved as I started down the drive.

I barely made it to the road before jamming the car in park and throwing open the door to vomit on the brick-lined street. Did Dylan Charter think I was his *girlfriend*? The very idea bucked my stomach once again, but behind that bloomed the idea, *I could use this.*

A girlfriend would be trusted, and more importantly, a girlfriend would be believed.

PART THREE

CHAPTER TWENTY

Saturday morning, Maris greeted Noel with an olive branch in the form of a cup of decaf. He still loved the morning-coffee ritual. Noel took it, bags under his eyes, and said he needed to get some sleep first, but maybe they could talk later. "Fair enough," she said, relieved when he bent down to kiss her on the cheek. It wasn't the lips, but she'd take it.

She'd dressed in an old Huskers sweatshirt and some paint-splattered jeans, figuring maybe she'd clean out the basement and see about hauling out the roof spider while Noel slept upstairs under the whirl of the white noise machine. It could be another olive branch, this one for Cody. She worked slowly, cautiously with her broken ribs, taking frequent breaks on her phone.

Late morning, she came upstairs to use the bathroom and found a note from Cody on the fridge saying she'd gone to hang out with Lynette. Maris knew she was making plenty of noise in the basement, and that Cody had sneaked out quietly and on purpose to avoid her. Maybe that was for the best; it would give Cody some more time to cool on the idea of going to Nebraska. That afternoon Maris took another break and checked her email to find a message from Beth Novak responding to her request to chat about Diane Garland and Hollis Grant. And jackpot, she'd sent her cell phone number.

Maris dialed, and after a few rings, the woman answered. "Dr. Heilman?" she said, and Maris was surprised by the timbre of her voice, childlike and high though she'd be in her fifties.

Maris was also surprised Beth knew who she was automatically. Maris had sent her cell number in her first email, and Beth must have programmed it into her phone. It was a good sign she hadn't wanted to miss Maris's call, and Maris felt a surge of hope that Beth had something important to tell her. A new lead panning out had always made her giddy, although where exactly it was leading, she couldn't say. She'd originally been looking into Hollis to build a case why he shouldn't vote on her tenure, but was there more here? *Could* he be tied to her blackouts?

"Call me Maris, please. I assume this is Beth Novak?"

"Beth, yes. I'm sorry it took me a few days to get back to you. I guess I had to think about it."

"Think about what?"

Beth's reedy voice rushed through the phone. "Oh, I don't know. Digging up all that history."

"What history?" Maris prodded.

"You like to answer questions with more questions, don't you?"

"Do I?" Maris joked, and Beth laughed. The sound was so open, Maris felt a small spark of hope that she could figure this all out, that answers were just around the corner.

"Yeah. You do." There was a clicking noise, quick steps. "I've got my dog on a walk, just a sec," Beth said, followed by a long pause. Her voice came back. "So you're having issues with Dr. Grant?"

"I am." Maris gave the short version regarding his attacks on her work, and how he now would be voting on her tenure case. Just a short time ago, her tenure had seemed the most pressing thing in her life, but she felt its importance abstractly now. "A colleague and I were talking," Maris said, stretching the truth on her connection to Eula, "and she thought something might have happened in Cincinnati, so I'm just following up. You were his advisee?"

"Yeah, his research assistant back in the early nineties, although I was hardly doing research. I was more like a monkey."

"So not a positive experience?"

"No, to put it mildly. I had plenty of negative experiences with male professors back when I was in the sciences, but no one was as . . . persistent in his beliefs about women's limitations."

"You're at the BMV now, correct? No longer in neuroscience?" Maris asked.

"Correct. I left before Hollis was fired, but that experience had a lot to do with why I left."

Maris's heart rate increased. "Fired?"

"I know that's not the university's line, but he definitely was. They swept it under the rug as a resignation, but he wasn't given an option. They even revoked his tenure." In her ten years in academia as a grad student and now assistant professor, Maris hadn't known someone to actually have tenure revoked.

"What happened?"

"Um." Beth paused. "I'll be honest, I don't feel comfortable talking about it over the phone, and it might not even be relevant—"

"It's relevant," Maris assured her.

"Maybe we could meet for coffee? Cincinnati is only about an hour—"

"Absolutely," Maris said. "I can come right now."

"That soon?" Maris could hear the panic in Beth's voice as she backpedaled. "Listen, maybe this isn't such a good idea," she started. "Talking on the phone, meeting."

"Beth, something is going on," Maris said urgently, fearing she was slipping away. "Something I can't explain." How would she begin to tell this woman about the blackouts when she couldn't even tell her husband? She knew how crazy she'd sound, but she needed to keep Beth on her side. "I think he's hurting women," she said. "Me and others."

Beth paused, and Maris heard her dog bark at something on the other end, the barks growing more persistent. "Fine. I'll text you an address," Beth said, and ended the call.

A moment later, an address for a Starbucks popped up on Maris's phone, and they agreed to meet at four, which didn't give Maris much time to get there. She snagged a brush through her hair and looked down at her stained jeans. She'd put them on to clean the basement, but they were also her only clean pair. She thought fleetingly of Cody. She hadn't picked up her new jeans and top at Macy's, just like she hadn't made it to career day, but the sooner she could find out what was going on, the sooner she could get her life back on track.

Thanks again for agreeing to meet, Maris texted as she grabbed an apple for the road, realizing she'd skipped lunch. I really appreciate it. She threw the apple and a bag of Cheez-Its in her purse and called it good. Her phone dinged.

You might not feel that way after we talk, Beth warned, and Maris's heart thumped, knowing she was on the right track.

Noel appeared in the doorway and Maris screamed, swatting a hand against her racing heart. "You scared me."

"I see that," he said. Only it wasn't with the jovial way he normally greeted her unreasonable startle response, but with coldness. For a second, she worried he'd found the camera. But no. What she was looking at was the slow disintegration of trust—first because of her drinking, and then, for the last eight months, because of her tenuous sobriety. She poured coffee in a travel mug and topped it with skim milk before screwing on the lid. Her mind raced with what Beth might tell her. She assumed it had to do with Hollis's unethical behavior targeting women, but could it be more? Could this be related to her blackouts?

"I thought we were going to talk," Noel said, and she started again, lost in her head.

She glanced at her watch: 2:54. "I've got to run to Cincinnati. For work. For an article."

He looked pointedly at her grubby clothes. "Dressed like that? And on a Saturday?"

"First time for everything," she tried to joke. What she wanted was to tell him everything, but it was happening so fast.

"How about first time for some honesty."

She took in his crossed arms and the resolute look on his face. "I swear, Noel, it's for work."

"Then what, exactly?"

She bumbled for a sec, then told a version of the truth. "It's about Hollis Grant and his attempts to deny my tenure."

"Okay," he said reasonably. "But you need to go to Cincinnati for that? Why the urgency? Isn't the university vote still a ways away?"

"It's complicated."

Noel laughed, but not really. "Complicated? What isn't?"

She looked up from Google Maps on her phone. "Fine. He used to work at Cincinnati University, and I just found out he was let go under shady circumstances. According to my source, they revoked his tenure, maybe even fired him." Noel's eyebrows rose; he'd been married to an academic long enough to know that was a big deal. "I'm heading out to meet with her. I promise, Noel: it's important I go, and now."

"What source?"

"An old grad student of his. Listen, I really do need to get on the road."

Her phone dinged with a text from Karen in all caps. I NEED TO TALK TO YOU!

Noel glanced at her phone upside down. "Is that Karen Patel from the hospital? Why's she contacting you?"

Maris turned with a twinge of pain and opened the garage door, saw Noel's car, and remembered: I can't drive. "Shit."

Noel stepped up behind her. "What is it?"

Shit. Another thing she couldn't get into. Why she wasn't driving would lead to another slew of questions, and for the first time in her life, she believed that she wasn't shutting down out of denial, but urgency. She needed to get on the road and find out what happened. "Nothing, I—" Who could she ask to drive her? Noel would ask too many questions and want to meet Beth. She thought fleetingly of Janice, but she couldn't drive either, for the same reason as herself. Then she looked over to Eula's Honda parked next door, hardly driven since Carl had died.

"Mare?"

She turned back. "I just remembered, I have to get something at Eula's."

Noel turned on his heel toward the kitchen. "Fine."

"Noel, I—"

"No. I thought you were actually telling me the truth right now," he said, his voice rising as he turned back to her. "But now you've got some bullshit about going to see our neighbor when you're in this big of a rush? And some emergency in Cincinnati? I don't even believe that's where you're going anymore. I don't believe anything you say to me." Tears filled her eyes, but she knew she didn't have the right. It was true: she'd given him little reason to trust her. "Go," he said.

"I'm sorry," she whispered to Noel, looking frantically again at her watch. Already she had less than an hour to get to Cincy, and skittish as Beth was, Maris worried if she was so much as a minute late, Beth would bolt. "But I have to go. I do."

"Noel—" she started again, but he went inside the house and slammed the door behind him, and what could she do but walk out the door?

CHAPTER
TWENTY-ONE

She pounded her fist against Eula's door until she heard scuffling inside, then pounded harder.

"Maris!" Eula said, swinging open the door. "What in the ever-loving world?"

"Can you drive me to Cincinnati?" she asked.

"Right now?"

"Ten minutes ago, actually."

Eula looked down at her own gardening jeans, then at Maris's unwashed face. "I take it we're in a hurry?"

Twenty minutes later they were on a stretch of interstate between towns, the afternoon sky a brilliant, cold blue. Eula had agreed to drive eight miles over the speed limit and not a penny more. Knowing they wouldn't get there any faster, Maris concentrated on the landscape ticking by: cornfields and wooded areas dotted by exits for fast food. Being a passenger reminded her of the road trips when she was a kid. The ones that would start at five in the morning, her father always determined to make it to their destination by happy hour. Was he still drinking as much as he used to? Still the life of the party? Last time she'd seen him he'd put on weight, his shoulders stooped. She'd hardly recognized him at the airport.

All Maris had told Eula was that she was meeting with an old graduate student of Hollis's from Cincinnati. When Eula looked at her questioningly, Maris reminded her that she'd wondered if Hollis had left Cincy because of a woman.

"So was this a girlfriend?"

Maris shook her head no. "I thought maybe in the beginning, but whatever her connection is, it's something more interesting than that." She gave a quick sketch of Diane Garland and her death, the nervousness Beth had about meeting her.

"It's good you asked me," Eula said. "I might be able to help decode some of what she says about the research."

Maris hadn't gotten that far. She was thinking she'd be meeting with Beth on her own and hadn't anticipated having to share this information with Eula, but it was the least she owed her. She nodded.

"Can I ask you about something else?" Eula said, and Maris was sure it would be about her digging into Hollis's background. She could not have been more surprised by what Eula said next.

"What happened back in February?"

Maris felt her stomach bottom out, and as Eula swerved to miss a car that had leaned too close to their lane, she thought she might puke. "Why do you ask?"

"I saw the tire mark in your yard," Eula said, righting the car.

Backing out of the garage that night, on her way to pick up Cody at the Lamberts', she'd swerved onto the lawn, the car jolting as she ran over the short rock wall around a hedge. That awful night, she'd been proud she'd made it onto the street with only one wheel crushing the grass.

"I'd been drinking," she admitted to Eula now. "And I swerved onto the lawn."

"Where were you going?" Eula asked, and the lack of judgment in her voice surprised Maris.

"I was supposed to pick up Cody."

Eula's voice remained steady. "And did you?"

The sick feeling in her gut came back as she recalled the night. Janice had ushered Maris into the living room where Cody sat in her winter coat and jeans, her packed bag on her lap. Maris kept her feet planted on the carpet, confident she wasn't going to sway, but aware of the possibility. She was okay to drive, wasn't she?

"Um," Cody said, and looked to Janice. "Can I talk to you for a sec?"

Cody followed Janice into one of the back bedrooms, and Maris felt a flare of panic, but certainly they didn't know she had been drinking—she was so good at faking! Her stomach bottomed out, and she turned and located the sink in case she needed to puke. Jesus, was this really happening?

When Janice came back and said it appeared she'd been drinking, Maris assured her, "I only had a glass or two," but heard the slur of *glass* into *glash*. It began to sink in, slowly, yet heavily, that she had made a drastic mistake, but what shot through her next was the terrible decision to double down. "I appreciate you being protective, but I think I know my limits."

"I don't," Janice said, and offered to order a Lyft.

Looking back on that night, Maris could so clearly see the mirror image of her dad waving her mom's concerns away, telling her, "Jilly, you're being a nag." All these years she'd wanted to be like her father, the fun one, but in hindsight she realized the clearest comparison had been to her mother: the one who knew they were endangering their child, but let it happen anyway. She was somehow the worst of both of them.

Maris leaned forward, teetering just a hair, wanting to look like a determined mother and not the drunk she was. "You will not tell me how to parent my kid."

"Okay," Janice agreed, which felt like a trap. "But Cody won't get in that car. She told me herself, and my job now is to respect those wishes." She looked at Maris. "Do you hear me: your daughter asked me to stop you from driving her home. Your daughter *does not feel safe.*"

She told Eula as much of this as she could—Cody figuring out she was drunk, Janice refusing to let Maris's daughter go with her—although she downplayed how much she'd fought Janice on the decision. A part of her had wanted to throw herself into Janice's arms, thankful someone had stopped her, but that wasn't the way it played out. That night, she could not bring herself to admit how much she'd fucked up, even if everyone in the room knew it, including her. Maris had steadied herself and clomped to the living room, the back of Cody's head flinching at the sound of her footsteps. Maris's chest had constricted even further.

"Code?" she said. Cody turned slowly and focused on a spot over her mom's shoulder, tears in her eyes. *She can't even look at me,* Maris realized. *My daughter can't even look at me.* Her mind linked to Saturday mornings on the farm, crisscross applesauce in front of the TV, her father sliding on his boots in her periphery, her eyes glued on Daffy Duck.

Janice followed her downstairs, offering once again to call a Lyft. Maris finally acquiesced, thankful in her own convoluted way that she'd been forced into a good decision.

"What happened the next day?" Eula asked, and Maris told her how she ran back the next morning at a punishing pace—eight-minute miles—to pick up Cody and her car. When Janice answered the door, Maris was ready to admit her mistake, but the words wouldn't come, and she pivoted. It was a move she'd internalized from those Saturday-morning conversations between her mother and father: her dad on the defensive, her mom trying to rally home her point. To the child sitting on the living room floor trying to watch *Looney Tunes*, her mother had been the bad guy: if she'd just stop poking, this could all go away.

Janice said, "I can help if what you want is help. But if you're going to lie to both you and me, there's not much I can do." But that was the thing: Maris didn't *want* her to do anything! She wasn't *asking* for help!

Cody said her goodbyes to Lynette and Janice, climbed in the car with her duffel on her lap, and clicked her seatbelt. Maris promised her daughter, "I'm done. I'm not going to drink anymore." She had said this to herself for years, decades, but this was the first time she'd said it to someone else. And not just someone, but her daughter. The person she was on this earth to protect.

Cody kept her eyes on the row of trees lining the street. "Okay," she said. "Whatever."

What Maris would have given to have that memory blacked out, to never have to think of it again.

"And what about Noel?" Eula asked now, zipping down the interstate. "What did he say?"

Later that day, Maris had downplayed the incident to Noel, passed it off as just a few too many drinks. What was the harm, Cody safe at the Lamberts'? Just a lady home alone on a Saturday night, eating too little dinner. She never told him she'd tried to drive with Cody in the car, or that by herself she'd driven drunk.

"So you never told him about the yard?" It was the first time Eula had a hint of judgment in her voice.

"He never asked," Maris said. "I wasn't about to bring it up."

"I get that," Eula said. "But if Carl had done something like tear up the lawn with the car, I would have pushed him for an answer and found out just what happened. I would have needed to know he was okay."

For the first time, Maris thought about it from that side. Sure, she'd screwed up, but shouldn't Noel have been more concerned? More anxious about her well-being? Why *hadn't* he asked her? But for too long, she'd shouldered the blame and thought of Noel as the good guy, the perfect one, while she struggled to be worthy.

"It's not his fault," she said, sure everyone could see it was all hers. She saw the Starbucks siren calling to them from the side of the interstate, and Eula turned on the blinker.

"You sure are concerned with fault, Maris," she said, and Maris thought, *Well, who the hell isn't?*

Chapter Twenty-Two

They arrived five minutes after four, and when they entered the coffee shop to the grating noise of the milk steamer, Maris swept her eyes over the large room. Everyone was bent over a laptop, engaged in conversation, or not the right age to be Beth. "Shit," Maris whispered, but then a woman in her fifties with gray, curly hair came out of the bathroom and waved, a cup of coffee in her other hand.

Maris's breath stuttered with relief as she held out her hand. "Thanks so much for meeting with us," she said.

"Us?" Beth let her limp hand be folded in Maris's. "I assumed you were coming alone." She shook her head. "I don't—"

"I'm no fan of Hollis Grant," Eula said, "if that's what you're worried about." A bray of laughter shot out from behind the counter, and a barista called out a tall mocha Frapp.

Beth took a step away from the counter. "How do you know him?" she asked, and Eula explained he'd worked primarily with her husband, but that she'd coauthored some papers with him in the late nineties after he came to Glenn State.

"What topic?" Beth asked, and Eula told her about her work in cellular tracking and oscillation identification. "You're Eula Moore," Beth said, and Eula laughed.

"I sure am."

Beth nodded. "I followed your work with him. I knew enough about Hollis's capabilities and specialties to see the majority of the work was yours." Maris was struck by her voice once again. In person, her voice was even more distinct, and she thought its childlike timbre probably hadn't done her any favors in the sciences.

"Yep," Eula said, and leaned forward. "And that prick still put himself as lead author on the papers." Beth laughed.

Maris pointed to Beth's coffee, and Beth put her hand over the lid. "No more for me, thanks."

Beth led them to her table, where Maris sat down, forgoing the coffee, and Eula took the seat next to her. "I appreciate you coming all the way to Cincy on such short notice," Beth said, and Maris waved a hand to dismiss the trouble.

"Seriously, our pleasure. I'm so thankful you took the time to talk to me."

"Maybe wait until you hear what I have to say before thanking me." Beth rotated her cup half inches at a time, the logo disappearing behind her fingers and eventually appearing out the other side. "I was nervous about digging this back up after all these years, but after you reached out, I did a little research. I read your articles about the Charter case."

"And what did you think?"

"That you're not afraid to tell the truth." Beth smiled and glanced at her watch. "I've only got about an hour before I'm due somewhere, so I guess I'd better jump right in." Beth let out a deep breath and started the story. "Like I said, I was a research assistant for Hollis back in the nineties. Fall of '91 through part of spring semester '93, to be exact. There were two of us, and Hollis was working on the separation of neural oscillations and their functions."

"Still is," Maris said cautiously. She didn't want to give away anything she knew about Hollis's work until she heard from Beth first, but that little bit could be read on his faculty webpage. Maybe Beth had read it there too.

"He was particularly interested in the effects of memory," Beth said, and Maris tried to show no response, though she was relieved they were at least talking about the same type of work. "He was trying to isolate specific neurons to figure out their functionality by recording a subject's brain waves, and from there, he was hoping to divide them further to isolate what each neuron did."

"Through electrodes?" Eula asked, and Beth nodded.

"And did he have subject permission?" Maris asked.

Beth smiled, and confirmed he did for that part. Maris thought from the smile that Beth took the question as encouragement they were on the same page. "But not for others?"

"No," Beth said matter-of-factly. "And I would know. I was one of the subjects, along with another female graduate student, Diane Garland."

"She was the research assistant who died in '93, correct?" Beth nodded again. "She was awfully young," Maris said. "Did she have a history of health problems?"

"No," Beth said. "Quite the opposite. She was a college athlete." Her voice hitched at the end. "All the promise in the world."

Maris remembered she was a swimmer and led Beth to the next knot in her thinking. "So you think her death might be connected to Hollis's research?"

Beth nodded and continued. "In the fall of '91, Hollis was recording brain waves through electrodes, like a one-way reporting system. It was all data collection."

"I remember reading the paper about that," Eula said, and it rang a vague bell for Maris based on his CV. The door to Starbucks opened, and a tall, old white man came through the door in a tweed coat and scarf; Maris blanched, sure it was Hollis, her mind playing tricks. Eula gave her a questioning look, and she shook her head just the tiniest bit: *I'm fine.*

The old man held the door for the elderly woman behind him, and they linked arms as they toddled toward the cash register.

"Did you see the research?" Maris asked.

"In the beginning we did. It was terribly unorthodox that we were working as subjects and not actual research assistants, but given our grad contracts we didn't have a lot of say about the kind of work we were doing. It was his research, not ours. Diane and I used to talk about how disappointed we were. We had friends in the cohort working with other professors who were doing *actual* research, their names coauthored on the articles, while we were just test subjects in the lab."

"Let me guess," Eula interjected. "You were the only two women in the program?"

Beth nodded. "I don't know if that's coincidence or—"

"It's not," Maris said. She certainly knew what Hollis thought about women in the academy.

"Either way." Beth shrugged. "We were given copies of the grant application that outlined the study, and we signed IRBs, but what we signed for was not what happened. For the first six months or so, the experiments went as outlined. We were basically getting paid to work on homework for other classes, hooked up to the electrodes at our desks while we wrote papers or read novels or whatever. But about six months in, something changed. I had a harder time concentrating during the trial time, and would sometimes just stare at the same page for hours. I asked Diane about it, and she had the same thing, but we just convinced ourselves we must be spacing out. As soon as the electrodes came off, we were back to ourselves. It took us a while to talk about it, because honestly it took us a while to realize it was happening."

"Did you feel like your mind was wandering?" Maris asked.

Beth shook her head no. "Maybe that's what we thought in the beginning, but it was more like we went . . . blank." The word *blank* made Maris shudder as she felt a mounting excitement. She knew that feeling.

Three teenage girls came in wearing ripped jeans and sweaters, and Maris wondered if Cody was home yet. "How long were the sessions?" she asked.

"Three hours, generally, although"—a blush crept up her cheeks—"one time, I peed myself, and after that, he shortened them to an hour and a half, and insisted we go to the bathroom before we were hooked up."

Maris reached over and squeezed Beth's hand. She'd peed on a couch one time in college, drunk at a stranger's house. She assumed at the time it would be the most humiliating moment of her life. "Did you ask for an updated IRB?" She'd filled out her share of research method paperwork for the institutional review board, which made sure people's rights weren't trampled in research.

"Short answer: yes. We asked, but Dr. Grant kept putting it off. Eventually, Diane and I knew something wasn't right, and we tried to talk to him about it, but he assured us we were just letting our minds wander."

"Did you believe that?" Maris said.

"Yes and no." Beth shook her head. "It's so hard to say. Diane and I speculated that maybe he was trying to disrupt the waves by sending signals back to them, not just to record the oscillations, but it sounded so . . . unethical, we didn't think it was possible." Maris nodded. For a month she convinced herself there was nothing wrong, all evidence to the contrary. It seemed no one was brought up to believe women, even women. She glanced at Eula, whose face was a mixture of incredulity and anger. It made Maris furious to think of the danger Hollis had put Diane and Beth in, but with each new piece of information she also felt a glimmer of hope: *if we know what he's doing, we can figure out how to stop this.*

"And he's a doctor and scientist," Beth continued in her high, reedy voice, "working on these multimillion-dollar national grants. We didn't think there was any way, really, until—" She paused and took a drink of her coffee.

"Until Diane died?" Maris asked, and Beth nodded. "Of a stroke, correct?"

"Well," Beth said, drawing out the word. "At least a stroke is what they called it."

CHAPTER TWENTY-THREE

Maris kept her eyes steady on Beth's, not wanting to give away the rapid slam of her heart against her rib cage. She had wondered how it was possible a college athlete had gone from prime condition to suffering a stroke, and this confirmed it hadn't been natural causes. What the hell had Hollis been up to?

"What do you think really happened?" she asked mildly as Eula leaned in closer, her brows furrowed.

"We came out of the session," Beth said, "and the first thing I noticed was that Dr. Grant seemed very agitated. He'd turned our desk chairs around and was standing in front of us, hunkered down and staring at our faces. Diane's in particular. When we woke up, for lack of a better phrase, he seemed so relieved. I remember him putting his hand to his chest and bowing his head, like he couldn't believe we were alive. It was clear something had gone wrong. I felt okay for the most part—a little fuzzy, like I was struggling to wake up—and Diane seemed a little out of it as well, but it wasn't until she began to speak that things seemed off. She was confusing words—she called a book a boat, I remember, and a tree a tribe when we left the lab. When I pointed it out to her, she tried to laugh it off like it was no big deal, but I could tell something was wrong. She also had a barely perceptible droop on the right side of her face. Or maybe it was the left, I can't remember, but by the end of the next week, it was like her face was made of wax and someone had tried to melt it. Hollis told her not to worry about it. He even said temporary paralysis was to be expected from the electrodes, plus we made so little as grad assistants she didn't want to spend the copay at a doctor's office. Then at ten days, she had her first seizure. She called me from home, and I could barely understand her, but I raced to her apartment and found her on the floor with her limbs frozen like sticks, yellow bile foaming at her mouth."

A memory swam up from Maris's childhood: tiptoeing into the living room for Saturday cartoons as the sun was coming up and finding her father lying on the floor, a sour pool of vomit near his shoulder. She yelled his name—"Daddy!"—and her knees hit the carpet. She pounded her tiny fists ineffectively on his plaid-shirted chest. Eventually she ran to find her mother in bed, and she stumbled to the living room and was able to rouse him.

Beth shook her head as if to erase the image on an Etch A Sketch. "It was awful. I called an ambulance, and by the next morning, she was dead."

"Oh my god," Maris said, a hand to her mouth. Hollis had let that woman die. And she could be next.

"After she died, I confronted Dr. Grant and said I thought something had happened in his experiment. He was furious. Said if I was going to make wild accusations like that, he'd get me kicked out of the program. He said he'd stop my career before it even started." Beth took another sip of her coffee, her hands trembling slightly. "I didn't listen to him. I went to the department chair and told him what happened, and he said he'd look into it, but in the meantime, since it was going to be under investigation, I shouldn't speak to anyone about it."

"And did you?" Maris asked.

Beth shook her head. "I figured they were going to handle it. Stupid of me, I guess.

"A week or two later, the chair called me into his office and said Hollis Grant had accused me of stealing his research and wanted me kicked out of the program. It was a two for one: he hid the records so I couldn't investigate, and got rid of me in the process. The chair even told me there wouldn't be much use in applying to other programs after this kind of a scandal and wished me well in my endeavors."

"He just destroyed your career?" Eula said, and Maris wondered if she was considering her own thwarted attempts as an ambitious woman. She couldn't imagine the fury she'd feel to be cast aside so carelessly, but hadn't that been the way? She was an object to men in her teens and twenties, competition to be squashed in her thirties, and finally in her forties when success was in her grasp, they would still find a way to destroy her.

"He did, and without a backward glance. I had straight As up until that point, which, as a woman in science, was no small feat. If men had to score a hundred percent for an A, I had to score a hundred and ten."

"And is there a record to back this up?" Maris asked.

Beth shrugged. "I don't know about my reason for dismissal. It was in the nineties, like I said, so much of the university was still on a paper system. I doubt they've kept files going back that far, especially for students who didn't even complete the program."

"What happened with Dr. Grant?" Maris asked.

"Nothing was ever announced formally, but he was gone from Cincy U by fall of '93. I went back to campus early that semester—they didn't have a restraining order or anything—and the nameplates were off his office and labs. I asked the department secretary what had happened, and all she could tell me was that Dr. Grant was on paid leave. I checked public records in 1994, and he was no longer listed as an employee of the university. When he started at Glenn State, it was as an assistant professor, and I know he had to go through the tenure process, even though he'd been an associate professor before."

"Sometimes if people transfer universities, they're not able to take the rank and title with them," Maris said, but Beth shook her head.

"It wasn't that. There was a board hearing for tenure termination. They voted for his removal, but they wouldn't say publicly what he'd done, so he was still able to get a job elsewhere. The president and dean swept it under the rug and basically let him become Glenn State's problem."

"He always led us to believe he left of his own volition," Eula said, and Maris felt a gash of raw fury. If they'd held him accountable, her life wouldn't now be in danger.

"Did you ever tell anyone about all this?" Maris asked.

"Other than the chair that ignored me?" Beth smiled ruefully and exchanged a look with Eula—two women in the sciences used to being ignored. "I tried reaching out to Glenn State when he started there, but was dismissed as a disgruntled graduate student. A hysterical woman who'd been kicked out of the program. But I've kept my eye on him for all of his career, wondering if he might try something again."

"Did you have any other lasting physical effects?" Maris asked.

"Not for a long time," Beth said. "But every time I'd get a headache over the years, I'd wonder if he'd found a way back in." Maris thought of her own migraines and the worry they caused. "I always worried he wasn't done yet." Beth looked up, tears in her eyes.

Maris squeezed her hand. "And was he?"

"I've been having these episodes," she said, her thin voice hitching.

"Like blackouts?" Maris asked, and Beth gasped. "Blank spots in your memory?"

Eula turned to her slowly. "How do you know that, Maris?"

Maris took a deep breath and told them both what she knew.

Chapter Twenty-Four

They were back on the interstate before either of them spoke, their minds reeling. Maris had hoped that learning about Hollis's past would illuminate something, but she hadn't anticipated he would be the linchpin, or that she'd discover a new victim. Whatever slim connections she'd found between him and the other women—Shelby Steele and Beverly Halberg—she had to keep digging. She was confident he could stop and start their memories with the press of a button, the looming terror always there.

She'd always hated horror movies—it was her hair-trigger startle response—and the creeping terror of something just around the corner or lurking at the top of the stairs. The scariest were the ones where the call came from inside the house, only now the house was her brain, and she no longer occupied it. She thought of all the rape victims she had interviewed over the years for different articles and essays, how they talked about the dissociative act of hiding in their brains during the worst of the sexual assault. How there was always that tiny part the man couldn't get to. Not anymore.

She rolled down the window, the cold air whipping in through the car at seventy-five miles an hour, and found three things to concentrate on: the compass suctioned to Eula's dash, the red billboard for a Honda dealership, the lone cloud in a blue sky. Many people held generational trauma in their bodies, the legacy of their ancestors, and she believed this was true of all women. The anxiety, the startle response, the vigilance. It lived in all their muscles and skin.

"What I don't understand," Maris said, finally calming as she closed the window, "is how he's getting into my brain if he doesn't have the electrodes."

Eula nodded. "You have me to thank for that." Maris looked at her, shocked. Were Eula and Hollis in cahoots? She did not think she could handle any more surprises. "Not on purpose," Eula quickly clarified, "but my research." She shook her head. "That son of a bitch stole that too."

"I don't understand," Maris said, a migraine starting behind her left eye. She had wondered if the severe headaches were related to the blackouts, an early warning they were coming, but she no longer thought so. They were related in that they were caused by stress, but when Hollis struck, there would be no question.

"Did you know that brain waves are more accurate for identification than fingerprints or a retina scan?" Maris shook her head no. "More accurate even than DNA, which is already at ninety-nine point nine percent. And brain waves are like any other wave we talked about with RFIDs—they're just electrical impulses firing between neurons. So my area of study was the overlap of using the brain as the processor instead of the chip *and* how the brain waves could be used as unique identification. If you had access to a person's neural patterns and a powerful enough signal, you could find anyone in the world."

"But how?" Maris asked. "How would you find them?"

"I did work with cell towers in the early aughts," Eula continued. "Think back to the RFID: if the brain could be the circuit that stores and processes, then a cell tower could be the conduit that receives and transmits the message. Add to that what Hollis was figuring out about specific neurons and how to disrupt them, and we're talking about mind control." Maris's face flushed hot, but Eula smiled gently. "It sounds awful, I know, but a layperson would be shocked to know all that scientists can do: genetic modification, cellular transformations. They can basically remake a person with a corpse and a pig's heart." She slowed for the white van in front of her, and Maris thought how it was like the ones serial killers drove in TV shows. What if Hollis was in there right now, tracking her neurons? It sounded ridiculous, but this wasn't paranoia; it was reality.

"But since my expertise was in bioengineering," Eula continued, "with a dabble in physics, I was able to theorize, but I wasn't able to apply it directly. For that I needed a neuroscientist."

Maris knew who that meant, her acrid stomach clenching. "Hollis Grant."

Eula nodded. "Carl was the one to originally tell him what I was working on. You might remember me telling you that Hollis came to Glenn State to work with my husband, and that's what we thought for a long time, but it was actually my work he was interested in. He'd read my thesis—crude, and written almost forty years ago—but the nugget of my ideas was there. And since my thesis, I'd expanded my theories about neural tracking into cell towers, which is an incredibly affordable and abundant option, and a replacement for the parabolic dishes. When Carl died, Hollis came over and gathered his research—from his faculty office and home—and told me he was working with the archivist at Glenn State to preserve his contributions, but he was actually after my work, which he copied as well."

"That's . . . awful," Maris said, knowing the implications were well beyond a case of plagiarism.

"You know," Eula continued, "I called the head archivist a few months later to let her know I'd found some more papers while cleaning out Carl's home office, and she said the archives hadn't been contacted about the donation. I assumed it was an error in paperwork and kept meaning to follow up." Maris knew all too well how easily you could convince yourself all was fine.

Maris felt like she'd found a Peeping Tom—not outside her window but inside her body. And there was still the question: Why her, and why the other women? Was this really over her *tenure*? Over articles he disagreed with? It seemed ridiculous he would care so much, and she knew there had to be a piece to the puzzle she was still missing. What he had was more powerful than killing her: it was the ability to turn her into someone else. If she couldn't remember what she did, was she even who she was?

"So you're saying for sure he has a record of my brain waves, and those of the other women?"

"He must," Eula said, "but I'm not sure how he got them. And honestly, my work was theoretical. Not something I could prove without lab time, and certainly not on human subjects. What's kept science in check has been the ethical implications and the regulating agencies. But if you don't worry about the ethical implications—"

Maris knew from her research into every issue of sociology that enough money could buy your way past nearly any regulation. "And you've got the means to bypass the agencies," Maris added, and Eula nodded.

"Exactly. With enough money and power, you can do anything. But yes, my guess is Hollis has used my theories on identification and paired them with your specific neurons to disrupt memory."

"Shit," Maris whispered. She thought back to the enormity of all those nights she'd blacked out on her own—the times she woke up in a frat house before she was dating Scott; those single years post-Scott and pre-Noel where she spent nights out with her grad school cohort, almost always waking up with a banging headache, not knowing until she opened her eyes if she'd be in her own bed or someone else's. She'd told herself this was sexual empowerment, and maybe it was, but it was also handing over her safety to random men, which she knew, based on everything she'd ever written, put women in danger.

And now? There wasn't even gaslighting or concern of consent, just a man in control of her mind and therefore her body.

She thought back to Beth telling her about the last experiment: Hollis kneeling in front of them, concerned they wouldn't wake up. The slight sag to Diane's face. Just what exactly had gone wrong?

She had thought when she first read Diane's obituary that it was odd a woman so young would have a stroke when it was something associated with much older people. Maris's grandfather had had one, and at the time she'd wondered whether strokes could be related to alcohol, but talked herself out of looking it up, another sign of her denial. It had been her companion for so long—*Wine moms are fun! No one noticed that fifth glass! Everyone throws up in their office trash at least once!* With her grandfather, she'd told herself that he was an old man, and old men have strokes. *Nothing to do with alcohol there!*

Maris thought again about her grandfather—old and stroke age. Why did that stick in her mind?

CHAPTER TWENTY-FIVE

It made sense when Maris got home that Noel's car wasn't in the driveway, but when she opened the kitchen door, and the house was the kind of quiet it was when they returned from a vacation—a musty smell, a thickness to the air—Maris felt her eyes well at the emptiness. She'd hoped she'd have a chance to apologize for leaving so abruptly and maybe start to explain.

She wanted nothing more than to see her family's faces, even if they were disappointed, distrustful. She wanted to run her hand over the hair on Cody's head. To bury her nose in the crook of Noel's neck. "Noel? Code?" she yelled, even though she knew Noel would have left for work by now. But where was Cody?

She ran upstairs, yelling their names again as she went, the house's eerie quiet causing panic. She peered in Cody's room, but it always looked like it had been ransacked and so looked the same as ever. Her and Noel's room also looked as it normally did—her robe on the back of the bathroom door, his scrubs in a heap next to the hamper. She checked the mirror: no note. There were two places she and Noel left each other notes: on the bathroom mirror (*thanks for a fun night xo*— although those types hadn't been left in a while) and on the fridge.

She bounded down the stairs. Nothing.

Running her hands through her hair, she scanned the kitchen and then the living room. Her stomach dropped when she saw on the small surveillance camera a Post-it note that read *watch me* in Noel's handwriting.

Maris pulled the app up on her phone, scrolled to the last video before she arrived home, and pressed "Play." It opened on Noel walking into the room and sitting on the couch where she now sat. He clasped his hands and looked straight into the lens, and Maris jolted as if their eyes had locked in real time. She hovered her thumb over the phone's home button, not sure if she could watch. She knew it was bad. So bad.

Noel shook his head and looked down, then wiped a hand under his eye before he started speaking. "I don't know what to say, Mare. I really don't. I don't know why you've been"—he motioned to the camera—"taping us, or for how long. And how long have you been faking going to work?" He held up a piece of paper and an envelope, and Maris thought she was going to be sick. "HR sent this, saying you've initiated a leave of absence." He coughed, and Maris felt her own eyes well with tears. "Where do you go?" he asked, and she wanted to scream, *I don't know!* But he didn't mean in her head, where the memories were blank.

"I don't know who you are anymore," Noel said, shaking his head. "I've gone through the spectrum of emotions these past few weeks, maybe longer—fear you were pulling away from me, or fear you were drinking. Anger about those same two things. Sadness. More anger. And I guess at this point, I'm pretty settled into worry. I think there's something really wrong here. Things have been better since February, but now they're not. I don't know if you're in trouble, or . . . if it's something else, but I know you're not the woman I've been married to for the last three years, and I know Cody feels like you're a stranger too." He looked at her again through the camera, and Maris winced. Why was he bringing up Cody? She shame pinched the inside of her arm so hard she cried out. She needed to feel something other than emotional pain.

Noel cleared his throat. He was crying now, too—big wet tears tracking down his vulnerable face—and Maris wanted to pull him to her through the phone screen and tell him she loved him, to explain away all that was going on, but where to start? A month ago, or eight? Back to when they both agreed for him to start the night shift? The student loans she racked up trying to claw her way to a career? The first beer with her dad in the garage when she was twelve? She wanted to tell him everything she could so he would know how much she needed him.

"I'm pretty worried about you," Noel continued, "but I'm also resigned that you're not going to talk to me, and I have to think about what I need to do for this family.

"I called Scott—"

Maris paused the video. It hurt too much. Noel had met Scott, Cody's dad, a handful of times, and they'd gotten along well, talking about home improvement projects or college football, or whatever else men in their forties talked about that wasn't craft beer. She squeezed her eyes shut as her lizard brain started up: *This is too much. You can't do this. There's a way to feel better.*

She pushed "Play," and Noel continued. "And he's going to pick Cody up at the Omaha airport tonight. I bought her ticket one way until we can figure things out." He gazed at her through the phone. "I'm not trying to take her away from you, Mare, but I have to do what I think is safest for her right now. I hope you can agree with me on that." He inhaled a deep breath as the voice continued in Maris's head—that voice that wanted what it wanted. *You've proven you could stop for eight months now. And what's your reward? An empty house.*

"I'm going to stay at Joe's for a few nights while I look for an apartment." Joe was another ER doctor, the one whose wife Maris had insulted while drunk at a party. "I have an appointment with a rental company next week, and I'm going to get one with a bedroom for Cody in case she needs to stay with me for a while."

Oh, how had she fucked this up so bad? Not only with Noel but with Cody. Not only with Cody but their family. *You need something to take your mind off this,* she told herself. *Off Noel and Cody. Off the hurt you've caused everyone.*

Noel looked in the camera again as if he could see her. She rested her fingertips against his face on the screen, tears falling on the back of her hand. "I love you, Mare. But I think the fact that I'm recording this through a surveillance camera in our living room shows just how disconnected we are from each other right now. Given how much you've shut me out lately, I assume I won't hear from you after you watch this." He paused. "If you watch this."

Maris was crying freely now, big sobbing gasps. Noel ran a hand through his hair. "But know I'm here if you want to talk." He stood up and walked away, and a few seconds later she heard his footsteps elsewhere in the house, then the sound of the front door opening and closing. She waited through the full minute until the screen went black, then looked up as if for the first time in an hour. Her neck hurt from the rigorous way she'd held it over the phone, her teeth clenched so hard her jaw hurt.

She couldn't take the pressure and grabbed her jacket and purse and ran out the door.

And it's not just your family, she reminded herself. *A crazy man is trying to infiltrate your brain. This is not just normal everyday stress. Can anyone be expected to stay sober during this? Just one. Maybe two.*

Your family is better off without you. Safer.

Turning toward Savory's, she tried to combat these thoughts with her higher brain and reason: *You'll feel like shit. It will mean you failed. You can't trust yourself to have only two. Noel will hate you. Cody will stay in Nebraska with Scott. You will want more than two, and you know this. You will want and want and want.*

But lizard brain knew her better than anyone, and how to push her buttons. *You deserve to feel like shit. You are a failure. You deserve to lose your family and can't be trusted.* Her feet moved quickly, pointed true north. Lizard brain knew that part of the allure of drinking was the gratification of proving herself right: she was just as awful as she'd always suspected. It had taken so much willpower to stay sober all these months, to say no and no and no and no, and where had it gotten her?

She rushed through the automated doors of Savory's Market and past the cash registers with their twee, short checkout lines and their impulse-purchase artisanal chocolates. A woman with orange-red hair and lipstick looked up from her station. "Can I help you find anything?"

Maris ignored her and looked up at the balcony bar. She'd sat there countless times before, pretending she was waiting for a friend, just a quick glass or two while she shopped for dinner.

But eight months. Was she really willing to go back on eight months of hard work? On the one hand, it struck her as stupid to think of it as work when the job was to do nothing. Don't buy the wine. Don't uncork the bottle. Don't pour the glass. But it had been the hardest work she'd ever done. With a sharp pang she could almost taste her bad decision, and the sensation brought tears to her eyes. Was she really willing to go back to day one?

Yes. She was. Because it seemed that her troubles hadn't started until *after* she quit drinking. Now there were great, gaping holes in her life, and they so resembled the blackouts from her drinking days, what was the point of staying sober? Why bother with all the work? Let the work be the uncorking, the pouring, the drinking. The slip out of consciousness, but on purpose.

She kept her eyes focused on the stairs at the back of the store, not willing to look around and possibly make eye contact with someone she knew. She thought how much she would hate herself. How much she would hate who she'd become. And still she had to will herself not to take the stairs two at a time.

At the top of the staircase, she took a deep breath, and slid her hip onto the well-worn barstool.

Chapter

Twenty-Six

"What can I get you?" the bartender asked, leaning his upper body toward the bar, elbows out. He was a harried young man in his twenties, single-handedly filling the orders of approximately two dozen people. The balcony bar had a smattering of tables for customers to enjoy their coffee or wine, or take part in buck-a-shuck nights when the market's seafood department ran the special on oysters.

Maris looked at the chalk menu as if assessing the white wines but really contemplating whether this was something she could do. What did she have to lose? Her family had abandoned her, and it was all her fault. A man was trying to destroy who she was. She glanced at the small camera in the corner, a steady red light trained on her. Who knew how Hollis was tracking her?

"Ma'am?"

Eight months. Eight months. Eight months.

She tried to answer, but nearly choked on her words. "Sorry," she said, in reference to the strange, guttural noise she'd made. "I'm getting over a cold." She cleared her throat and smiled at him. "Kendall-Jackson chardonnay, please." She told herself just because she ordered it, that didn't mean she had to drink it; he was impatient, a line forming behind her. No reason her indecision should slow him down. In a way, she was just being thoughtful.

He pulled the half-full bottle from the ice as he grabbed a wineglass from the rack above him. The cork came out in a smooth motion, and he set the glass on a napkin, poured the wine in, and slid it toward her, sloshing dangerously close to the rim. She held out her credit card, and he swiped it through. "Start a tab?"

"Please."

He handed the card back. She tucked it into her wallet and put her wallet in her purse before she allowed herself to pull the glass even closer, smoothing the napkin as she brought the drink to her mouth and opened her throat.

The first sip was much sourer than she had expected. She grimaced, blinking her eyes. This was what she'd been missing all these months? This was what she hadn't been able to give up a million other times? The taste lingered, like a penny at the back of her throat.

She brought the glass back to her mouth and rested it on her lip. It had been horrible, right? But that didn't make sense. She tilted the glass for another swallow. Better.

And the third, better still.

In the fourth large swallow, she found it: the warmth started in her chest and slipped toward her stomach like a low-grade hum. Oh sweet Jesus, there it was. She'd missed this feeling. Needed it, even. Her brain, now at the slightest delay, was able to think over what she'd learned that afternoon: Hollis had killed a woman and destroyed another. Any chance she had of reasoning her way out of this or winning her case had disappeared; he would need to be stopped. She held the question in her hands—*Will I have to kill him?*—as if turning over an algebra equation.

She looked around at the other drinkers, wondering what they were thinking. Tonight was the regular, middle-aged crowd at Savory's with women dressed in expensive name-brand athleisure wear and men in button-down shirts with fleece vests in navy, green, and gray. It was a crowd Maris could usually slip into unnoticed but in which she still felt like a spy. She was dressed in her paint-splattered jeans and grubby sweatshirt from that morning, unshowered, and she gripped her wineglass tighter and downed the rest. Toward the back of the long, narrow balcony, a woman with curly gray hair was watching her, and her pulse bolted—Beth had followed her—but then the woman began to laugh at something her friend had said, and Maris saw it was just an anonymous woman.

The bartender came over and asked if she'd like another. Had he flinched at how quickly she'd drunk the first glass? She had to get a hold of herself. Maris turned over her phone and fake-checked the clock. "Sure. My friend should be here any sec." He smiled, and she wondered if he heard that day after day from women at the bar who were clearly there by themselves. "Let me order one for her as well."

"Of course." He reached down and pulled the bottle back out of the ice as he grabbed a second glass. He emptied the bottle between the two glasses without spilling a drop, evening out the generous pours before tossing the bottle with a clank into the recycling. These were not the five ounces served at classy restaurants, but that good ol' midwestern pour. Maris took a greedy sip from one of the glasses and asked him to tab her out. She signed a generous tip and picked up both glasses.

"Don't forget which is yours," the bartender said, and she looked back at his handsome, bland face. Did he know both were for her? Was that a snide remark? He pointed innocently enough to the one in her right hand. "Your cold. You don't want to pass it to your friend."

Her face grew warm. "Yes. Thank you."

She carried both glasses to an alcove in the corner where she could drink in peace. Had the bartender been judging her? she wondered as she sat down at the small café table, but reminded herself there were people who had much more serious problems than her when it came to drinking. Much more. She liked to drink, sure, but what was so wrong with that? Why had she felt the need to suppress this part of herself for so long? Hidden away in the corner, she drank her second glass in three gulps, pinching the thin stem between her fingers as she tipped her head back with the glass to her mouth so the last drop could roll down the side and land on her tongue. Zing!

She picked up the third, that liquid heat seeping now to her limbs. It wasn't just heat, but tingle. My god, how had she gone so long without this, and why? What for, really? This was who she was—a person who loved to drink—so why had she tried to deny herself for so long? If Noel didn't like it, he could piss off. He hadn't married only his favorite parts, but all of her. Every freaking bit.

She peered through the railing slats to downstairs and watched the shoppers, a glorious haze invading her brain. A haze *she* had created, not some batshit scientist who had it in for the ladies. She giggled at the thought. A white woman in produce picked up a green pepper, turned it in her hand, then set it back on the pile. She picked another and another before finally selecting one to her standards and setting it in the front basket of her shopping cart. In the basket-y thing with the leg holes where you had to flip that red plastic flap up to keep the peppers from rolling out. The child's seat! A man spun the greeting cards and stopped, picked one up, opened and read it, then plucked an envelope and started for the cashier. Maris wondered if it was for an anniversary or a birthday or maybe even a dead aunt, but either way! Oh, how lucky he was to find the right card on the first try!

Her phone started bleating, and she saw an incoming call from Eula. *Oh no,* she thought. *No, no, no.* First rule of drinking: never talk on the phone. She'd violated it last February, and look where that got her.

Her head was starting to fog, and she knew if she opened her mouth to speak to someone, her voice might sound thick. That first slur from word to word, always catching on the *t*'s and *sh*'s. When was the last time she'd eaten? She remembered the apple and Cheez-Its in her purse, now long gone. She looked again at the clock on her phone:

it was almost seven thirty. She'd left home less than forty-five minutes ago; she was less than an hour into this mistake. She could turn this around, go home and drink a big glass of water. No one would ever have to know. Maris pushed the thought from her already hazing mind. She didn't want to consider her better options; she wanted to drink and drink and drink.

She had the spinny sensation she always got when she was first getting drunk, a swirl inside her mind that made a noise like holding a seashell to her ear. Some nights she used to lie in bed drunk with her eyes closed, and in the morning, she'd still be able to remember this sensation—the darkness, the sound of the ocean—and think, I must not have been too bad last night.

She thought about Hollis; he was just an abstract problem. She was in charge of creating her problems now.

She looked through the slats again and saw the thinning hair of her chair, Tammy Lerner, as she pushed a cart toward the frozen foods. Maris was going to have to leave. There were too many people here in this well-lit market, and it was only a matter of time before someone she knew spotted her back. She carried both wineglasses to the plastic tub so the bartender wouldn't find them empty when he wiped the table. Her phone secured to her ear, she faked a call as she walked by his station. "No really," she said loudly, careful with her words. "It's fine. We'll catch up another time." She faked a convincing pause as she waved goodbye to the bartender, who wasn't looking up. "Sounds great. I'll see you then." She held the phone to her ear until she was halfway down the stairs, to be sure the bartender couldn't glance over and see the black screen.

Outside the market, Maris threw her purse over her shoulder and walked the few blocks to the Treasure Club, holding her arms against the chill. It was still a few weeks before Halloween, but twentysome-things were on their way to parties, never passing up an opportunity to blend alcohol and disguise. On the way she passed Sonic the Hedgehog, Elle Woods, the fisherman's sweater from *Knives Out*.

Maris had always hated Halloween; she was too much of a scaredy-cat. When she was nineteen and in college, she went through a haunted house run by a fraternity on campus. At a particularly frightening stretch, where the zombies reached for the crowd, she fear-farted so bad the frat bros broke character. One boy put a hand over his nose and loudly exclaimed, "Who farted?" Thank god it was dark in there. Thank god she was with a group. The girls all started laughing and shrieking, sure it was part of the haunted house, and when they got outside, the girls collapsed in giggles, so Maris did, too, relief thrumming through her body. *My god,* she thought now. That had been over twenty years ago. Had she had a hair-trigger startle response all this time, or did it go even further back?

Shortly before Maris reached the bar's door, two teenagers rounded the corner. One was dressed in a white hoodie, a curly-haired wig, shower shoes, and a HELLO MY NAME Is sticky name tag that read DYLAN.

"What the—?" she started, shifting her eyes to his buddy dressed in a short skirt and a crop top, his hairy belly showing between the two, an awful ratty wig on his head. His name tag read JANE. Jesus Christ, they were dressed as Dylan Charter and his victim, Jane Doe. The man dressed in the skirt grabbed a pumpkin from a next-door florist shop and threw it in the street, the splat like a head opening. Maris leaned over thinking she might puke, and waited for both the men and the nausea to pass. She thought: *I could go home. I can still make a good decision.*

And then she opened the bar door.

CHAPTER TWENTY-SEVEN

The Treasure Club was actually a restaurant, old-fashioned with a wrap-around bar, tufted red-leather booths, and dark lighting. It was a place built for boozehounds. In its heyday, back in the fifties and sixties, the restaurant used to have a dress code—no jeans; men in jackets—and you could still see the hangers-on from days gone by littered among the booths: mainly oldsters in their seventies with a stiff drink and an iceberg lettuce salad, a squat of cottage cheese in the middle.

But the real clientele now was at the bar. Mainly men in their forties and fifties with bloated faces and button-downs, or golf shirts tucked into khaki pants. They were prosperous looking (this was still Oak Park), but with signs of lives hard lived. Burst blood vessels on their noses, the puttylike skin, a puffiness to their cheeks. The few women were thin, but they, too, showed their drinking in their faces. She guessed that every man here had grown up in Oak Park. They'd taken over their fathers' businesses and kept up the family tradition of coming to the Treasure Club every Friday and Saturday night, with or without the missus.

Maris sat down at the curve of the bar in front of a bowl of Gardetto's and another of Goldfish: free snacks to keep the drinkers going. See, she didn't need dinner! Two women were laughing, leaning against each other and deep into their cups. It was one thing to get drunk on your own, but another altogether when you were in smart shoes and silk blouses, with $200 jeans and a BFF by your side. Nothing desperate to see here! Just two ladies cutting loose; can you believe how naughty we are?

An attractive bartender in her early thirties came over and pointed at the two bowls. "You want another bowl to mix them?"

"No thanks," Maris said, and ordered a chardonnay. The bartender set it down on a napkin, and what the hell, Maris ordered a shot of vodka. "Grey Goose, if you have it." She could give two shits what kind of vodka she had, but knew ordering top shelf would make her look less desperate. She did a full body scan to check in with herself. Heart rate: normal. Thoughts: still got 'em. Fizzy feeling: excellent. She was sure she would remember being here, how fun it all was. How much she loved being out on a Saturday night, even if the bar was packed with losers. She thanked the bartender as she set the vodka in front of her, and Maris shot it in one gulp. She pointed at the empty shot glass, and the bartender nodded as she passed two Warped Wing beers to a customer.

Her phone rang, and she looked down at the blurry screen, seeing Karen's name this time. She rejected the call and looked at the time: 7:58. Down the bar, the two women pointed their ears at a cell phone as a rumbling voice Maris couldn't understand trumpeted through the speaker. One of the women started laughing while the other blushed, or maybe that was from the empty highball glasses in front of them.

In what felt like no time at all, her two shots and wine were gone. Oof. She never did well without a pace car. Nights she and Noel went out before she quit drinking, she'd stare at his glass, willing him to drink the last half inch so they could order another. When he went to the bathroom, she always sneaked gulps from his side of the table. And speaking of the bathroom, Maris could feel the tightening in her bladder, that pinch of unease as she realized she was going to have to go soon.

She squinted toward the back and could see the discreet sign for the restrooms, but it seemed an awful long way away. She planned her route, how she would weave through the tables and booths, but first she had to make it down from her barstool. What an amateur mistake! Always pick a chair closer to the ground when you're committing to a long night. She tried once again to remember the tipping off point, that moment where consciousness stopped. She held up her hand for another chardonnay but put her palm over the shot glass. No vodka. She could keep this going longer if she drank only wine, and if she really, really concentrated on remaining sober.

The bartender brought her a fresh glass filled an inch from the lip. God bless Ohio.

The two women across the bar leaned their heads together, and one sneaked a look at Maris. She glanced down at her decade-old sweatshirt and dirty jeans, not quite self-conscious but aware she should be. "I'll tab out," Maris said, careful to enunciate each word, extra emphasis between the *b* and *o*. She would go back to Savory's and get a bottle for home. Maybe two. She would drink them in peace, without judgment, and she remembered suddenly the joy of being in her room as a teenager, away from prying eyes.

She took the receipt set in front of her—when had that appeared?— squinted one eye, times two-ed the amount, and signed her name. God she had to pee, but first: finish the wine. Make that bathroom trip worth it.

An older woman came out from the dining area in slacks and a satin blouse. "Ma'am?" she said, and Maris put a hand to her chest. The woman had an air of authority and a take-no-shit attitude, and Maris intuited from all her time in bars and restaurants that this was the manager. Maybe she'd won a free drink! Or Customer of the Year for her tip! *Or maybe,* she thought, looking down at her wobbly outfit, *they think I'm a bum.*

She squinted, her wineglass halfway to her face.

"I'm going to have to ask you to leave," the manager said. Maris tried to concentrate on the woman, but it was like watching a 3D movie without the glasses, two identical images jumping against each other. "You're being disruptive."

But as drunk as Maris was, she knew this wasn't being disruptive. Drunk, yes, but not disruptive. She'd gone down that path more times than she wanted to admit, especially in her younger days, and this wasn't it.

"You're kicking me out?"

The woman nodded, and set a guiding hand on Maris's elbow, but Maris ripped it away. This was a misunderstanding! She opened her mouth to explain she was a professor—a professional!—but the woman leaned closer. "Other customers have requested you leave."

Maris heard another voice behind her, a woman's voice. "I've got her," the woman said. Maris turned, a throbbing starting now in her head that made it difficult to turn too quickly.

"Karen? Were you at Savory's?" It sounded like *Salffory's.*

"I've got her," Karen said to the manager.

"We need her to leave immed—"

"I *said* I've got her," Karen repeated roughly, and Maris started to laugh. Karen didn't take any shit.

The manager leaned in. She was a leaner, too much perfume. It mixed with the smell of sautéed onions from the kitchen, and for a moment Maris thought for sure she'd puke.

"Thanks for returning all my calls and texts," Karen muttered. "I see you've been really busy." Maris was pretty sure that was sarcasm. No calls when drunk! Didn't Karen know the rules?

◆ ◆ ◆

They were on the sidewalk now, the world at a tilt, most of her weight held up by Karen. Maris kept an eye on her feet. Not a straight-straight line but close. There were footsteps next to her. Maris looked up and saw Karen's determined face, a jaw that could crack a walnut. Maris laughed. She leaned forward, the sidewalk rushing up to meet her, but Karen yanked her back. They were in front of an ice cream diner-thing now, two blocks away. How'd that happen?

"My car's just over here," Karen said, and Maris wanted to explain that she couldn't drive but couldn't find the words.

"Hey!" someone yelled behind them, and Karen stopped as Maris's stomach hurled upward from the change in direction. Whoops! "Hey," the voice said again, an angry, secret whisper. "Here." She reached for Maris's purse—*good job remembering that!*—and shoved a piece of paper inside.

Maris squinted at the person. A woman. She stepped toward her, and Maris instinctually flinched. Up close she could see the woman's eyes, pupils big in the dark, the skin around them pale and taut. Chestnut-blonde hair and a smoky eye. She was the kind of together person who could keep their lipstick on while they ate a full meal. Dressed for Instagram in a floral dress and ankle boots, a leather bag on her shoulder. *I know her,* Maris thought.

"Do I know you?" she said, but words were getting harder, longer, fully made of vowels.

"Make sure she gets home safe," the woman said to Karen, and turned the way she'd come, running back to the Treasure Club on chunky-heeled boots.

◆ ◆ ◆

Maris's eyes were closed, or at least she thought they were. Things were swimmy and shimmery and dark. She heard a voice. Karen? "I'll get her some water."

"Do you think she should throw up before she lies down?" It was a different voice now, and boy did they seem worried about something. Maris winced open an eye—was she on a couch? A bed? There was a desk. A chair. She rotated her cheek and found she was face-to-face with a picture of Michelle Obama, ready to give her a kiss. She shut her eyes again as an acidic wave crashed in her stomach. She tried to sit up in a panic—*Where's Code?*—but a hand on her shoulder gently pushed her back down, then two sets of hands rolled her onto her side.

CHAPTER TWENTY-EIGHT

I had my back to Maris but could see her in the mirror, and it was only a matter of time before the Charters noticed she was there. I wasn't too worried she'd recognize me, because along with me wearing a different disguise than the other times I'd seen her—that of the perfect girlfriend—it was clear the good professor was drunk. She rested her sloppy elbows on the bar top as she poured wine down her throat, a Goldfish cracker stuck to her cheek. *This* was the woman I thought might be able to help me?

"Oh dear," Carol Charter said, and set her fork with an uneaten bite of salad back on her plate.

"What is it?" Eric Charter asked.

"It's her," Carol whispered, and Dylan's dad looked up.

"Jesus Christ," he muttered. "Isn't she ever going to leave us alone?"

"Of course she would want to ruin my birthday," Dylan groused.

Poor baby, I thought, and had to keep my face neutral. Adoring. Sympathetic that he might not get the perfect twenty-fourth he'd dreamed about, no matter that the media reported anonymously that Jane Doe already had two suicide attempts under her belt.

Eric Charter held up a finger for the waitress, beckoning her over with a crooking finger. We had the largest table in the restaurant with nine people: the Charters, me, an aunt and two uncles, and two cousins, both preppy assholes like Dylan in untucked button-downs. Dylan had asked his parents not to make a big deal, but they insisted on coming to the Treasure Club, a birthday tradition for generations, and one they'd been robbed of celebrating last year because of that awful ordeal.

"Yes, sir?" the waitress said, bending closer to Eric Charter to hear his request.

"That woman at the bar," he said. "She's clearly drunk and making a scene. I'd like her to be removed."

The waitress's brows furrowed. "That one?" she said, pointing toward Maris.

"Yes. She did something . . . unsavory," he said, and made eye contact with the waitress.

"I didn't see anything," she admitted. "But I'll keep an eye on her and ask the bartender to as well," she started, but Eric cut her off.

"Get Lucy."

The waitress looked confused. "Lucy? My manager? Sir, I'm trying to—"

"Now," he said, and she took a step back and nodded, her tip slipping between her fingers. The article Maris first wrote about Dylan, "The (White) Boy Next Door," talked about how rich communities and families raised boys to be men who thought rules didn't apply to them. That was certainly the Charters.

"Right away, sir."

She disappeared into the kitchen, and a moment later an older woman in a satin blouse and neat trousers appeared. It was the exact wrong outfit for working in a restaurant, and I knew it was a fuck you to the waitstaff and cooks, or anyone else who actually had to get their hands dirty at a shitty job. She was signaling she was better than them, an equal to the rich and elite who came in, although the rich and elite wouldn't see it that way. To them she was a glorified waitress, a concierge for their dining experience.

As she approached, she put both hands on Eric Charter's shoulders, leaning in to give him a squeeze. "How's my favorite family?"

I gritted my teeth at her affection, but plenty of women just wanted a seat next to the power. And this was good for me. The more people at the Treasure Club who saw me with the family, the better. There would be witnesses to confirm I was Dylan's girlfriend, a nice girl, and when I made allegations, there would be voices to back me up.

"We were having a great time until that woman started up," Eric Charter said, and the manager followed his arm down to his fat finger, pointing at Maris.

I pouted at Dylan: *How dare that drunk woman ruin your night!* He sneaked his hand into mine and rested it in my lap as my body went still. There was only a thin layer of cotton and a floral dress separating him from my naked skin. I focused on the shiny tines of my fork, the tight points of metal, and imagined grinding them into his hand until I hit the unyielding wood of the table. I allowed his hand to remain as long as I could—maybe two seconds—until the bile climbed my throat and threatened to erupt.

"I'll take care of it, Mr. Charter," the manager said, and nodded to every individual at the table, addressing most by name. She even nodded to me, then looked approvingly at Dylan and winked.

As she walked to the bar, I watched her lean forward and say something to Maris, the cracker dropping from Maris's cheek.

"I can't believe that woman would even show her face in here," Eric Charter said, and shook his head.

"She wouldn't have known we'd be here," Carol reasoned, but Eric sneered.

"Please. She probably had Dylan's birthday marked on her calendar, just ready to ruin it. It's probably her Christmas."

"Dad—" Dylan started, but Eric held up his hand, and Dylan obeyed.

"No matter," Eric said faux pleasantly, and rearranged the napkin on his lap. "We'll put a stop to her soon enough, won't we?" He bent to wolf down a piece of his steak.

A stop to her? "What do you mean?" I asked, and Eric turned his gaze on me for the first time all night. "I mean, I would love to see her shut up as much as the next person given what she's said, but how can you stop her?" I paused. "Free speech and all."

Eric leaned forward. "So you know about her? *Dr.* Heilman?"

I had to tread carefully. "I mean." I shrugged. "I admit, I looked up Dylan when we started dating." I reached over and took his hand again. "I read all those terrible things she wrote."

"But how do you know it's her?" Eric said. "How did you recognize her?" He laughed, then said something that made no sense: "It's not like she has a new faculty picture." One of the men at the table started laughing, the other bent over his cell phone, while Dylan seemed as confused as I was.

At the bar, the manager put her hand on Maris's arm, and Maris yanked it away.

A woman approached, and I watched her negotiate between the manager and Maris as Maris started laughing.

"Let's just say," Eric continued, "she's not going to be writing much longer."

"Why not?" I asked, unable to stop myself.

"I've taken care of it," he said, and laughed as he lifted one of the bottles on the table. "Now. Who wants more wine?"

The third woman escorted Maris out, and I pushed my chair back abruptly, nearly colliding with one of the attentive water boys, who sloshed a cold wave against my arm. "I'm so sorry!" he said as I gave him a shaky smile and then turned it on the table.

"Will you excuse me, please? I'd better get a towel."

Right before the bathroom, I bolted left for the front door. I knew from the way Eric Charter had laughed that Dr. Maris Heilman was in danger. Real danger. This was already a family that condoned rape, so who was to say what the next leap would be? What was it he'd said? She wouldn't be writing much longer?

Between the double doors of the restaurant, I scrabbled through my designer purse for a pen, dug a receipt from the bag, and scrawled a note. Outside, the wind whipped my hair in my eyes, and I looked left to right and left again, finally spotting a wobbly Maris and the other woman holding her up. Maris threw her head back and laughed, and I felt a spark of irritation. *Doesn't she know how much danger she's in? What is she doing getting drunk?*

The hypocrisy of my statement nearly stopped me short as I echoed the very voices that had been in my head since the rape. *What did she think would happen when she drank at a party? What did she think would happen when she was already willing to fuck two guys?*

I sped down the sidewalk. With Maris on unsteady feet, they hadn't gotten very far, and I grabbed her by the elbow and spun her around, tucking the note in her bag.

"Make sure she gets home safe," I said to the other woman, and turned and ran back to the restaurant. Already I imagined Eric Charter would give me a dirty look for being in the bathroom an unladylike amount of time.

Back between the double doors, I smoothed powder over my face and lip gloss over my mouth. I dabbed at the wet sleeve from the clumsy water boy. Sliding into my seat, I left a sticky lip gloss print on Dylan's cheek and smiled with my capped teeth at his father.

I just wanted to look good for your son, that smile said, and Eric smiled back, satisfied.

He lifted his glass, and the table quieted for the patriarch. "To a bright future," he said, and clinked with Dylan's uncles, Dylan, and eventually his wife.

Dylan hadn't been the only one with a bright future once upon a time, I thought, but I held up my glass and clinked with my boyfriend.

"To a bright future," I echoed.

PART FOUR

CHAPTER TWENTY-NINE

Pain crackled through Maris's skull like a live wire, and she knew if she opened her eyes or moved her head, the electricity would burn down her body. Sour chardonnay coated her tongue, swollen like a dead slab in her mouth.

She carefully opened one eye.

Her cheek was on the edge of a green floral couch cushion and the floor was an industrial linoleum, and as she glanced up, she saw a desk and two chairs—too much furniture for this small room. She moved to sit up but winced and gently rested her head down the two inches. Her dehydrated heart thumped in her chest.

Where the hell am I?

She wasn't home, but it was somewhere familiar. She had been here before. The sound of two sets of footsteps echoed from the hallway, and Maris leaned up through the bolt of head pain as Karen came into the room, a paper cup in her hand along with a paper bakery bag, followed by Eula. It clicked together: she was in Karen's office at the hospital.

She winced as she sat the rest of the way up. "What time is it?" And more importantly, was Noel still on duty? *How in the fuck did I end up here?* Maris frantically shifted through last night's shoddy memories.

The last thing she really remembered was being blotto at the Treasure Club. The bar manager had thrown her out, and Karen had shown up—was that right?—and helped her stumble walk out of there. And then home but not home, her thudding head on a pillow. She looked at the couch where she now sat: same one as last night.

Had Karen taken Maris to her office, or to the ER? "Did I talk to Noel?"

Karen shook her head. "I brought you in the service entrance."

Maris was about to ask where Cody was, but then dropped her head in her hands. Of course. Cody was in Nebraska. She dug her phone out of her purse, now almost out of charge, and found text alerts from Cody.

Landed in omaha. 10:51 p.m.

In lincoln at dads 12:23 a.m.

Did u call school? they know I'm gone Monday? 12:41 a.m.

Oh, for the love of god, could she not fuck up for one day? She tucked her phone back in her purse knowing she'd have to face it soon. She winced and squinted at Eula. "And how did you get here?"

"My car," Eula said smartly.

"No, I mean *why* are you here?" Maris struggled to keep from crying. Eight months down the drain.

"You insisted I call her instead of Noel," Karen explained. "You said you didn't want Noel to know you were drunk, so you asked me to call Eula instead." Maris remembered now that she had met Karen originally through Eula, that she'd been at one of the annual cookouts in the Moores' backyard. Which also meant a potential connection to Hollis. Could she trust Karen? Or for that matter, Eula? She was so tired.

"And I picked up when I saw Karen's name," Eula said. "She was one of Carl's students years ago."

"And don't forget how Eula and Carl first met." Karen laughed. Maris remembered: Eula had been his student, and he was married at the time.

"I always encouraged Carl to have the students over to the house for a party at the end of every semester," Eula said, "so I could suss them out, see who might be my competition." Maris remembered some of these in the spring: older students mingling in the backyard over sangria, always seemingly able to keep it to one or two. "I loved that man dearly, but he had a wandering eye. Every now and again I'd hit it off with one of the students, and we'd stay in touch. One of them was Karen."

Karen sat in one of the empty chairs and Eula the other. She stuck her hand in the bakery bag and pulled out a slice of cakey bread, and as she unwrapped it, spongy and damp, the smell of overripe bananas wafted from the plastic. Maris's stomach lurched, and she shook her head as Karen held out the slice but gratefully accepted the extra cup of coffee, hot and bitter.

"I'm sorry I stole the folder," she said, remembering bits of Karen's muttering about not returning her texts last night.

"Not cool," Karen admitted, "but after talking with Eula, I have a bit better idea what's at stake."

"How are you feeling?" Eula asked as she unwrapped one of the bakery items, this one thankfully a blueberry muffin.

"Not great."

"I would guess not," Karen said, but it was not so much judgmental as a biological fact. She wondered how many drunks Karen saw each weekend in the ER, how many people were hospitalized from accidents and mishaps and near-death blunders. *She'd* never been hospitalized because of drinking. Although she'd sprained her ankle once and had to ice it for three days, and there was that one time she'd tripped on the sidewalk, her head making a walloping splat noise like a cantaloupe when it hit the concrete.

Maris drank a scalding gulp of coffee. "I don't know what happened. I only had two glasses of wine," she lied, shame thick in her throat. "Maybe it's just because I haven't had anything to drink in so long. Or maybe someone slipped something in my drink." Karen gave her a patronizing smile. Tears formed in Maris's eyes. "I'm sorry." She wasn't even sure who she was apologizing to, or what for. "How did you even find me?"

"Julie and I were out celebrating our anniversary," Karen said.

Maris lowered her head in her hands. "So I ruined that too." She looked imploringly at the two women. "I swear, last night was the first time I've had a drink since February."

"You've had a lot to process," Karen said, and moved to the couch to squeeze Maris's hand. "I'm glad you're okay."

The awful memories from the night before flashed through Maris's brain: Trying to sound sober and trick the Savory's bartender into believing she had a friend when he hadn't even bothered to look up. Teetering on the high stool at the Treasure Club. Pouring large piles of Goldfish into her palms and shoving them into her mouth; at least one or two ricocheted off her face and onto the dirty bar, where she pinched them between her clumsy fingers and ate them anyway.

Maris leaned her head back against the sofa cushion and closed her eyes, the guts of her brain pushing against her skull.

"Clearly you aren't feeling your best given last night's activities," Eula reasoned. "And I'm sympathetic to that, Maris, I am, but we do have bigger problems than you finding your way to the bottom of a bottle of chardonnay." Maris was tempted to laugh—such an unimaginable sound burbling up in her—and she burped it back. When had a problem ever seemed bigger to her than her drinking? "Karen and I have had some time to compare notes and get a sense of what's going on."

Karen jumped in. "I think we're both clear enough on what Hollis is doing as far as brain waves and cell towers, and that he's implemented Eula's theories to put things into practice, but Maris? Why *you*? Why the other women?"

Maris scooted forward, gripping her coffee, and shook her head. "It doesn't make sense. He's been pretty vocal about hating my work and thinking I'm an impostor in academia"—as if Maris needed anyone to tell her that—"and he's fighting against my tenure, but *this*?"

"Exactly," Karen said. "That can't be the real reason. And if it is, why Beverly? She directs the Women's Center here at the hospital, and I get he doesn't like women, but again, why her?"

"And Janice Lambert?" Maris said. "She doesn't even work with women but children."

"And Shelby Steele is little more than a child herself in her twenties," Eula said.

At the mention of a person in her twenties, Maris remembered the strange woman chasing them down the sidewalk outside the Treasure Club. She'd always been good with faces (when sober), which had served her well as a teacher, and she was sure now she hadn't had her in class. She knew she'd seen the woman before, but something didn't add up. Something was out of context. It could be as simple as she'd waited on Maris at a restaurant or took her package at the post office, but the moment gnawed at Maris until she remembered. The woman from office hours and the library. The woman last night had the same crackle of energy and unease but had been polished like a stone—the right outfit, chestnut-blonde hair, expensive makeup.

She whipped around to look at Karen, hangover be damned. "The woman. The one last night."

Karen furrowed her brows, and then her face lit up. "That's right. I'd kind of forgotten about her."

"Do you know her?"

Karen shook her head. "She just seemed like another Oak Park rich girl."

"But the thing is," Maris said, "I don't think she is." She explained about the odd run-ins, the unease she felt, the sense the other times that the woman had been in disguise.

"Okay," Eula said, "but what does that have to do with Hollis Grant?"

"What does any of this?" Maris asked. "It doesn't make sense why he'd have it in for me or really *anyone* to the point he'd want to stop their memories."

"And stopping memories is only part of it," Eula said cautiously. "My concern is that's not the end goal."

Maris looked at her expectantly, and Eula raised her shoulders in a shrug. "I'm not sure what he has planned next."

"Can you figure it out?" Maris asked.

"Probably not without a good look at his current research."

Maris nodded. "Then I guess we need to figure out how to get our hands on that."

But for now, she needed to sleep. Her hangover was barreling down, a bill about to come due. "Give me a few hours," she said, "then I'll get to work." She needed to figure out how the women were connected and how to get her hands on Hollis's research. She leaned her head on the sofa back, a plan taking shape.

"I'll drive you home," Eula said.

Karen walked them to the door, stressing how confidential this information was, how important it was they keep it within this small circle and not tell anyone else.

"Stealing the folder was one thing because I wasn't culpable, but we're talking about my medical license now," Karen said. "You can't tell Noel about this. If he knew I was involved, he'd have to report me to the AMA. I'd lose my license for good, not to mention any access we might need to hospital records."

Maris didn't have the stomach to tell Karen it wasn't a concern. Noel had moved out; Cody was gone. Her only chance to get them back was to stop all of this.

Eula pulled in the driveway, and Maris climbed out, her body now sore from the hangover in addition to the broken ribs and bruises.

At her front door, she opened her purse and moved aside her phone and wallet for her keys, and that was when she found the note.

CHAPTER THIRTY

Maris locked the door behind her and brought her purse to the sofa, taking a big breath before pulling out the note and unfolding it.

It was a receipt to a liquor store, delicate at the folds where Maris's palm sweat had dampened the paper. Had this odd woman been following Maris? And had that started at the Treasure Club, or the library, or months before?

She unfolded it carefully, reading the three lines of block letters in blue pen.

Charters are DANGEROUS!!!

and they are after you

BE CAREFUL!!

What in the ever-loving hell? Who was this woman, and what danger exactly did she know about? Maybe she was just trying to scare Maris into going after Dylan? The note seemed like it had to be related to the blackouts, but as unhinged as Maris felt right now, she also wouldn't be surprised to know there were other dangers out there, lurking around every corner, her entire life a sinking ship. Maris felt her sanity was being held together by a string of dental floss.

She smoothed the note against her knee and tried to be rational. Was this note a threat or a warning? Her weird run-ins with the woman confirmed she had a hatchet for Dylan Charter, one Maris, too, had to an extent, but that didn't mean she could just frame him. Was that what the woman was trying to do? Maris realized for perhaps the first time just how alone she felt, how adrift in her own fears.

Maris wanted to dig into Hollis's research, but she knew she wasn't going to make any good decisions now, or be able to piece these clues together. First, sleep.

She tucked the note back in her purse, double-checked she'd locked the door, and stumbled upstairs. Tired as she was, she peeled off the sweat-stained clothes she'd been wearing for almost thirty hours and climbed in a too-hot shower, leaning against the tile as she allowed herself to cry. She half dried off, then slipped on one of Noel's Old 97's T-shirts and climbed into the cool bed, the sheets in need of a wash but welcoming.

It was almost noon now, and Maris was aware Noel would be home from the hospital, home to Joe's anyway. He was probably asleep, and still, she debated texting but didn't know what she'd say. How had things gotten so bad? She knew the answer was that they just hadn't faced things as they'd come: the distance, the drinking, how much they both hated his awful work schedule. Wasn't that what they'd done with their finances? When they'd gotten together, between the two of them they still had nearly $50,000 in student loans, but for the first year or two—the second adolescence—they'd ignored what was too big to look straight at and added weekend trips to the credit card, a surprise trip to San Francisco to see Wilco. It wasn't until notices started coming with red ink on the envelopes that they turned things around and got serious. Now their marriage seemed covered in red ink, and she felt helpless to fix it.

She plugged her phone into the extralong charger by her bed—the one long enough so she could lie on either side and catch up on Twitter rather than getting the sleep she so desperately needed—and after a deep breath, opened the texts from Cody.

Thanks for keeping me updated, she wrote, and sorry I didn't answer sooner. I'm sorry you're gone Code. I miss you. I will call the school and take care of it but there's much more to say than just that. Please know I love you and I want to be better. She stared at the words, then erased the last bit after *I love you*. Even in the state she was, she couldn't bring herself to put in writing to her daughter how much better she needed to be.

◆　◆　◆

When she woke up hours later, it was from the deep-tissue sleep of the hungover—limbs and tongue heavy, mind still throbbing but from a distance, and every cell craving water. She gulped two bottles and sat down to pee, her underpants at her ankles and her mind finally clear.

What in the ever-loving fuck had she stumbled into?

Although she hadn't stumbled into it, had she? She'd been targeted.

Perhaps one of the weirder parts was how relieved she was to not be the only target. Relieved this hadn't been connected to her drinking, and that she wasn't alone, because with Noel and Cody gone even less than a full day, she certainly felt alone in other ways.

She checked her phone and found a text from Scott saying he didn't know what exactly was going on but he was here to talk and hoped she was okay. Had he figured out it was connected to her drinking? She'd wondered for a long time if what they had been attracted to in each other was the damage—their mutual love of alcohol—but it wasn't just that. He was a kind and good man, and she was lucky to have him still in her life.

She texted back thanks, I'm fine and then, or I will be. She hoped to god it was true, and vowed again that if she made it through this, she'd find ways to be better.

She called and left a message at Cody's school that she'd be out the following week and asked that her teachers email the assignments to herself. "I'll be sure she gets them," she said, and recognized it was a way to force Cody into contact with her. She wanted that much connection to her daughter if nothing else. Cody hadn't responded to her earlier text, but Maris sent another. Thinking of you. Free to talk anytime.

As for Noel, she hadn't heard from him at all. What she wouldn't give for one of the idiotic texts that was just an excuse to be in the other's thoughts. A month in, he'd sent a picture of the cereal aisle at Kroger asking what kind of cereal he should buy. As if she didn't already know he ate Special K every morning of his life. A box of it stood in the pantry right now, and my god what if Noel never came home and she had to look at that box every day? Even in the blackouts she'd felt tethered to her family, but maybe that hadn't been true. Maybe there had been problems stretching back further than she realized as she tried to convince her family as well as herself that she had it all together. She reached for her phone to text him but felt the guilt of the night before would come through in her words and he'd know how much she'd messed up. Plus, he was the one who had left, so why should she be the one to contact him first? Instead she turned her volume all the way up, waiting for the special *bing-bong* notification she'd assigned to his texts.

She thought of everything she'd gone through in the last twenty-four hours, some of it at her own hands and some of it not. As the memory of last night at the Treasure Club came rushing back, she wondered what about drinking had ever appealed to her while at the same time she knew that if someone handed her a glass of wine right now, she'd drink it.

Her father's saying reverberated in her head: the sun comes up, the sun goes down, and here you are.

With her father's drinking, she'd long wondered about nature versus nurture and what generational trauma she'd passed on to her own daughter. Was Maris herself drawn to alcohol because of something encoded deep in her DNA, or was it all those afternoons and weekends when she'd watched him drinking with his buddies, laughing at some raucous joke above her head, as the Huskers won on TV? She hadn't understood that the surly mornings were a part of the drinking, too, or that her mother's sternness had tried to protect Maris from her dad's actions. One time, her father had drunk the last six-pack in the house and was going on an ill-advised beer run when he told Maris to hop in as his copilot. Her mother voiced that she didn't think that was a very good idea, and her father said, "Take a chill pill, Jilly."

"Yeah," Maris echoed. "Take a chill pill, Jilly." Oh, how her father howled! She was so proud of his approval. Now she burned at the way it must have hurt her mother when she did that, undermining what small shred of authority she had, and also burned with anger that her mother ultimately let her get in the car with a drunk driver.

In the kitchen she heated up some shrimp-flavored ramen—*Cody's favorite,* she thought with a pang—and tried her daughter on FaceTime. Her heart leaped as Cody answered, the phone held at arm's length, and Maris could see she was sitting cross-legged on her bed in the room her father kept decorated for her year-round, the same blue-and-gray quilt on Cody's bed that Scott had on his own bed when he and Maris were dating. "Hey, sweetheart." It was their first time talking since Noel had put Cody on the plane.

"Hey, Mom." Cody shuffled some papers in the well between her knees, and Maris told her she'd have assignments starting Monday. She didn't want to talk about homework or logistics. What she wanted was to tell her daughter a truth, but how to do it without getting into exactly what was going on? What was the deeper, generational truth?

"I haven't been a very good mom lately," Maris said. "I've been too caught up in my own life. My job, my problems. Those things are important, and I want to model for you that women can have careers and accomplishments or anything they want, but nothing in the world is more important to me than you." Cody kept her eyes steady on her mother, and Maris let it all pour out. "I want you to know how much I love you. I'm going to change, Cody. I need you to trust me on that."

Cody narrowed her eyes. "And why would I do that? How much did you trust me and Noel when you were recording us?"

Her daughter had a point. Maris hadn't given Cody a lot of reasons to trust her, and it went further back than the video camera or the blackouts or the night at the Lamberts' house. How many times had she had one too many glasses when it was just her and Cody in the house? When Cody could have fallen or choked and Maris wouldn't have been able to drive her to the hospital? Or what if Cody had cut herself with a knife slicing vegetables, and Maris hadn't been able to react quickly enough? She'd always gone by the what-if principle, played the odds nothing bad might happen. Only now did she realize it wasn't just about being prepared for the emergencies, but being present for the good times: How often had she snapped at Cody because she didn't feel well in the morning, or fallen asleep reading her a bedtime story because she'd had one too many glasses with dinner? How often had she spaced out on her phone without the energy to do a dance party in the kitchen or make bookmarks at the dining room table?

Maris cleared her throat. "You were right back in February to not get in the car with me," she said. "I shouldn't have been driving. And I certainly shouldn't have been driving with you."

Cody looked straight into the camera, a jolt to Maris as she felt them lock eyes almost eight hundred miles apart. "Then why'd you do it?" Cody asked, and it physically pained Maris to hear those words. She thought, *If I can just remember this horrible moment, if I can just remember this shame, I'll never want to drink again.* But she knew now that wasn't how it worked.

She went with the simplest answer, which was also the truest. "I'm an alcoholic." It was the first time in her life she had said it out loud. It happened almost in slow motion, the word hanging in the air. She imagined the two silhouettes from *The Electric Company* pushing out the syllables: *Al. Co. Ho. Lic.* "That's the reason, but it's not an excuse. I made a mistake. And I'm so sorry, Cody. You have every right to be mad about it."

"Thanks for the permission." It was the same line and tone from just over a week ago when Maris arrived at the school the day Cody got her first period. It was a huge event, and yet she hadn't asked any follow-up questions, or checked in with Cody about questions or supplies, or even offered to make her a special dinner, one they could cook together. It made her realize it wasn't just the drinking that had been her issue; it was putting too many things in front of her daughter. She should have always put Cody first.

"I haven't always been a good mother," she said. "I've been selfish, and judgmental, and haven't prioritized the way I should have. You're the most important thing in the world to me, Cody, and I'm going to be better," she promised. She would find a new way not to drink—not just through white-knuckling, but by asking for help. She felt for the first time she might have the tools and perspective to make that happen. Cody looked down, her body still, and Maris used her stillness like a screen to flash all the different versions of her daughter onto: toddler, middle schooler, baby, eight years old. How could one person contain so much?

"You haven't been *all* bad," Cody said, and the teenage surliness of her sarcasm gave Maris a ping of hope.

"I want you to come home," she said. There still lingered the threats from Hollis Grant, but she and the other women were getting closer. "It doesn't have to be tomorrow, but soon, I hope."

"I'll think about it," Cody said, and Maris admitted that was probably better than she deserved.

CHAPTER
THIRTY-ONE

Rejuvenated, she got back to work.

It was early afternoon on Sunday, her local library closed, so Maris pulled on a pair of Noel's wool socks and a cardigan and settled into a nest on the couch. She'd debated taking a Percocet for her injuries and hangover, but flushed the pills instead. She couldn't afford a foggier brain than she already had.

She was getting ready to dig for the connection between the other women again when she thought about her earlier talk with Beth Novak. They'd been so freaked about the blackouts themselves when they met for coffee, they hadn't had a chance to discuss if she knew Beverly, Janice, or Shelby.

She dialed Beth's number, and after three rings, Beth answered, a question in her voice as she said hello.

"It's me. Maris," she said, but Beth didn't say anything. "Dr. Heilman."

After a long pause, Beth responded. "I'm sorry, who?"

Maris's stomach tightened. Hadn't Beth programmed Maris's number in her phone? "Maris Heilman." She felt a drip of anxiety as it became clear Beth didn't recognize her name, but she knew she was talking to the same person based on the voice. "From Starbucks yesterday?"

"I'm sorry, but you have the wrong number," Beth said, and Maris heard the two beeps as the call disconnected. She felt a bolt of panic shoot up her back and called the number again, standing up to pace the living room.

"Beth! Don't hang up," she said, almost panting.

"Who is this again?" Beth asked.

Maris explained: Maris Heilman, from Glenn State. "I met with you yesterday?"

"I'm sorry," the woman said, her voice dubious and maybe a little frightened. "I don't know what you're talking about."

"What did you do yesterday afternoon?"

The woman paused. "I'm not going to tell you that. I don't even know who you are. Goodb—"

"Wait!" Maris yelled, and luckily Beth hung on. The video camera on the shelf caught her attention, and she walked toward it, her reflection in the black lens like a funhouse mirror. "One more question. Do you know who Dr. Hollis Grant is?"

"Dr. Grant?" Maris couldn't tell by Beth's voice if she knew who he was or not. "I don't think so."

Maris gripped her cell phone tighter. "When were you in graduate school?"

There was another long pause, and Maris heard what sounded like a dog barking somewhere in the distance over the line. "I only got my BA."

"Did you know a Diane Garland?"

"I have no idea who you're talking about," Beth said, and Maris's heart nearly stuttered to a stop. "And please don't call here again."

Already Maris was gathering her laptop and notebooks, and telling Beth thank you for your time.

She sprinted across their lawns and pounded on Eula's door.

"What the—" Eula said, and Maris cut her off.

"It's Beth," she said, and told her about the call—how Beth had no memory of their meeting over coffee, that someone had been asking about Hollis, or, it seemed, much about working with him at all. She certainly didn't remember Diane Garland and her stroke. Was it possible she was lying? But to what end? She had been so willing to talk yesterday. Maris remembered her irrational thought that Hollis could be in the white van next to them on the interstate, and while she doubted that was the case, he'd obviously been tracking them. She stopped short: *Of course.* He would have located Maris and Beth together through the cell towers.

"He must have figured it out," Eula said, her voice full of terror and awe. "The next phase. He's not just stopping memories from forming but erasing older ones."

"How difficult would that be?"

Eula shook her head in wonder. "It's hard to say if it was luck or patience, but he got there."

Maris thought she might be sick. It had been one thing for him to put her in a blackout, but to wipe out memories already in the brain was another. Had it just been chance that he had gone after Beth first and not her? How much time did she have? Maris put her hands over both sides of her head as if to hold in the memories, seal them away. She wondered for just a second if she might be able to wear a helmet to keep them protected before the next logical thought struck, that cell reception penetrated buildings and earth. But for a second she understood why people might wrap their heads in tinfoil hats only to be called crazy, when in reality it wasn't that crazy after all. She took stock of her body—heart rate, breath—as if she could feel a stroke coming on. Someone else she knew had a stroke. Who was it?

And then she remembered: Carl, Eula's husband. Hadn't he died of a stroke?

"Do you have Carl's medical records?" she asked, and Eula said just the death certificate. "But he went to the hospital, correct? Which one?"

Eula named Karen's hospital, and Maris sent her a text asking her to get a copy of his records and come straight to Eula's. "What are you thinking?" Eula asked.

Maris took Eula's hand and pulled her to the couch. "Tell me again what happened."

"I was in the kitchen with him," Eula reminded her, and Maris remembered: toasting a bagel.

Eula went on. "It was like someone severed the strings on a puppet. He didn't faint, or fall, it was more that he literally crumpled. I checked for a pulse, breathing, but everything had stopped. A bit later—before the ambulance arrived—he woke up, but was completely disoriented and had lost the ability to speak. He died the next day in the hospital." Eula reached for her tea, spilled some over the cup, and set it back down. "It was Hollis, wasn't it?"

"I think so."

"I always knew something was off," Eula said. "Carl and Hollis had fought the day before—he'd been angry all night about something. I think now it must have been about Hollis moving forward." She shook her head. "Carl would never have agreed to testing human subjects."

"Oh, Eula," she said, and pulled her neighbor in for a hug. Natural causes was hard enough to accept, but this? "Do you think if you had access to his research, you could figure out what he was doing?"

Eula nodded. "It's all based on my theories, so yes."

"So we get access to his research," Maris said.

"I was close enough to academic channels to know things move at a glacial pace. It'll take too long to cut through all that red tape."

Maris nodded. Her tenure process took almost a year. "Whatever we do," Maris said, "we have to keep this all contained. It's not just a matter of exposing Hollis, because if we do, that research becomes public knowledge. It's not something we want in the wrong hands." It had taken her only one or two logical leaps to realize the wrong hands would end up being the government, the very governing agencies that were supposed to protect them. "The next step might be to see if we can get copies of his research. His lab will be secure, but what about his office? We could at least see what he's got on his hard drive. Hopefully the data from the experiments and some of the financial records." Maris knew the best way to get answers was to follow the money.

"I don't know anything about computers," Eula said.

Maris thought of Janice, who, in addition to working part-time as the counselor at Horace Valley, taught computer programming. "I have just the person."

CHAPTER

THIRTY-TWO

A half hour later, Janice and Karen were both in Eula's living room with cups of tea, Janice's boot cast elevated on the coffee table. Maris and Eula had filled them in on Beth Novak and Diane Garland, and Maris's theory that Carl's death hadn't been a stroke but related to Hollis's first attempts at blocking memories. And if she'd learned anything from Diane Garland, it was that he often didn't get things right on the first try.

Eula shook her head. "If there was one person Hollis respected, it was Carl, but maybe I should have known."

Janice fidgeted with the sleeve of her sweater, worrying free a thread of yarn on the cuff. "I don't—" she started and shook her head. "It's just so *out there*."

Maris reached for Janice's hands to steady them. "Janice. Look at me." Janice slowly lifted her eyes to match Maris's. "You know as well as I do it's real. We know it better than anybody." Neither woman blinked. "We need to be strong for our daughters." At her worst times, Maris thought Cody would be better off without her, but deep down, she knew that wasn't true.

Slowly, Janice squeezed her hands back. "For our daughters."

Karen pointed to the medical file she'd set on the coffee table. Over the phone, Maris had filled Karen in on the large sweeps of her conversation with Beth, and saying the words out loud had made them more real yet. Hollis was really doing this: he could kill her at any second.

"The medical records aren't as helpful as you might hope," Karen said. "Carl was old and he had a stroke, so it was standard that no one would have ordered an autopsy. But the way Eula describes it, it sounds a lot like what happened to you two on October 8," she said, indicating Maris and Janice. "His autonomic systems just shut down."

"So you can't say for sure?" Eula asked.

"No," Karen said slowly, "but it's an awfully big coincidence."

Tears filled Eula's eyes. "I could have had more years with him."

"I'm so sorry," Janice said as Eula reached for a tissue.

"As am I, but for now, we need to concentrate on what's next." Eula looked at Maris, who explained to Janice the plan to copy Hollis's hard drive while he was out of his office.

"So breaking and entering?" Karen asked, and looked at Maris skeptically. "Is that really the only option? I could lose my medical license for a felony."

Maris thought fleetingly of her tenure case. It almost seemed laughable that had been the most important thing in her life just a month ago. "It might sound ridiculous, but your job is nothing compared to this. Hollis gets his way, you won't have a life, much less a career."

Eula dabbed under her eyes. "Carl was his best friend, and even he wasn't safe."

"If we can get a copy of his hard drive, I should be able to crack any kind of firewalls or security," Janice said.

"And I should be able to make sense of the research," Eula said.

"What about the other women?" Karen asked. "When do we call them?" She grimaced. "Those are not calls I'm looking forward to making."

"Let's see what we find out first from Hollis's research," Maris said. "All we need is to make sure he's out of his office."

"And how are we going to do that?" Karen asked, and Maris knew the answer: she was the perfect bait.

She reached over and squeezed Eula's hand. Maris realized that each day, more and more women were counting on her. "We're going to get him," she said. "I promise." The unspoken words rattled in her brain: *or die trying*.

◆ ◆ ◆

Maris did her best to put aside her terror over what might happen. Hadn't she lived much of her life this way? With the constant question of whether her future would destroy her? What if she drank now? Or now? The constant threat of her drinking and its guilt was like a malevolent cloud that followed her around, only one of her own making.

As it had always been, her work was an escape.

She addressed an email to Hollis Grant and Tammy Lerner with the subject line Tenure Process. She was requesting a meeting with the two of them for the next morning to discuss her case and her concerns regarding discrimination. She lied and said her lawyer was filing the paperwork against the university the next afternoon, and the morning would be their only chance to plead their case. Her real motive in requesting a meeting was so that Hollis would be guaranteed out of his office and Eula and Janice could gain access. It would make more sense to wait for another weekend when campus was nearly empty, but given the looming danger, they didn't want to wait.

Maris reviewed the university's policies on discrimination and highlighted her concerns Hollis would deny her tenure based on his biases against women. She knew there was discrimination at work, particularly in relation to what her predominantly male colleagues classified as scholarship, but like most of her female colleagues, she'd choked them down. The exception had always been Tammy.

She'd coauthored enough articles to get promoted to associate professor, then stopped publishing and became chair. In that position, over and over, Maris had watched her kowtow to their male colleagues' requests while she wielded her administrative powers against women. In her email, Maris described her fear, quoting from the policy, that he would "deprive [her] of educational or employment access, benefits, or opportunities on the basis of sex or gender." She couldn't call Hollis on the violations he was *really* committing: criminal offense, danger to the health and safety of others, impinging upon civil rights. There was even language in the policy forbidding incapacitation and blackouts, defined as "a period where memory formation is blocked," although the assumption here was that it would be accomplished through drugs or alcohol, not the blocking of neural capacities. But Eula was right: academic channels weren't going to help them. The meeting was a distraction.

Karen stood over her shoulder and watched as she typed the message.

"Are you sure he's going to agree?"

Maris nodded. "He won't be able to resist an argument. He'll want me to know his opinion and why it's the most important one. He'll try to put me on the defensive."

She hit send on the email, and seven minutes later, her phone rang. She looked down to see Tammy's name. It reminded her of the old sales mantra "always be closing," but in Tammy's case it was "never in writing."

"Maris, good. Glad I caught you," she said after their hellos. "Listen, I saw your email to myself and Dr. Grant, and I'd just like a little more heads-up so I'll know how to prepare for the meeting." That was academic code for, what the hell is this about?

Maris cited Hollis's personal attacks against her as proof he'd been gunning for her for years: in his classes, over email and LISTSERVs, in local and national papers. "There's no way I can get a fair shake if he's on the university committee for my promotion," she said. "Obviously he's biased."

"I hardly think a few opinion pieces and emails are enough of a reason to worry," Tammy said. "Are you sure you're not feeling unconfident for other reasons?" Whether she was alluding to Maris's medical leave or her scholarship wasn't worth pursuing.

"I want to have the meeting," Maris said. "I'd like to talk to him face-to-face and see what he has to say about my case, and I'd like you there as mediator." She needed someone there so she wouldn't be alone with Hollis. She didn't trust him, and at this point, wasn't sure she could trust herself not to lunge across a table and punch him in the throat.

"This is highly unprecedented," Tammy tried again, and she was right: for the most part, those up for tenure pretended their lives weren't held in someone else's hands. If you passed that colleague in the hallways, it was best to act like you didn't know they were on the committee, even though anyone up for promotion would have studied that committee list and burned it to memory like a love letter.

"I know you believe that, Tammy, and if I wasn't so concerned about discrimination in my case, I'd let it be." She had to convince her. "If you'd like to skip the meeting, I can tell my lawyer to just file—"

"No, no," Tammy interrupted. "Let's meet." The last thing she'd want was the higher-ups thinking she couldn't handle the faculty problems in her department. Was it odd Tammy was so invested in stopping this meeting?

They ended with pleasantries, and an hour later, an email from Hollis confirmed he would attend the meeting.

CHAPTER
THIRTY-THREE

Maris knocked on her neighbor's door the next morning. Eula answered in black leggings, a black crewneck sweater, and a black peacoat, with a black hobo bag slung over her shoulder.

"A little on the nose, don't you think?" Maris said.

Eula shooed her as she turned to lock the door. "When else am I going to get the chance to break and enter? Let an old lady have her fun."

They climbed in Eula's Accord, the plan being to swing by Janice's house to pick her up, since Janice had also quit driving the day of Maris's accident. Janice had been lucky just to collapse at work and sprain her ankle—again, what constituted lucky for a woman—but recognized driving was not a possibility right now. She'd called in sick to work today and would help Eula capture all of Hollis's files on a thumb drive while Maris was in the meeting. Eula was impressively confident with a lock pick, but less so with computers.

Maris was surprised to feel butterflies at the prospect of her meeting. At this point tenure was a distant concern, but being trapped with Hollis in a room wasn't. She thought back to seeing him at DiSalvo's restaurant, the snide way he'd sent over wine, knowing what he was doing to her. She'd had little problem rejecting that glass. She couldn't believe she'd screwed it all up by drinking again, the guilt like a crushing weight. Eight freaking months.

Eula turned off Peach Orchard and onto Shroyer. They were well into October now, what Maris thought of as feather-quilt weather. Her favorite fall tradition was switching from cotton to flannel sheets, from a well-worn crispness to a cozy hideaway. At night she cracked the window so her face was cold to the touch as she slept, but now she questioned how enjoyable that would be without Noel there to reach for when she started to shiver. She missed him. Even though he'd only been gone two nights (one of which she'd spent drunk in Karen's office), it was the closeness she really missed, the intimacy. Same went for Cody, who felt much more than eight hundred miles away.

She glanced at Eula in the driver's seat and asked how she was doing regarding the new information about Carl's death.

Eula confirmed: it was like losing him all over again. "Last night I kept replaying all the times we had Hollis over for dinner, the evenings they'd work until late in the night and he would sleep over on the couch. They went to Reds games together, and to the Schuster Center for shows. They were *friends*." She looked incredulously at Maris. "I'm going to assume it was an accident, but as you found out, not the only one. Hollis knew the risks and did it anyway." She shook her head and tapped on her blinker. "I knew he was dangerous, but I don't think I fully understood how much so." She glanced at Maris. "To him you're expendable. No more important than a lab rat."

Maris sat on her hands to stop their shaking. It was impossible for Eula to fully grasp how much Maris understood this. Hollis had put a bomb in her head and started the countdown, and even he didn't know when it would blow. If she were to die, she guessed he might feel bad about it (or not), but it would provide more data, get him that much closer on the next test case, while she'd just be dead. Gone. She always assumed she'd have more time—to spend with Cody, to make things up to Noel—but now time was finite, a door starting to close. "I'm here now," she said to Eula. It was the only way she could keep going. "All I can think about is next steps."

"Are you ready?" Eula asked. "Do you know what you're going to say?"

"I've got the faculty LISTSERV emails on my phone, the *Times* op-ed on female academics, and his published letter to the editor of the Oak Park paper." She patted the side of her bag where she'd packed them that morning. "And I know I don't have to make my case as much as keep him in the room. He's not a man who's going to change his mind. If he looks like he's going to leave, I'll change tactics."

There was a stretch of sunlight as they passed a few blocks in silence.

"So can I ask how you're feeling today?" Eula asked, and glanced at Maris. "About the drinking?"

"I think you just did." She smiled at Eula, her neighbor's red lipstick a brighter shade than her regular coral. "I'm okay, I guess. Physically recovered." That wasn't quite true. Her back still held some soreness from the alcohol, as if her skin were bruised.

"Did you talk to Noel?" Maris shook her head. "Why not?"

"I'm too embarrassed, I guess."

"You need to get over that," Eula said matter-of-factly. "One time I had the flu so bad I passed out on the toilet with diarrhea and hit my head on the bathroom counter going down. Carl heard the racket and came in and found me with my drawers at my knees, my bottom still a mess." She laughed. "And he had the flu too. It smelled so bad, he threw up in the bath."

"Oh god." Maris laughed in horror. There were so many ways the body could betray you: illness, addiction. But it was just the body being a body. She remembered her one good therapist, the one with the cute shoes, saying to her that her drinking wasn't a moral failure, but an act of wiring. She'd burst into tears. The last time she'd seen her was when she and Noel were getting serious, when'd she felt confident enough in her happiness to try for even more.

It wasn't just her drinking but the lies and denial that had caused her rift with Noel. She'd wanted to believe she could handle all her problems on her own, but that wasn't feasible, and it wasn't even really what she wanted. It was bad enough she might have finite time left; did she really want to spend it lying to herself?

Eula clicked on her blinker again and slowed for the corner. "Are you going to tell him about Saturday night?"

On the sidewalk a woman walked three corgis, their wiggling butts in a happy row. "I don't know." On the one hand, if he found out it was true—she'd been drinking—would that seal his distrust, or would that happen if she were to lie about it? Maris shook her head. "I can't believe I just pissed away eight months. I can't believe I'm back to day one."

"Oh, I don't know," Eula said. "I wouldn't say that."

"How so? I screwed up eight months of sobriety. Yesterday I was literally back to day one, and I'm not sure the hangover day counts."

"What you did," Eula reasoned, "was ruin one *night* of sobriety. It doesn't take away from the fact you were sober for eight months."

"Yes, it does. If I was in AA, they'd take away my chips," she joked.

Eula glanced at her and rolled her eyes. "Please. Aren't you the feminist here? AA was established by a bunch of white men."

Maris snorted, then laughed. They pulled up in front of Janice's apartment building, and Maris was amused to see she was also dressed in all black, all except the white cast on her foot. "You're right. Why should I let those men tell me what to do?"

◆ ◆ ◆

Driving down US 35 on the way to Glenn State, the three women went over the plan. Eula would drop Maris at Marr Hall and park near Engineering. Once Janice and Eula were done, they'd text Maris and let her know they were out of Hollis's office; if Maris finished first, she'd warn them he was on his way.

Walking into Marr, transitioning from the fall smell of dried leaves to the wet odor of old radiators and stale coffee, Maris was surprised to be hit by a wave of nostalgia. This was the first fall in six years she wasn't on campus at least a few days a week, teaching her classes in the overly hot building before the heat evened out for winter. She missed her students. Two had emailed her to say Dr. Scanlon had fallen asleep at the front of the class while they were taking a test and had farted himself awake. She missed their earnestness and humor. How excited they grew as they found their voices. She'd made it her mission to get each of them to care in a larger way about the society they lived in, even those who told her point-blank they were there for the GE credit, not the content.

Early on in pursuing sociology, she'd decided teaching was a necessary evil—she needed insurance, and freelance was just too unstable—and was surprised as a PhD candidate to realize how much she enjoyed it. As soon as this was behind her, and assuming she survived it, the first thing she would do is get back in the classroom. She would Lyft to work every day if she had to. Getting the job at Glenn State had still seemed a means to an end, but faced with the reality she might not be in front of students after this year brought tears to her eyes. She tilted her head back, willing them not to fall.

Collected, she slid lipstick across her lips and smoothed them together, then blew her mouth open with a satisfying pop as she approached the conference room.

The first power move happened as Maris walked in: Hollis Grant neither turned toward the door nor stopped talking. Tammy waved to her and raised her eyebrows—*Hi, hi there!*—but kept her head tilted toward Hollis and what he had to say. Maris was struck immediately that Hollis felt entitled to Tammy's attention as well as her own. He was just the type of man she'd been intimidated by all her life. But even so, she would not let him win.

CHAPTER THIRTY-FOUR

Maris settled into a seat across from Tammy and Hollis and cursed herself for not reserving a space with a round or at least oval table. Sitting across from them felt like being on trial or in the principal's office.

She took off her coat and draped it across the back of her rolling chair, her purse and workbag next to her. As Hollis continued—something about a colleague in his department and his latest grant—she pulled out her notebook, pen, and phone. She did her best to appear nonplussed, but underneath, anger boiled. This was a man who had been figuratively inside her head, who had been able to power down the very memories that made her Maris Heilman. She opened Twitter and scrolled without reading, anything to keep from giving him her attention.

Eventually Hollis quit speaking, and as silence settled in the room, she looked up from the screen. "Are you done?" she asked, setting her phone screen-down on the table.

He motioned toward the phone. "Are you?"

He actually sounded somewhat amused, and she and Hollis both took a moment to size up the competition. He wore a tweed blazer with elbow patches and four gold buttons on each cuff, a maroon-and-blue bow tie choking the collar of his white oxford. He had an open ceramic mug of black coffee in front of him, and it struck her as an odd kind of chutzpah to walk these halls as if it were your house, unmindful of spills. He was balder than she remembered from when she'd run into him at the restaurant with Noel and Cody. He had the look of someone whose hair had been thinning strand by strand for years. She supposed it was like anything else: at some point you passed the threshold from one thing to another without noticing—young to old, hair to no hair— that magical last lock still lying on your pillow.

She wondered, just briefly, what he thought when he looked back at her. She'd worn a green-and-black wrap dress with tights and black riding boots, her hair flat ironed and down, the swipe of lipstick on her mouth. Getting ready that morning, she'd pulled a delicate gold cross necklace from the back of her jewelry box: a gift from her mother for her Lutheran confirmation when she was fourteen. She'd put it on as if warding off a vampire.

"Where's this high-powered attorney you mentioned?" Hollis asked, amusement dripping in his voice. "Did he realize you didn't have a case?"

"*She* is at the courthouse," Maris said. "Waiting for my call."

Tammy jumped in, paperwork splayed in front of her. "I think it might be a good idea for us to each be reminded of the bylaws regarding tenure and promotion before we begin. As we all know, the university's vote comes after the department and college votes, but before the Board of Trustees'. It's highly unusual for the vote to differ from the contingents before it." She looked at her notes. "An 'extraordinary event,' it's referred to, and one that requires a letter of explanation from the provost." She folded her hands over her notepad. "Maris, you surely remember your vote was twelve-four—twelve for, four against—at the department level." Maris nodded. Duh, she remembered. She glanced at Hollis; would he know she could remember that? What exactly did he think he was doing to her?

She opened her mouth, but Hollis beat her to first response. "I understand we have to work within certain bureaucracies, and I'm thankful there are women like you, Dr. Lerner, who are willing to keep up with these niggling details so faculty can focus on the larger picture, but the real question that matters here is: Does this assistant professor deserve promotion?" It was almost breathtaking how insulting he could be while seeming so logical. The jab at bureaucracies, the slight regarding Tammy as separate from the faculty and little more than a paper pusher, and of course, his ego that he should be the one to judge.

Here he was holding her life in his hands, smug as ever, but rather than feel completely intimidated, Maris felt a sense of calm. What would happen would happen, but she was fighting back and now had Janice and Eula and Karen on her side. She glanced at her watch. They'd be in the office by now, Janice working her magic. How long would it take to copy everything, she wondered. She thought of all the times she'd be duplicating her simplistic word files and the computer would give her an estimate of two minutes, then switch to twenty-five. *Please, let it not take that long*, she thought.

Maris pulled two copies of her CV out of her bag. She'd emailed it to both Hollis and Tammy the night before, but would bet money neither had looked at it. She was proud of the work she'd done, despite what these two thought of it. She'd told people's stories while weaving in social context well beyond one's personal experience and concluded larger truths about the world. And she knew that was important.

She handed the pages across the table. "As you can see, I've more than met the criteria for scholarship."

"More than," Tammy said with air quotes, "might be a little grandiose given the votes."

Hollis kept Maris's eye contact, not looking down at the pages. "I've seen your scholarship."

"Have you read any of it?" she asked.

"Enough."

She crossed her fingers on the table—*here is the steeple*—and leaned forward. "And what did you think?"

"I am . . . not impressed."

She noticed with a spark of triumph he had crumbs on his shirt. Tortilla chips? Crackers? It made him seem less invulnerable. "And what would be impressive to you?"

Hollis leaned back in his chair, crossing his hands over his stomach. "Science."

"I'm in the sciences," she started, and Hollis chuckled.

"Real science. Not the soft sciences you dabble in."

She knew he was baiting her but gulped her mouth gladly around the hook. *Keep him in the room.* "Dabble? I've published dozens of articles. I have a PhD in sociology."

"Yes," he concurred. "In sociology. The word *social* is right there in the field's name. What you do is more akin to a hen party than science."

"Well now," Tammy ventured. "The field itself isn't what's up for debate here. There's been much important work to come out—"

"Your work is irrelevant," Hollis said to Maris. "It's only words. There's no discovery or change. You just make up these complaints about people you don't even know, but you have no real power to change anything. Your work doesn't *do* anything."

The last thing she could do was expose what she knew about his own work and how he was literally trying to change her future. His influence over her tenure was the least of it, the absolute least, and with that she was able to keep her semblance of control. Her phone buzzed next to her, screen down.

"Do you need to get that?" Hollis asked—a taunt. "What if it's your social media?" The phone buzzed again. It could be Eula or Janice, but she shook her head to the question. "Well, then, what if it's your doctor?" Hollis said. "My understanding is you're on medical leave right now." She saw spots in her vision. "Nothing serious, I hope."

Tammy darted glances between Maris and Hollis, and it reminded Maris of when she and Noel used to have conversations above Cody's head when she was younger. Cody was aware of an entire stratosphere of air too high for her to breathe, but also that she could do nothing about it.

Her phone buzzed again.

"Or maybe it's this female lawyer who has yet to appear," Hollis said. "I don't believe you really contacted someone. I think you just made that up, and this whole meeting is a bluff." He began to stand. "We're done here."

In the room, in the room, in the room. "I think I can influence the future plenty," she said, and picked up her phone, pausing a millisecond to see the text from Eula. Need 10 more minutes.

Impulsively, Maris swiped quickly to Twitter and tapped the plus-feather at the bottom and began a tweet thread. An endowed male prof wants to stop my tenure. What's @glennstate going to do about it? 1/

She was lucky she'd started social media in her late twenties when she had a modicum of sense and had built a professional reputation as one who backed up her claims, but there was no time to pause.

"Are you on Twitter?" she asked Hollis and Tammy. Hollis hovered for a moment, then sat back down.

I've pubbed dozens of articles in reputable online venues w huge audiences but he says not scholarship? 2/

"It's a waste of time," Hollis said, but he leaned forward to look at her phone, which she tilted away from him.

Outstanding student evals, numerous service commitments, but it's all for nothing if 3/

Sociology not science but "hen party" 4/

"What was it you said?" she asked Hollis. "Sociology is just people complaining?" She tweeted it with 5/.

"What are you doing?" he said, a touch of dubiousness in his voice now, the power dynamic shifting in the room. "You can't post that without my consent."

Consent! As if he had any room to talk.

She thought about fake news and how reasonable rhetoric had been flushed down a gold toilet. Things didn't have to be accurate; you just needed to shift the story. "Well, you said it, so I should give you credit." It's Dr. Hollis Grant @glennstate "What's your office number?" He looked at her suspiciously, and she waved a hand. "Never mind. The hens can type with their little hen feet and look it up." She added 6/ and then Let's let Professor Grant know what we think of his opinions! 7/

"Let's just see if I have any influence over the future." @glennstate is this how you allow female junior faculty to be treated? Devalued for their disciplines and name-called?? 8/

Every tweet she sent, she felt the power growing from her phone. No wonder young people tweeted such outrageous things—the dopamine hit was incredible.

> @glennstate is it fair to be evaluated by male colleagues if this is their opinion? How will you #protectfemalefaculty? 9/9

"Listen," Tammy said, "this meeting has perhaps escalated—"

Hollis's pocket buzzed, and he pulled out his phone. "Yes?" A long pause followed. "Who's saying it?" He glanced across the table at Maris, and his eyebrows furrowed. "How did they get the num—" He was cut off by the voice on the other end.

Maris's own phone buzzed. Janice: we're out. Relief flooded her limbs; they'd done it.

"It's clear I'm not going to persuade you on any of my points," Maris said, and scooted to the left to pack her notebook and pen in her bag. "We're done here."

Hollis disconnected his call and leaned across the table with his mouth open. For an irrational second Maris thought he was going to bite her, but his lips steadied into a thin smile. He leaned back and folded his spotted hands against his stomach again, briefly flicking away a crumb from his chest. "None of it will matter in the long run," he said. "Your tenure, your very self. You don't matter at all."

Maris stood, bumping the seat of her chair with the back of her knees as she leaned over the table. "I might matter yet," Maris said, grasping her bag to her chest and leaving Hollis with his mouth agape. "We'll see what the future brings."

CHAPTER
THIRTY-FIVE

The cold air slapped Maris's face as she scurried outside Marr Hall. She felt like she was burning from the inside out as she clawed open the neckline of her dress and walked briskly toward the parking lot. She looked behind her a few times, making sure Hollis wasn't following her, but all she saw was a pack of college boys in cargo shorts playing hacky sack and a harried student running toward the library.

She was queasy thinking about a Twitter dustup with half-assed accusations and little proof to back them up. This was just the kind of thing she'd worked meticulously to avoid in her career, double-checking resources and facts before she'd even send 280 characters out into the ether, and there would be little coming back from it down the line. But realistically, what was there to come back *to*? Going back on the job market having been denied tenure? Starting a six-year tenure clock again in her forties? Even if she were to find a job, what kind of university did she think it was going to be at? She'd be lucky to end up teaching five classes a semester as an adjunct.

The Honda idled at the curb, and Maris flat-out ran the last few yards, opened the back door, and jumped in. "Go."

Janice turned around, her hand gripping the side of the passenger seat as she peered at Maris. "And here I thought we were going to be the ones flustered after the break-in."

"Did you get it?" Maris asked.

"Eventually," Janice said. "But let's just say Hollis might find out about it."

Maris asked what happened, and Eula turned left out of campus with a screech. "I should have anticipated people would remember me. I used to visit Carl on campus for lunch at least once a week. I ran into Hollis's department administrative assistant on our way in, and she wanted to know how I was doing, whether I was still in contact with Hollis, what I'd been up to." She shook her head. "If she only knew what contact I had with Hollis and what I've been up to."

"Shit," Maris said, and bit her lip. "I bet that's the same person who called at the end of the meeting." Maris's big concern had been that her tweets could blow what career she had left sky-high if the university came after her with a libel suit, but now what if the administrative assistant mentioned seeing Eula? Would Hollis piece it together?

"What happened with you?" Janice asked, and Maris told them how Hollis had balked not only about her scholarship but her whole profession, and her retaliation on Twitter. "I at-ed Glenn State so they're in the conversation, and I'm already up to—" She glanced down at the app on her phone and sucked in a breath. "Shit, I'm already up to four thousand likes and almost five hundred retweets." Her first viral article had taken a day to see that much of a response, and of course from there, the momentum kept building. She watched in real time as the numbers jumped higher and higher.

"Read us what you said," Janice said, and Maris read her tweets back.

Eula laughed. "For all the advancements in science, that man barely knows what social media is, so my guess is this is going to come as quite a surprise."

"But will he put together that you were there at the same time I was in a meeting with him? Is there any evidence you were in his office?"

Janice winced. "I had to disable his password, so there's a chance."

"We're going to have to act fast," Maris said as Eula accelerated into the turn.

◆ ◆ ◆

Karen was waiting on the porch as they drove up to Eula's house, a bag from Submarine House at her feet. Eula and Maris filled her in on the mission as Janice set her laptop up at the dining room table. She snapped the thumb drive in place and unwrapped an Italian sub, clicking away on the keyboard with one hand as she took a large bite of her sandwich.

Maris watched the Twitter notifications continue to pile up, faster than she'd ever seen before. She'd already gained four thousand followers since that morning. She hated to admit what a heady rush it all was, all those people interested in what she had to say. No wonder people tweeted such incendiary stuff. She flipped to email and saw a message from the *Guardian* asking if she was interested in writing an article about #protectfemalefaculty. We'd love to hear your specifics on what Hollis Grant has done to endanger your tenure, and how this ties in to other movements in the culture at large, the editor had written. This was the first time Maris had been approached by an outlet without pitching first—a career landmark she'd looked forward to, just like the blue check on Twitter, which she'd celebrated two years ago by getting drunk. Now her sobriety seemed more important.

"Are you in?" Karen asked, and Janice smiled wryly.

"It's not quite as top secret as all that," she said, then paused. "This guy knows something about computers—he's got things behind a firewall—but most of my high schoolers could crack it." Janice pointed at a folder on her desktop. "I think this is the bulk of the research, but we're talking thousands of pages of notes and spreadsheets and simulations. It's going to take me a couple of hours to sort through what I'm looking at and send it to each of you. It's written in code, but again, nothing very sophisticated. You could crack it with a decoder ring out of a cereal box if you had the right one, but I still need to figure it out. Plus, there's just bullshit like on any hard drive. Old lesson plans, conference papers." Janice grimaced. "Wait."

Maris leaned closer. "What is it?"

"This folder is further encrypted, but I'm not sure why. It's going to take a little more time."

Maris read the folder name—Charter—and her stomach looped. "It's got to be my articles. They're what started him after me in the first place."

"I'll make it a priority," Janice said as her hands flew across the keyboard.

"Send it to me as soon as you can, along with any spreadsheets and IRBs," Maris said. Janice looked at her blankly. "It's the paperwork for the institutional review board saying he has approval to work on human subjects. And see if you find folders on the other women too."

"I already searched for my name," Janice admitted.

"And?"

"Nothing."

Maris nodded and set her own laptop at the table. She would focus on the money and legal trails, as well as patterns in the spreadsheets. While she was far from a neurologist, she'd done plenty of research in the social sciences wading through data to detect repeated traits or anomalies. While she waited for Janice to send her files, Maris would continue to look into the other women, digging for a connection. At some point they'd have to contact Beverly and Shelby and let them know what was going on, but she wanted to wait until they'd at least had a chance to digest what was buried in Hollis's research. Maris felt the key to piecing this together was just out of reach, like a popcorn kernel tucked behind the last tooth in her mouth.

"I'll take anything on cellular information or identification," Eula said, and pulled out the seat next to Janice. "And I'll try to make sense on next steps for research."

"I'll take a stab at the neuroscience," Karen said, and pulled her own laptop out of her bag and grabbed a tuna sub.

Maris looked around the table at the group of women and for an amused moment thought they looked like they were playing Battleship, a game she and Cody played obsessively when Cody was ten. She felt a pang for her daughter, but also energized by the idea of a war room, these smart women fighting on her side.

"Great," Janice said, taking another huge bite of her sandwich. "Let's get to work."

CHAPTER

THIRTY-SIX

Shelby Steele, Janice Lambert, Beverly Halberg, and herself. It made sense why Beth was in the research, but surely there had to be something connecting the rest of them. If she could just figure this out, it would all make sense.

She had ties already to Shelby and Janice. She taught at the university Shelby had attended, and Janice taught her daughter and was the mom of her daughter's best friend, but she didn't see a link between those two directly. And she'd looked into their connections to Hollis, and they were tangential at best.

She started on her university's learning management system, digging through five years of classes looking for Shelby as one of her students. No luck. She was a mathematics major, a department Maris had little crossover with. Shelby ran track in high school and attended Glenn State on scholarship, but it wasn't renewed after her junior year. That was about the time she deactivated her Facebook, but Maris could access the dormant account. Shelby had worked at Forever 21 in high school, and had a few short-term girlfriends and what appeared to be one serious boyfriend her sophomore year of college (Greg, also a grad

of Glenn State, but never in Maris's classes). The last birthday she celebrated on social media was two years ago.

After a bit, Maris made an excuse to go home and get some more
snacks for the group, but really to use the desktop they kept in the
living room. It was the one Noel used to play video games, and was
where Maris had downloaded and hidden Tor to access the dark web.
If Cody ever borrowed a computer, it was Maris's laptop so she could
take it to her room, and she hadn't wanted her daughter stumbling
across the VPN.

At the small desk behind their couch, Maris fired up the computer
and clicked to Tor. In graduate school, there had been the legal, inves-
tigative routes taught in class, but each student had learned their tricks
for leads that were less than on the up and up. Digging into Shelby,
Maris found she'd been a good and steady student up until spring of her
junior year, when her grades plummeted to mainly Ds along with one F
and one C. What had happened that semester? She knew there were the
normal ups and downs in college, but a drop that steep usually meant
something serious—a breakdown, a death in the family.

Shelby had rallied again but never fully recovered, graduating with
a 2.65 GPA. Maris was able to hack her cloud storage and see pictures—
she appeared to have been dating a woman for the last six months or
so and was working an entry-level job at LexisNexis here in Dayton.
Deeper, darker still, she found Shelby had an average amount of student
debt (meaning outrageous) and carried about $6,000 between various
credit cards. Maris hacked her Citibank card and felt a twinge of guilt
at the invasion of privacy, not to mention the potential felony charge,
but they were running out of time and needed answers.

Looking at the category breakdowns for the past year, she found
an unusually high amount of spending on services, whereas most girls
in their early twenties spent on merchandise. There were charges for
meditation retreats, breathing classes, yoga lessons, acupuncture, and
even hypnosis. Whatever had happened that semester when her grades

plummeted, Shelby was still trying to heal from it. They'd downloaded Hollis's calendar from his computer, and she checked back to see if there was anything out of the ordinary for him that semester. There wasn't—just his two classes and lab time were listed—although it was likely he kept a paper calendar for social engagements.

Beverly Halberg was a bit easier to stalk. She had a social media presence that was active on Pinterest, Facebook, and Goodreads. She was a voracious reader, tending toward women's fiction and true crime; there wasn't a Laura Lippman out there she hadn't rated at five stars. Pinterest contained curated lists of knitting projects, sourdough bread, and felting, and Facebook had been overrun for the last six years with pictures of her grandkids interspersed with women's marches, Black Lives Matter protests, and #MeToo proclamations. There was less to learn about her as a person from her online footprint, and a quick look at her financials for the last ten years showed nothing out of the ordinary: she'd been beefing up her retirement, she had paid off her house, and she and her husband had cosigned on a Winnebago.

—

—

—

She could smell garlic from the dinner she'd cooked a few days ago, and she fluttered her eyes, still shocked as she emerged from a blackout. She glanced at her watch; she'd been out only two minutes. Her breath caught, and it reminded her of the times in the night when Noel's breath would catch in a snore and she'd lay a hand on his back to ease him back to sleep. Her eyes filled with tears. She would never take her family for granted again.

She sent a quick text to Janice—did you have one?—and Janice texted back no. Did that mean Hollis was singling Maris out now? What about the other women? They had to check in with them soon. What frightened Maris in particular, along with everything in general, was not knowing with each blackout if they were doing cumulative damage, chipping away each time at her sense of self. It was so similar to drinking—killing brain cells one by one—she shuddered to think she had done it voluntarily. Each blackout could be the last, Hollis finally taking the plunge to end her.

◆ ◆ ◆

She hurried through the rest of her dark web searches and remembered to grab some granola bars and oranges before she ran next door.

Back in Eula's living room, Eula's cell phone rang and she told the others, "It's him." The room stilled as she answered.

"Mm-hmm," she said, and Maris could hear Hollis's voice murmuring from the other end. "Oh, you know me, Hollis," Eula said, her voice strained but jovial. "I was there to have lunch with one of Carl's old students and got turned around." Hollis said something, and a flash of panic crossed Eula's face. "You don't know her."

He continued, and Eula signaled scribbling in the air; Janice lunged to grab her a pen. "What about her?" Eula said as she scribbled across her notepad and turned it to the others.

asking about maris.

Janice linked arms with Maris.

"I haven't seen her in ages," Eula said. Hollis kept talking, long paragraphs it seemed. "I'll keep an eye out," she said, and it sounded as if Hollis was saying goodbye when Eula said, "Hollis? I found some more papers for Carl's archive. Should I drop those at the library myself?" He said something else, and she added, "You're too kind." She said goodbye and hung up. "Prick," she muttered.

"What'd he say?" Janice asked, and Eula told them he had heard she was on campus and wanted to say he was sorry he missed her. She wasn't completely convinced he believed why she was there, but he had also asked about Maris—"whether I'd seen her lately or heard anything about her. He said you were on medical leave for mental health reasons."

"Prick," Maris echoed.

"But whether or not he believed me, he's suspicious, and the clock is ticking."

Maris turned back to her research, her fingers flying over the laptop as she picked up where she'd left off on Bev's feed.

She checked LinkedIn and found professional connections between Karen and Beverly—obvious enough, since they both worked at Miami Regional—but none for the others. There was, however, a professional Twitter handle listed for Beverly's job position that was posted to sporadically and appeared to have a social media handler that wasn't Bev. She already had enough sense of the woman's voice based on her Facebook posts to know these bland tweets about improvements to the Women's Center or the hospital's national ranking weren't from her. Still she scrolled back, and back, and back, until there appeared an anomaly that lasted a few months from approximately three years ago. Whoever was running the account then was sub-tweeting about rape kits backlogged through the police station, how victims were treated with care and confidentiality at the hospital, and the social and mental health services available to women in the community. She checked the date, and Bev had started tweeting about backed up rape kits just days after Dylan Charter's rape of Jane Doe.

Fire lit up her spine: that had to be the connection. Dylan Charter, the name that had haunted her life for three years. She would bet money that Beverly Halberg had been working at the Women's Center the night of the rape and had worked on the case. She inhaled sharply. Was the victim Shelby?

The other women stopped what they were doing and looked up. "What?" Janice asked, and Maris turned to Karen.

"Was Dylan Charter's rape victim a patient at Miami Regional?"

Karen paused long enough that Maris could imagine the gears in her mind chewing through HIPAA. "I can't give out that information," she said reluctantly, but Maris could tell by her hesitancy that the answer was yes.

"Was his victim Shelby?" Maris asked, and to her surprise, it was Janice, not Karen, who answered.

"No," Janice said.

"Do you know Dylan Charter?" Maris demanded. Her whole body was tingling, sure she was on the right track, the focus on Dylan narrowing to a pinpoint.

"I don't," Janice said.

Maris's shoulders deflated, but only for a second: *Trust your gut.* She knew he had attended Oak Park High and not Horace, but there had to be something. "Did he visit the school, or maybe try a semester there? Maybe you knew him from basketball games?"

"I've never met him," Janice said. "I would remember."

"Why?" Maris pushed. "Why would you remember?"

Janice lowered her eyes. "Because I knew Jane Doe."

Maris was dizzy with triumph—the connection was Dylan Charter. "Who is she?"

"I can't tell you her name," Janice said resolutely. "She's worked so hard to stay anonymous."

"Is it Shelby?" Maris asked, doing the math in her head: that awful semester when her grades tanked had also coincided with the rape. Janice looked confused and shook her head no. "How do you know Jane Doe?" Maris pushed, and Janice crossed her arms.

"Tell me why you thought it was Shelby."

Maris told her about Bev's tie to Jane Doe's case and Shelby's bad semester. "And you? What's your connection?"

"This is completely confidential, but she was a student at Horace and always a favorite of mine. She used to come to my office between classes, that kind of thing." She turned to explain to the other women.

"Along with teaching computer science, I do some advising and counseling for the students since I have a social work background, and she was one I helped with her college applications. Never had much drama to speak of—got along with her folks, liked her siblings as much as a teenager could—but after the rape, she was a mess. An absolute wreck. She contacted me out of the blue—I had no idea she was the victim—and asked if we could talk. I began kind of unofficially counseling her at least once a week. Somehow Hollis must have figured that out." Maris remembered the strange conversation with Janice about career day—how she had asked Maris not to reference the case directly—and wondered if Jane Doe's siblings were still at the school.

"But it wasn't Shelby?" Maris said. She could hardly believe she was wrong; she'd been so certain.

Janice shook her head no. "But she had a good friend named Shelby. I remember that. They met in college. My guess is that's her." Maris thought about all those services on Shelby's credit card, and she wasn't even the victim, just part of the fallout. Jesus. "We need to contact the other two women," Janice said.

Maris nodded. "It's time." She felt guilty she'd dug so deeply into the women's lives without their knowledge, but was glad at least they had as much to tell them as they did.

"You're right," Karen admitted. "And as much as I don't want to, I should be the one to make the calls, since I was their attending physician." She picked up her cell phone and waved it in the air. "Wish me luck."

Maris thought about how convinced she'd been that Shelby was Jane Doe, for it to turn out she was just another young woman damaged in her twenties. She thought fleetingly of the girl who had found her in the library and chased her down with the note. She certainly seemed less than stable. As sure as she'd been that Shelby was the victim, she turned her attention to the mystery woman, digging through her purse for the note.

Chapter
Thirty-Seven

Dylan came back from the kitchen with a bowl of popcorn, two open cans of Fresca on the coffee table. I tried to hide my revulsion when he sat right next to me, our hips and thighs touching, as I reached for my soda can and shifted a millimeter away as I did so.

"I told you I was fine to take it slow," Dylan said, obviously noticing. But there was weariness in his voice. Resignation. As if he could guilt me into feeling sorry for him.

This was only our third "date," but I'd let him know over the phone that I was coming out of a serious relationship and not ready to be with someone new. More than once at the restaurant, I'd had to hide a shudder of disgust when he touched the sleeve of my dress or grazed my hand reaching for his water.

The night of his birthday, I'd planned to come home with him and crush his mother's Zolpidem in a drink—not enough to make him suspicious, but enough that I could get my hands on his phone and laptop—but after running into Maris Heilman, I'd been too thrown to go through with it. When Dylan offered to drive me home, I told him my aunt was coming to pick me up.

He leaned forward and put a chaste kiss on my lips. I bit the inside of my mouth to keep from crying out. "I can't believe I found someone like you. Someone who can see I've changed."

"It's so obvious you have," I cooed, and leaned back to drink the rest of my soda so I had an excuse to get us more. "Let me," I said when he started to stand.

In the kitchen, I cracked open two more cans and pulled six white pills from my pocket, crushing them under my thumb. I could hear Dylan's voice from the couch. "I'm in therapy, you know," he admitted.

What the hell, I thought, and crushed two more, enjoying the sharp bite of chalk against my skin.

"I'm going twice a week," he said, and his voice grew louder as he approached me, rounding the corner just as I swept the last crumbs into the open top. I covered the hole with my palm and gave the can a quick swish to mix in the sleeping pills before handing it to him.

"Thanks," he said, and took a drink as he slid onto a stool at the breakfast bar. "My folks said I didn't need to go, but my parole officer thought it was a good idea. I haven't really told them I'm doing it."

My heart was still stuttering from the close call as I took a sip of my own drink. It tasted bitter, but it could have been the grapefruit and the tickle of the carbonation. Or had I given him the wrong can?

"What do you guys talk about?" I asked.

"What happened," he admitted.

No shit, I thought. "But what about it?"

"About how I didn't really see her as a person." I felt tears sting my eyes and hoped it looked like I was soppy from his vulnerability, but it was rage leaking from my eyeballs. "And how it's hard for me to think of myself as the person who did that." He put a hand to his chest. "That's not me. I would never hurt someone." *But you did!* I wanted to scream. *Just look at me!* "My therapist says it's because I'm still thinking of it as sex, not violence." He shook his head. "My family keeps telling me I have to stop talking like that."

"How so?"

"That I have to stop thinking everything's my fault, and that the judge should have taken into account that woman's actions. Dad says it's all the press around the case, and that it's been blown out of proportion. He says what I did is no worse than what's been happening forever." He couldn't meet my eyes now.

"And what do you think about that?"

He took another long drink of his Fresca. "There's a woman in town who writes about me. All these articles about how awful my family is and how I'm a spoiled brat and an awful person." Now his own eyes were wet with tears. "Since the arrest I've looked back on a lot of my actions, not just that night, and I've got shit to be sorry for. I told my family maybe I should try to make some amends, but they said that can't be the face of the company. They said: no apologies, ever."

I watched his chest wobble slightly to the left, and he put a foot on the ground to steady himself. Shit. Had I overdosed him?

"You ready to keep watching?" I asked, and nodded toward the living room, Bradley Cooper's blue eyes paused on the seventy-five-inch TV above the fireplace.

"That sounds good," he said with a slur in his voice as he slid off the stool. I gritted my teeth as I put my arm around him to escort him to the couch.

Ten minutes later, his eyes fluttered shut, and I eased myself from under his armpit, slid to the ground, and grabbed his phone from his hand on my way down. I held his thumb to the "Home" button until the lock screen opened, then sneaked into the bathroom.

I scrolled quickly past the restaurant and sports apps, the streaming video services, the dumb games. In Notes there were mainly lists of things he needed to do at work. I checked his search engines next, and was surprised to see he'd bookmarked all of Maris's articles about him. I wondered if he read them regularly to feel worse about himself and hoped so. I swiped through the home pages for social media, but the apps had been deleted.

I'd saved Photos for last. It was where I would most likely find the evidence I needed, but what if they were photos of me? My thumb hovered above the app, shaking, and then Dylan pounded on the door. "You okay?"

The phone slipped from my hand and clattered to the tile floor. "Fine!" I yelled back.

He pounded again. "I don't feel so good."

I grabbed his phone. Relief rushed through me when I saw the home screen hadn't locked. "I'll be just a sec!"

I clicked open Photos and scrolled my thumb up and up, past more pictures of the golden retriever, his parents, the dinner at the Treasure Club. Screenshots of LeBron and other players I didn't know. A bowl of curry from Thai 9, a picture he'd taken to send me.

"Can you let me in?" he said through the thick door. "Seriously."

Too quickly I was at the end of the photo roll. There was only a month of pictures, the phone cleaned out while he was at prison. I grunted with frustration.

He knocked on the door four more times, and I flung it open. Dylan rushed past toward the toilet, his head bending over the bowl as vomit rushed out of his mouth. He heaved a second time, and I felt a rush of power seeing him so vulnerable, so incapacitated. I wanted to kick him in the gut.

He turned around, wiping his mouth with his sleeve as he tumbled the few inches to the floor. He scrunched his face. "Is that my phone?"

I looked down, the phone still in my hand, my pulse racing. "You must have left it in here."

He kept his eyes on it and shook his head. "I don't think so."

I leaned over to help him up from the floor, setting his phone on the counter as I did. "Who looks like they know what's going on here, you or me?" I teased. "You aren't exactly a hundred percent."

"I guess," he agreed.

I knew a real girlfriend would help him into bed and make sure he was okay, but I could not enter that back room with him. I would not. I lied and told him I also wasn't feeling the greatest—it must have been something we ate—and that I'd better get home before it got much worse.

"You could stay here," he suggested, and the look on my face made him flinch. "I just meant—" he started.

"I know what you meant," I said, and the tension held between us.

What the hell was I going to do? He was getting suspicious; the phone had been a dead end. Whatever was next, I needed to keep him on my side. "And it's sweet," I added, "but we are way too early in a relationship for me to get sick in front of you."

His shoulders sagged as relief flooded his face. "Yeah, okay." He chuckled. "I get it."

I told him to get some sleep, and I'd call in the morning to check on him.

"You're the best," he said, and smiled wanly. "I don't know what I did to deserve you."

You'll know soon enough, I thought.

PART FIVE

CHAPTER
THIRTY-EIGHT

By evening, Janice had decoded enough of the files that they could share what they'd learned, and they took a break for dinner and ordered Indian. Laptops pushed to the side, Maris passed the naan and opened the yellow chicken curry as Karen relayed her conversations with Shelby and Bev. "How did they take the news about Hollis?" she asked, and Karen said both women were relieved to have some answers, no matter how far-fetched, and believed her more readily than she'd hoped. "And their connections to Dylan?"

"We were right about Shelby being close to Jane Doe. Turned out she recognized Dylan at a Starbucks and threw her hot coffee on him. He ended up with third-degree burns."

"And Beverly?" Maris asked.

"She's working with legislators on new rape kit tracking systems and has used Charter's case as an example of mismanagement."

Maris loaded another piece of naan on her plate as the box came back around, anxious to fuel up for the long night ahead. The blackout earlier nipped at her heels, reminding her Hollis was circling closer and closer, and she shuddered to think what he had planned. "Thanks for the update, Karen," she said, and turned to Eula. "Why don't you fill us in on what you figured out from Hollis's research."

Eula took a bite of lamb biryani and explained with a hint of pride that her theory was in fact correct regarding neural oscillations, identification, and cell towers: once brain waves were identified and linked to a specific individual, the waves could be used like the chip or circuit in an RFID model, with the cell towers in place of the parabolic dish. "Based on his research, Hollis's contribution on that front wasn't a contribution so much as a test study. He confirmed my theories that the neural oscillations could be used as identification anywhere. All he had to do then was access the brain waves with the cell tower, bounce them to the responder, send a signal to interrupt transmissions in the brain, and voila."

Maris had learned more in the past few days about synapses, memory encoding, and the molecular levels of the brain than she would have guessed possible. "So the blackouts are interrupted transmissions," she clarified, and Eula said that was right.

"So what happens to the memories?" Janice asked.

"Nothing," Maris said, spearing a bite of chicken. "They're never stored, because with the disruption they never formed." It was similar to what she'd learned researching drinking after she quit: that those memories aren't lost but never take root. The difference was that when she was drunk, all brain functions were impaired, while in one of the transmission blackouts, implicit memories were still intact.

"And what are implicit memories?" Janice asked when Eula brought them up, and while Karen explained them as general knowledge people have, Maris wanted to say, the things you know in your bones: the musk-and-paper smell of your husband, the time of day your daughter was born. They were more than the automatic functions of what you knew, but who you loved. "So that's why we still act like ourselves?" Janice said. "Because the implicit memories are intact?"

"Exactly," Eula said. "You were still you, but the you in that moment wasn't storing. Does that make sense?"

Janice nodded, tears in her eyes. "I mean. It's as bad as we think it is, isn't it?"

Maris felt the first lightning strike of a stress migraine and put the heel of her hand over her right eye socket. She glanced at Janice, who was taking shallow breaths, like the ones Maris had been taught in Lamaze class. "You okay?" she whispered, and Janice shook her head as she shrugged her shoulders: *But what can you do?* She was the other one here who really understood the horror.

"My guess is when he started zapping, he wasn't really sure what he'd be interrupting," Eula said. "In a way, you women were lucky he perfected disrupting memories and something deadlier didn't happen." It did not feel that way to Maris. "I think what happened to Diane Garland back in the nineties was akin to nicking an artery during surgery, but he's moved beyond that."

"The short blips you've had?" Eula said, and Maris and Janice both nodded; Maris knew them well. They were the ones that helped her convince herself nothing was really happening, that it was all in her imagination. That she was just another hysterical woman run amok. "Those were the ones where he was figuring out how to home in on the correct oscillations. When all goes right, the blip will be no more than a nanosecond, so it won't be detectable to the subject, but for now he's moving on to the next step, such as with Beth Novak." Maris recalled their eerie conversation: Beth with no memory of their meeting or their call, no memory of Diane Garland. She wondered how sloppy Hollis had been, how much more he'd wiped out. Her husband? Her job? Was Beth still Beth at all?

"Which is?" Janice asked.

"Not just memory disruption," Maris said, "but erasure. He's not just stopping memories from forming, but attacking the ones you have."

She squeezed her eyes shut until she saw spots. Who was she without memory of Cody and Noel? Or her work?

"Has he done that to you?" Karen asked, and Maris shook her head, confident he hadn't. There were the usual black spots in her memory from drinking—nights she'd forgotten due to her own failures—but that was it. "Why not?"

"He took too much from Beth," Maris said. "He was going after certain memories about their work and meeting me, but he took huge swaths, like all of grad school. From the research, it looks like what he wants is for the extraction to be unnoticeable. But to do that, he needs to home in more on the correct neurons before he can try it again."

Eula grimaced. "But that's not the worst of it. I know now from the research that isn't the end goal. It's implementation of new memories. It wouldn't just be that you didn't remember who you were, but that you remembered yourself as someone else."

"And that person would be decided by Hollis Grant," Maris realized. He could create women as he saw fit. All free thinking could be taken away, replaced with submission . . . a scientific gaslighting. It wouldn't just be reverting back to the old ways of seeing women as inferior, but a literal dark age where women would have no free will.

"Exactly," Eula said. "But you have to remember how long these things can take to figure out. I worked on my theory connecting cell reception and brain oscillations for decades before it was proven. This next step for Hollis could take years."

"Or it could take a week, right?" Janice said, her voice muffled as she put her head between her knees. "I mean, it's possible?"

Eula sighed. "It's possible."

One week until Maris's thoughts would no longer be her own. Still one thing nagged at her. "I can't figure out how he identified our brain waves originally."

"Even looking through the research, I'm not sure," Eula admitted. "My guess is a portable EEG. The man isn't without talents."

"But how could he do it without us noticing?"

"The technology could be quite small," Eula said. "And it could be that someone else recorded them. The mechanism itself wouldn't be hard to run."

"How small?" Maris asked.

Eula picked up a piece of naan and ripped it in half. "It's like any other technology. Remember when computers were these huge blocks that sat on your desk? Or cell phones that were the size of phone books?"

With the mention of phones, a memory clicked for Maris: the day of her first blackout, before Maris left work to get Cody, Tammy had taken a series of quick photos of her to update the faculty webpage. Now she opened a browser on her phone, found the Sociology Department's home page, and scrolled to her faculty picture. It was still the old one.

"Could it have been an app?" she asked, and Eula said it was possible. Maris told the women her theory that Tammy had captured her brain waves with her cell phone, and Eula nodded. "That could be it, it really could, but that makes things even worse," Eula said. "It's not *just* Hollis."

And *why*? Why would Tammy be working with Hollis? She thought of all the times Tammy had bent to the will of the male professors, giving them the better teaching schedules and nominating them for awards, all in the hope that they'd one day respect her.

Janice leaned forward. "The day of my first blackout, I attended a morning conference downtown, and they told me I needed a picture for the temporary parking pass. I thought it was weird, and never got a copy of the picture, but by the end of the day I had bigger concerns."

"Do you know who took it?" Maris asked.

Karen shook her head slowly. "Just some woman."

Maris flipped to Tammy's picture on her department website, outdated but recognizable, and turned it toward Janice. "Her?"

Janice hiccuped and then gasped for breath, panic clear on her face. "That's the one." She waved her arms in front of her chest then tumbled forward, her knees on the carpet. In a heartbeat she was panting on all fours.

Maris recognized this for what it was and knelt beside Janice and slid a hand over her back and another under her belly, applying gentle pressure between them. *You are here. You are solid.* She used to get panic attacks back in graduate school. Her first was after her adviser had come out in the hallway to let her know she'd passed her comps and was ready to begin her dissertation. The reward for a job well done was more work, an impossible road ahead. The impostor syndrome already a heavy cloak, like the X-ray vest she wore at the dentist.

Karen knelt on the other side. "Janice," she said matter-of-factly in her calm, authoritative doctor voice. "You're having a panic attack. Can you hear me?" Janice nodded.

"We're here," Maris said. "And we're going to do our best to keep you safe."

The enormity of her statement hit her: they would do their best. She wanted to go on long enough that Noel and Cody would know it too: that she did her best. And no matter what happened to her, these women would always know that she had done everything within her power to look after them and keep them safe.

The question now was how.

CHAPTER

THIRTY-NINE

Well into the night, Maris worked with her spine bent like a question mark over her computer at Eula's dining room table. Every hour or so, she'd replenish with dried apricots or sesame crackers or a new pot of tea as the other women slept in short shifts on the couch with an afghan tucked under their chins. They had agreed early on that the best way to proceed was to gather information and present it in a chunk, or the horror, the never-ending shock of their discoveries, would continue to sidetrack them.

Maris waded through financials—document after document of legalese and LLCs, trying to follow the trail from Hollis down numerous rabbit holes to the backer. After six file folders and thirty-six different files, on page ninety-seven of a multipart corporate charge that listed seven funding sources she could legitimately identify with overseas bank accounts, she found the company that was supplying the money: LanTech Corporation. She stared at the name, nothing but pixels on her computer screen, and felt like it had been written in her own blood. She'd found where the buck stopped, but who was behind it? She scoured the internet for word of the organization and found nothing.

She also worked her way through the data, matching the women to the test subjects. Based on the dates of her blackouts, she was confident she was test case #5, with the first blackout recorded the second week of classes. From there, it appeared they happened with the frequency she remembered, and frighteningly enough, a few times when she was sleeping and would have been unaware. She looked through the medical histories Karen had recorded for Shelby, Bev, and Janice about their memory issues and assigned them to test cases #3, #6, and #4, respectively. On October 16, Hollis had run three quick tests on Maris and test case #8, and while those on #8 were successful, there were three anomalies in a row where it appeared Hollis was unable to locate her brain waves. She was pretty sure #8 was Beth given her memory loss when next they talked, but why had Maris been spared? Jesus, he had come so close!

Unaccounted for were #1, #2, and #7. Test case #1 began much earlier—in March—and had only one entry, and with a sickening feeling, she glanced at Carl's medical records and confirmed the date he died. The other test subjects were all included in the simultaneous blackout on October 8, and she called Eula over to run her theory by her.

"Here," she said, pointing at the spreadsheet. "October 8, when our bodies shut down." It was the day of Maris's car accident. The day she woke with an EMT over her, and she'd ended up at Noel's hospital. "What's this look like on your end?"

Eula scrolled through her cellular data. "It looks like he was trying to cluster the different waves to see if he could block them simultaneously from different cell towers but with the same responder."

Maris nodded. "My guess is he was seeing how it worked as something of a group block as a precursor to a groupthink, and it backfired. A bad deal for the women that day—particularly me, with the car accident—but good in that we might have a clearer sense of what he's trying to do before he does it." It was almost unfathomable that she could talk about herself—test case #5—in such removed terms, but it was the only way she could push through without going crazy.

Eula looked at her, impressed. "And to think, Hollis believes women in the social sciences are hens."

Maris pointed again at her screen. "See here? Test case #7's tests ended on the eighth." She grimaced. "It ends. Just like Carl's did on the day he died. I don't think she made it."

"I can see if we have her records at the hospital," Karen volunteered. Another body to add to Hollis's count.

"And this one?" Eula said, pointing to #2. She was in compartmentalization mode, too, barely flinching at the mention of her husband, but Maris knew how deeply that cut. They each were living with tight coils in their blood of stress and grief and rage.

"As of now?" Maris said. "Unaccounted for."

Eula blanched. "You don't know who she is?"

Maris shook her head. "Not a clue." She remembered the early days when her blackouts started, before she'd met up with Karen in the ER and talked to Eula, before these women confirmed she wasn't crazy. The hours she spent researching what might be happening, how she was certain she was dying and it was all her fault.

"But I can tell you this," Maris said. "There's a woman out there somewhere who is certain she's losing her mind."

At six in the morning, Maris slipped quietly out of Eula's guest bed after sleeping three fitful hours, Janice still asleep beside her. Maris had waited until Janice's eyes had drooped shut and the hand she held loosened before she'd allowed herself sleep. Now, as she tiptoed past Karen on the couch to make coffee, she was careful not to make too much noise.

It was still dark out as she stared out the window over the kitchen sink sipping her first cup, the beginning hints of gray in the sky. Something still bothered her about those anomalies in Hollis's disruptions of her brain, the night the responder didn't find her.

According to Eula, the most obvious explanation was that she'd been out of cellular service. It could happen, say, if you were in a dead zone, like some places still left in rural Nebraska, but even if she'd blipped down a side road and dropped a call, it wasn't anything that would have been ongoing. It wasn't something that would have happened three times in a row over the course of the evening, because as tied as she was to her cell phone, Maris would have noticed if she'd lost service.

All of her interruptions had gone as planned until October 16, when Hollis tried to disrupt memory function at 8:41 p.m., 8:54 p.m., and 9:18 p.m. but wasn't able to connect. She thought back to the first time Eula had explained the three parts of an RFID: a receiver, a responder, and a chip. It couldn't be the responder, because she would have known she was out of service. She quickly checked the other test cases, and at least one had been recorded at that time so it couldn't have been the receiver, which was the equipment Hollis would have in his lab. So that left the chip. But how could it have been her brain? How could that have glitched?

She bit into the granola bar she'd brought back from her house after using snacks as an excuse to go home, when really she'd wanted to get on the dark web. She remembered sitting at the desktop researching Shelby when her world went blank—the first blackout since her accident—and remembered suddenly she'd been in the living room. With the security camera. She'd been so upset after Noel left his video, she hadn't taken the time to disconnect it but ran, one bad decision after another, to Savory's and then the Treasure Club.

She pulled the security app up on her phone and clicked through to the last video, hoping it could offer some insight into her state during a blackout. The video clicked on as she entered the room and sat at the computer. She was horrified to see how bad her posture was as she clicked away at the mouse and keyboard, but other than that, nothing caught her attention. She watched in 4x speed, and only slowed to regular speed as she got closer to the time the blackout would have happened. She watched intently as new screens she didn't recall seeing appeared on the monitor, and she studied her profile for any changes: nothing. She looked exactly as she had before. Frustrated, she watched it again, but still there appeared nothing different about her, and she realized she had expected it to be like a blackout when she was drunk, those small clues that gave it away: a slack mouth, droopy eyelids. Something. But it was just her. Just regular, sober her.

As the first morning rays started to spread through the living room, a new idea began to bloom. Maris clicked out of the security app and into the calendar; it was October 19. October 16 was the night Hollis was unable to disrupt her memory with a blackout. Last Saturday. The day she and Eula went to talk to Beth, and the day she came home and found Cody and Noel both gone.

Pinpoints of light blurred her vision as it sank in: the night of October 16 was the night she'd gotten drunk.

She woke the women frantically one by one, not caring about her sour breath, her teeth still unbrushed, so quickly she raced through Eula's house to assemble the women and tell them the news. Karen had slept on the couch and swung her feet to the floor, making room for Eula and Janice. They settled into the living room, tea or coffee in hand, and Maris took a deep breath.

"Looking through the research, I found a pattern, one Hollis might not have been able to recognize." She took a sip of her milky coffee. "Like we talked about last night, we can't disrupt the responder because he's using cell service, and there's danger to stealing the receiver because he might access our brain waves, but what if we made it so he can't recognize them?"

Eula looked at her, confused. "Like brain damage?" She wore a Glenn State sweatshirt two sizes too big, and Maris wondered if she'd been sleeping in Carl's clothes since he died.

Maris winced. She wasn't wrong. "Yes, but temporary." She pulled up the data on her laptop and showed her the disrupted transmissions when Hollis wasn't able to find her wavelength. "Think of it this way: brain waves are as individual as fingerprints. If you have a little to drink, it's going to affect your brain—your speech slurs, your coordination starts to drop—but you're still 'readable' by the scanner. It still shows as your brain. Two drinks are akin to a smudge in your fingerprint. But when you drink enough to black out, the waves are altered to the point of unrecognizable. It's not just that the alcohol smudged the fingerprint, it's like it burned it off or covered it with a glove. For that moment in time, you had no fingerprint." Maris had to work to keep her voice steady, thinking about how willingly she'd been erasing her own life.

"Okay," Karen said slowly. "So maybe someone can get drunk and break into his lab and disrupt the responder?"

Maris almost laughed. It was a bitter irony to think the one thing that had seemed like her biggest problem was now the one thing that had saved her. But it wasn't her biggest problem; that was how she handled it. She should have talked to Noel about her drinking. She should have been honest about how hard quitting had been. She

—

—

—

Image of Noel and Cody laughing together in the kitchen.

"Maris?" someone said. "Are you okay?"

—

—

—

"I don't think she can hear us!" Eula said.

Noel turning toward her in his sleep, his breath sour yet sweet. Cody sitting with an art project at the kitchen counter while Maris made dinner.

—

—

—

"Maris!" Janice yelled.

The three of them in the car belting out Fountains of Wayne.

—

—

—

Maris fluttered her eyes open and saw the other women standing above her. She was on the floor and could smell the bitter coffee along with Eula's floral carpet freshener. "What happened?" she asked as Karen held her elbow and guided her to the sofa.

"You blacked out," Karen said. "Only it wasn't like the other times. We could see it. You had three quick blips, right in a row."

"You could see them?" Maris asked.

"It was like a heavy blink," Karen said, "and then you collapsed." She took Maris's wrist to feel her pulse and rested the back of her other hand against Maris's forehead. "Your vitals seem normal."

"Do you remember anything?" Janice asked as Eula opened her laptop and clicked on the keyboard.

Maris shook her head. "No?" She *didn't* remember anything, but somehow felt the presence of her family. Or not so much their presence, but that they'd just left, as if the ghost of them hung in the room. She tried to remember why she thought that, to hold on to something specific, but nothing would come.

"Look at this," Eula said, and swung her laptop around, pointing at the Excel sheet open on her screen. "Three quick blinks. It's what happened when Carl and the unknown subject died."

Eula's cell phone rang, and Eula screamed, a short burst of noise in the early morning.

"It's him," she whispered, and Maris rolled her hand like, *answer it.* Eula tapped the screen. "Hello?"

The women watched intently as Eula mm-hmmed her way through the conversation. "I still haven't seen her." There was a long pause. "It's too early now, but I'll be sure to check on her later." She grimaced and locked eyes with Maris. "Of course. I'll give you a call."

A moment later she said goodbye and hung up the phone, collapsing her head on her knees before taking a big breath and sitting back up. She looked at Maris.

"He wants me to check on you and see if you're okay. He'd know from the scans you're not dead"—fear slammed through Maris's nervous system as she realized how easily she could have been—"but he said he's afraid you're unstable from your medical leave and had a feeling something had happened."

"How long do I have?" Maris asked urgently. "How long until he comes and checks for himself?"

"I'll call him in an hour and tell him I talked to you but you seemed a little off. Maybe a slur to your speech. He'll think you had a stroke. I'll tell him I took you to the hospital."

"I can cover for you this afternoon," Karen said. "If anyone asks, I'll say we admitted you for an MRI and some tests."

"There's no way he'll be bold enough to try something while he thinks you're being monitored," Eula said. "My guess is we can buy you the day."

A day. It wasn't much time before your life disappeared. Maris tried to remember again why she'd woken up thinking of Noel and Cody, but the reason remained just out of reach. Had Hollis zapped something? Taken away a memory?

Either way, Maris knew what she had to do with her precious time left and pulled up the Lyft app on her phone.

Chapter Forty

Maris stood on Joe's porch step. She'd found his address from an old party Evite, the same party where Maris had insulted his wife, and had ordered a Lyft. She'd slipped her driver a twenty to take her through the McDonald's drive-through on the way to Joe's, because while she loved Starbucks in all its basic glory, Noel had always been a Mickey-D's man.

As she rang the doorbell, she concentrated on the cold cement under her feet and the hot coffee pressed against her thumb. She imagined Noel warm and asleep on the other side of this door.

Maris held three Egg McMuffins and three hash browns in a paper bag tucked in her armpit, the hash browns' grease soaking through, and four large coffees in a cardboard to-go carrier. If she only had a day left, it was time to tell Noel the truth.

Joe's wife, Lana, answered a long pause later, wearing a sky-blue terry cloth robe held closed with one hand, the other rising to smooth out the cowlick on the back of her head. At the party, to her great embarrassment, Maris had drunkenly insulted Lana's weight and her hair. She wondered if Lana had remembered, or if the motion was instinctual, answering the door with bed head.

"Maris?" Lana squinted against the weak sunlight as she tied the belt at her waist. It was just after eight in the morning, and if Lana was surprised to see her, she didn't let on. The party Maris and Noel had attended was for the couple's twenty-fifth wedding anniversary, and

Maris guessed that after that long you understood marriages had their rough patches.

"Here," Lana said, and opened the door wider, stepping back so Maris could enter. "I'll get Noel."

Maris followed her inside, took two coffees out of the to-go carrier, and dug a sandwich and hash brown out for Noel. She handed the bag and other coffees to Lana. "I brought an apology breakfast for you and Joe. Sorry to wake you up."

Lana looked at the food in her hand. "And you assumed because I'm fat I liked McDonald's?"

"No, I—" Maris stammered. "It's Noel's favorite. I brought him some too." So much for questioning if Lana remembered.

"I'm teasing you," Lana said. "Of course I like McDonald's. Look at me." She waved a hand over her typical fifty-year-old body, which looked like it had lived a good life, a healthy and a happy one. Maris realized Lana didn't remember (or maybe had never heard) the rude comment she'd made when she was drunk; this was Lana's own defense mechanism against her insecurities. How had women gotten so concentrated on the wrong things, so apologetic about their places in the world?

Noel walked into the foyer rubbing his eyes, his hair in disarray. "Mare?" Panic flashed across his face. "Is Cody okay?"

"She's fine," Maris said, and held the food out to him. "I brought you some breakfast. I was hoping we could talk." She knew she had to clear the air with Noel before she and the other women went any further. Even if he rejected what she had to say, she needed to tell him she was sorry about the drinking and the lies and the lies of omission. He was right; she'd given him lots of reasons not to trust her, even if they weren't exactly the ones he thought.

Lana held up her bag and coffees as thanks and gave Noel a meaningful look as she passed to the back of the house. Noel walked toward the dining room and sat down at the end of the table in an uncomfortable straight-backed chair as Maris tried to hide her disappointment. She'd hoped they'd sit somewhere more intimate, like the couch, but she knew they were at a formal-seating crossroads in their relationship. She took the chair across from him, three feet of doily tablecloth between them.

He unwrapped half the sandwich and took a bite, chewed methodically, and then took another. "Well?"

Maris cleared her throat; he wasn't going to make this easy on her. "I watched the video."

He paused with the McMuffin halfway to his mouth, then set it back on its paper wrapping. "And?"

"And you're right. I have a lot I've been keeping from you." She let out a shaky breath. "I guess I should start with the big things. Or at least the things that make sense." She looked up and held his eyes with hers. "You're right, I drank. Last Saturday night." He kept his face neutral, a doctor trained in not showing too much emotion so patients couldn't see how bad the news really was. "The day you and Cody moved out was an exceptionally hard day." He opened his mouth, and she held up a hand to stop him. "I'm not at all saying it's on anyone but me, not even a little bit, but I was so devastated, I thought, why not keep rolling with the bad decisions." She kept going, three licks to the truth-y center. "But it wasn't just that I was devastated, or feeling awful, or even wallowing in self-pity. I was also looking for an excuse to drink. I had been for months, just white-knuckling it not to. But I swear that's the only time since February." She would not have guessed that admitting she drank would feel so good, but it was a lightening, the words leaving her body.

"And?" He dragged the word out.

"And what?"

He crumbled the sandwich paper and dropped it on the tablecloth, pushing the hash brown away. "There's more to it," he said. "I know there is." He started ticking things off on his fingers. "You lied to me about going to work. You haven't been driving. Something's going on with Eula." He picked up the wrapper and squeezed it even tighter. "And Cody. There's no way you'd let her go to Nebraska without a fight." Noel ran a hand through his hair. It was thinning just a bit at the top, his widow's peak holding strong, and she could imagine him as an old man, old like Carl had been, out in golf shorts and a T-shirt mowing the lawn. Her heart squeezed; she wanted so badly to be at his side to see him age. "Whatever's going on here . . ." He shook his head. "It's not just from one night. It's something ongoing. For a while I thought it was an affair, but that seemed so out of character for you I couldn't believe it."

She looked at him, surprised he trusted her that much. "You don't think I'd have an affair?"

He side-eyed her. "You asking that doesn't inspire a lot of confidence, but no. I don't think you would. You're not that kind of person." Tears welled in Maris's eyes. "What?"

"Just that you think I wouldn't do that. That you think I'm a good person."

He stared at her incredulously. "Of course I think you're a good person. I married you, didn't I?" He moved a seat closer to her and put a hand on hers. "And I'm right, right?"

She squeezed back so tightly he winced. "Yes, of course. I would never cheat on you. Ever. There is no one I could ever want over you." She saw his face soften just the tiniest bit. "For as long as I've known you, I felt like I got the better end of the deal. I feel like that about a lot of things. I ended up with this job I doubted I could do, and I have this great kid who deserves a mom who can stop at two drinks, and then I lucked into this perfect husband who, if he knew the real me, would see what a mistake he made."

"Is that what you think? That we made a mistake?"

"No!" she said vehemently. "That's what I worry *you* think." She held her arms out like, *look at me*, then reached forward and grabbed his hand again. "Do you know how much I think about drinking? Do you?"

"I mean—" he started, but she cut him off.

"I think about it every day. Every morning I wake up hopeful I won't want to drink, and every afternoon I start counting down how many hours I need to get through before I'm asleep and not obsessing about it. And then I lie in bed and think, I could still go downstairs. I could still go to Savory's for some wine." She dug deeper, each shovelful like a weight released. "It's the reason I wanted you on night shift at the hospital. It's the reason I used to let Cody stay at Lynette's so much. Why I never took you up on the offer to buy groceries, because I wanted to be in control of how much wine we had in the house. I—" She cleared her throat; she had never told anyone the details like this, and tears blossomed in her eyes.

Noel shook his head, confusion on his face. "Why didn't you tell me any of this? Why would you try to do this all on your own?"

She threw up her hands. "Because who else was going to do it? You can't quit drinking for me."

He slapped his chest. "I could have helped you! Jesus, Mare. This was not something you had to take on by yourself."

"But—"

He shook his head. "If you carry a burden, *I* carry a burden." He squinted at her. "Do you honestly not see it that way?"

"All my life I wanted to be a person who didn't want to drink."

"But, Mare." He squeezed her hand and looked imploringly in her eyes. "You're *this* person." He fiddled with the wrapper of his breakfast sandwich. "Besides, it wasn't all you. I saw the tire mark in the yard last February." Maris thought back to that awful night, how she'd steered the car onto the lawn, proud in her drunken way that it was one tire and not all four. Even Eula had eventually asked her about it, but not Noel. "I figured something had happened, and then you didn't bring it up but had stopped drinking, so I just wanted to act like it was all fine. I should have talked to you about it. It takes two to communicate, Mare."

They sat a few moments. She'd always assumed he was too perfect to understand someone with her kinds of problems, but maybe the real disservice had been not understanding he had problems of his own. That he wasn't a saint, but her partner. Perhaps she hadn't given him enough credit for just being human. "Do you remember when we first got together and talked about maybe having a baby?" Noel asked as a dog barked down the street.

She conjured a picture of them in the bed in his old bachelor pad: a stipple of early-morning light across the pillows, their cheeks resting on their hands in prayer. "I do." They'd only been together a few months by then, and it seemed way too early to be talking so seriously, but they both knew they'd have a future. "You asked me if I wanted more kids."

"Do you remember what you said?"

She cleared her throat. "That I got it right the first time and knew not to push my luck." She pulled the thread in her mind, more memories opening. "You brought it up a few more times after that." A quick dip through the baby aisle at Target, or a story about a delivery in the ER. Anytime they were out running errands and saw a stroller, Noel would ask the mother's permission, then bend at the knee, eye to eye with the baby to say hello.

"I did," Noel said.

But those had been hints, small crumbs in a larger conversation. "Why didn't you bring it up for real with me?" Even as recently as building the closet for his pregnant coworker he'd mentioned the width of a baby's defenseless shoulders, and she'd made a crack about how that width didn't seem so defenseless when it was ripping through your hinterlands. He had tried to bring it up, she realized now. The best way he knew how.

"Why didn't you tell me why you quit drinking?"

She grimaced at him. "That logic's so sound it hardly seems fair," she said, and he smiled.

"I should have told you I wanted to have a child, and at least we could have made the decision together. It wasn't like it was my lifelong dream to be a father, but Cody was so great, and I had friends having babies, and it seemed like something I would have been good at."

She squeezed his hand. "You would have. You *are*."

"I know, and I love Cody like my own, but it would have been fun to have one from the get-go. To see their first smile, first steps. All of it."

Tears filled Maris's eyes. "We could still try," she said. "I'm in my forties, but—"

He put a hand to her cheek. "I appreciate that, Mare, and we can talk about it, but not right now. I bring it up not to reopen the conversation so much as to say that I held secrets too. I don't know what it's like for you to quit drinking. My guess is it sucks. You and I are just wired differently that way. But I *do* know how much it sucks to keep a secret from you. To feel like you can't show all sides."

Tears filled her eyes. She leaned forward and gave him a sloppy kiss on the mouth, just the slightest tip of tongue. "I'm going to try to be better."

He kissed her back.

"I don't need you to be better. I just need you to be you."

She threw her arms around him, a sob caught in her throat. *I am worthy,* she thought. *I am loved.* And then, *My god, it's like I finally understand bumper stickers,* and she hiccuped out a laugh. Noel took her chin between his thumb and forefinger and started laughing, too, although she doubted either of them could say exactly why.

Eventually he wiped a thumb across her cheek. "This doesn't fix everything, you know." She nodded. "I'm glad you've opened up to me about the drinking, but that doesn't explain the last two months. The driving. The leave from work." He shook his head. "There's more to it."

She nodded again and swiped her other cheek. "You're right, and it's not for any of the reasons you might think." She put her hands on his neck, his skin cool against her palms. "Just listen. Let me get it all out."

She started with the first blackout back in September, the day Tammy came to her office and captured her brain waves with her phone. She told him about the blackouts continuing, ratcheting up with the car crash and her trip to the ER. The meeting with Beth Novak in Cincinnati and Beth's inability to remember any of it. Eula's involvement. The connections to Dylan Charter. The neural oscillations and the cell towers. She told him truth after truth, holding his hands the whole time, certain if she got any lighter she'd float away.

He interrupted with a few questions—So Janice, Lynette's mom? That sweet old lady next door?—but for the most part he listened. And at the end he slouched sideways, an arm slung across the back of the hard chair, the other still holding her hand.

"It's a lot to take in," she said as he looked at her, stunned.

"It is." Her heart seized, and she worried all the trust she'd built in the last hour would crumble to nothing. For a split second she thought, *You shouldn't have said so much!* But no. She wanted those days behind her. He shut his eyes, and Maris studied the planes of his face, willing herself not to fill the silence no matter how much she wanted to blather on and take it back. She stared at the hand over hers. Noel had always kept his hands in pristine condition for his profession. They were clean with square nails, the skin dry from constant washing.

He opened his eyes. "I'm sorry you didn't feel you could tell me any of this sooner," he said. "When you quit drinking last February, I didn't know what to make of it, but I'd always thought of you as so strong, I assumed it was easy for you. I should have supported you more. I want a relationship where you feel you can tell me anything." He looked at her for so long without blinking his eyes began to water again. "As for all this"—he motioned a circle with his arm indicating what she'd told him—"I believe you."

"About the drinking?"

He shook his head. "No. All of it."

"How?" she asked, stunned. She had been prepared to bring in Karen as witness, for Eula to explain the research.

"Because you're my wife. And I know when you're telling me the truth."

Maris leaned into him, her mouth against his. How had she ever thought alcohol was the most intoxicating drug?

Chapter Forty-One

What Noel said earlier about this not fixing everything held true, and Maris knew it. She was done with easy fixes. They finished their coffees with their unoccupied hands entwined; she was aware now every minute could be her last, and this was how she wanted to spend it. Only Cody being there could make it better.

Her phone dinged with a text from Janice. **Finally cracked Charter folder.**

Noel threw on a fleece and said he'd drive her over. "I know you can't just move back in," she said as they loaded in his car. "My life was in danger, and I decided I'd rather risk it than tell you the truth." She let herself feel the pain of it and acknowledge it and accept it, knowing they could work together to fix it.

"I know," he said, his arm thrown over the passenger seat to back out of the driveway, even though he had a perfectly good back-up camera. "But this is a step in the right direction."

She leaned her head back and thought about his tear-filled eyes on the video. "Did you sign an apartment lease?"

"No," he admitted. "But Joe and Lana say it's fine if I stay a little longer."

As he turned toward their neighborhood, he asked, "Mare? Are you safe?" and Maris admitted, not at all. Was safe even possible now with Hollis in control? At any moment he could shut her real self down, not only by blocking memories but by inserting new ones. There was the terror of not remembering what she'd done, but also the escalated terror of not even realizing it. She rotated her cheek into Noel's warm hand. Every second mattered.

◆ ◆ ◆

When Karen answered Eula's door, Noel widened his eyes like, *WTF?*

"I know," Karen said. "It's a lot to take in. But, Noel? Every word of it is true." She shut the door behind him and Maris.

"I'm glad you're here," Janice said, looking up from her computer and nodding at Noel. "I finally got the Charter folder open."

Maris hustled behind Janice and bent over her shoulder as she pulled up the finder window. There were mainly PDFs, and Karen opened them one by one. As Maris had suspected, they were scans of her articles about Dylan. Some Hollis had printed, underlined certain phrases, then scanned to upload once again. In "The Best Get Out of Jail Free Card? Be Born White," he'd underlined many lines twice. *The best defense has nothing to do with innocence, or even alibi, but the ability to convince a jury that people like you don't do things like that. It isn't a defense of a man as much as the defense of a race and a set of assumptions.* She read these words now from Hollis's point of view and saw them not as a damnation but a blueprint: how to keep white men free. Other articles had similar markings. *Entitlement has warped men into believing they are untouchable . . . In a world where women aren't believed or trusted, all basic human rights are threatened . . .* And in "How is Rape Up for Debate?": *There are two options: stop men or silence women.* That one had been underlined three times.

She clicked on a file named LTC. It was a 533A tax form for Ohio, Article of Organization for an LLC. Company name: LanTech Corporation. She scrolled to page two of the form: *Hereby appoint the following to be the Statutory Agent, Dylan C. Charter.* She scrolled down to find his acceptance of the appointment and his signature, followed by the date. Dylan would have been eighteen at the time LanTech was formed and started funding Hollis's research, but where had the money come from?

"What are those?" she asked Janice, and pointed to a cluster of JPEGs. Janice double-clicked the first, and as it filled the screen, Maris's vision wobbled.

It was a young boy, no more than seven, in red shorts and an Ohio State basketball T-shirt, standing at a concession stand with a bucket of popcorn, the biggest money could buy. Hot dogs cooked behind him next to a neon-red Coca-Cola sign. He smiled a gap-toothed smile, and Maris knew without a doubt this was Dylan Charter as a child.

They clicked through more: Dylan as a toddler dressed in a suit holding a pillow in front of him, two rings tied to it with a ribbon. Dylan as a preteen, a basketball tucked in his sweaty armpit. Dylan on the college court before his scholarship was rescinded, and finally, what must have been a more recent picture with a crowd at a table. She recognized Dylan's mother and father, his dad smug as ever with what looked like a glass of whiskey in his hand. Maris recognized the Treasure Club with a sickening lurch. Dylan had a bottle of Coke in front of his plate, his arm around the chair to the right of him, and the girl in the seat was the one who had been stalking her—office hours, the library, that night at the Treasure Club.

"Karen," she hissed, and Karen bolted to her side. "That's her, right?" she asked, pointing to the screen. "From Saturday?"

Karen sucked in a breath and nodded. "Same outfit and everything."

Maris called over Janice and stabbed at the screen. "It's her, right? Jane Doe?"

Janice shook her head.

"It has to be!" Maris insisted. "Maybe in a disguise?"

"I'm sorry," Janice said, "but it's not. She actually moved away a few months ago." Maris shook her head furiously. "Maris, I'm sorry, but you're wrong."

Maris scanned the photo again looking for other clues—fall decorations, a telling centerpiece on the table—the picture fading in and out as she finally saw the biggest shock of all.

Across the table from Dylan and the mystery woman, in profile, sat Hollis Grant, a grin on his face, a raised glass in the air.

Maris grabbed her purse and scrabbled through for the scrap of paper the strange woman had given her. It was a receipt for a local liquor store—Maris knew it well—and she scanned the note.

Charters are DANGEROUS!!!

and they are after you

BE CAREFUL!!

She turned it over again. The receipt was from 5:21 p.m. October 10. Below that was the purchase—two bottles of Skyy vodka—and a credit card number. It was a local shop without the encryption, and she shot out the door for home, logging on to the dark web.

There, she entered the credit card number, paid an exorbitant fee, and a moment later the name Lolly Sawyer appeared, along with an address only a few miles away.

CHAPTER
FORTY-TWO

Noel drove, and Maris researched Lolly Sawyer on her phone, a trickle of sweat sliding down her spine. She'd graduated high school six years ago in a local suburb, no mention of college, and worked at a UPS copy center on Main where Maris sometimes dropped off packages. Was that how they'd originally come in contact? In images there were two pictures of Lolly, barely recognizable now, a mousy brunette who had participated in the high school choir and a STEM immersion day at Glenn State. Was that where she'd met Hollis? And was it that Lolly was in danger, or was the danger? Had the note been a warning or a trap? Maybe she had fully expected Maris to hunt her down.

They drove from their safe, middle-class Oak Park neighborhood to the industrial side of town where Lolly lived, her building squeezed between a convenience store and a Dollar Tree. Noel pulled into the apartment parking lot—little more than a gravel pit in need of resurfacing, the car lunging over potholes—and they raced to the third floor. Maris pounded on the door, aggravating her side.

"Hold it," a muffled voice said from inside, accompanied by a shuffling noise. The door was stamped hardboard, cheap, with no peephole to check who was there. Lolly answered the door in baggy jeans and a flannel shirt, no makeup, her hair held up in a messy ponytail that didn't look messy on purpose. As soon as her eyes clocked Maris, she went to slam the door, but Maris blocked it with her foot.

"Nope," she said, and with Noel's help, they pushed their way into the apartment.

She took in the studio in a quick glance. There was a futon folded down against the wall, a pile of well-worn clothes—mainly flannels and sweats—at the foot of the bed. Two bottles of vodka sat on the kitchen counter along with a cheap Mr. Coffee. Just looking at the bottles gave Maris a pang. A rolling hanging rack pushed against the opposite wall looked like an Instagram story in rose golds, earth tones, and denim. The sweaters looked like cashmere, and the jeans were expertly ripped. An open box of Honey Smacks sat on the counter next to a bowl of milk.

"You shouldn't be here," Lolly hissed.

"I gathered that." Maris moved to the futon and sat down, crossing her legs as if she had all the time in the world. It was the only furniture in the room. "Does your boyfriend like your place?" she asked, and Lolly flinched. "Or let me guess. You spend most of your time at his house."

"You need to get out," Lolly said again.

Maris leaned back on her hands, her heart thumping with adrenaline as she tried to appear calm.

"I can't be seen with you," Lolly said. She kept sneaking looks at Noel, who was still standing by the door like a bodyguard. Maris could read the energy in the room—how Lolly kept making sure he hadn't moved, how she was slowly inching her way away from him. She was scared of Noel, or at least uneasy around him. "You'll ruin everything if someone catches you here," she said to Maris.

"But exactly what kind of danger am I in?"

"The deep-shit kind," Lolly said. "Those articles you wrote really pissed off the Charters."

Maris was careful not to react, but even hearing the Charter name spiked her pulse. She remembered the girl in her office, angry about Dylan's sentence. She'd thought it was because the sentence was so light, but was she remembering that wrong? "And how do you know that?"

Lolly looked nervously at the door.

"I'm not leaving until you tell me."

"Fine. That night I gave you the note, I overheard Dylan's dad talking about how he'd taken care of you, that you wouldn't be writing much longer," she said.

"Who was he telling this to?"

The woman glanced at Noel again, uneasy. "Does it matter?"

Maris turned to Noel. "Why don't you wait for me in the car," she said. She knew the only way this woman would talk would be if they were alone. She needed to gain some modicum of trust.

"Are you sure?" Noel asked, and she nodded. He took another sweep of the apartment and pulled his phone from his pocket so they'd both see he had it if he needed to call 911, then left the room. It confirmed what Maris was hoping: he could still trust her judgment.

After he shut the door, she turned back to Lolly. "Of course it matters. I'm trying to verify your credibility. It seems odd to me that a woman invested in Dylan Charter's sentence just happened to overhear his father talking about his vendetta against me."

Lolly picked at the open hangnail on her thumb. "Fine. He said it to his family."

"So you think that the Charter family is upset I've written some articles"—*understatement of the year*—"and they want to get back at me. Any idea how they plan to go about it?" It was the question she was most curious to know the answer to: Did Lolly know what might *really* be going on?

Lolly's eyes darted away quickly, and Maris knew she didn't know. "I know they're feeling pretty confident about it. His dad said he'd taken care of it, not that he would. You were right about his family, by the way," she went on. "They're just as entitled and oblivious as you wrote. They don't care at all about what he did. They don't care if he's out there raping girls as long as he takes over the family business. As long as he keeps the fortune growing."

"But you don't know how they plan to stop me?"

"Not exactly," Lolly admitted, "but I think we both know they're the kind of people who are determined to get what they want. Little Dylan has certainly proven that."

"Okay," Maris said, trying to follow the logic. "So why did you risk giving me the note?"

Lolly stood in silence, but Maris could be patient. Even with Hollis scurrying around her brain like a rat in a maze, she could outlast a silence: it was the best pedagogical tool in her arsenal. Tears formed in Lolly's eyes. "Because I wanted to help you. I didn't want them to hurt you too." It was the first time Maris felt she was looking at the real Lolly and not a disguise.

"One more question." Maris grabbed her phone and pulled up the photo she'd snapped of the Charter dinner and zoomed in on Hollis. "Who's this?"

Lolly peered at the photo. "His uncle Hollis."

Triumph slammed through Maris's system, the adrenaline of an answer. But how had she not discovered this connection in her research? "But different last names, and the age difference," she said, and Lolly looked at her like, *duh*.

"He's Carol Charter's uncle, actually."

Maris scrambled to think what she'd learned about Hollis's family tree beyond that he'd never had children. She'd assumed there weren't family connections in Dayton and that he'd moved here for the job at Glenn State, but she should have thought more about his financial backing. Many of the older guard in academia came from money, the intellectual pursuit available only to the upper crust. "And he's close to the family?"

"He's the one with the purse strings," Lolly elaborated. "He and Eric Charter want Dylan to take over the family fortune, but only if he's willing to fall in line."

"And who are you in all this?" Maris demanded, standing up as Lolly took a step toward her. She wanted to ask her if she'd been having blackouts, but there was still the chance Lolly was working with the Charters and not to be trusted. Maybe she was laying the trap.

Lolly pressed her lips into a thin line. "I'm not answering any more questions. I've told you enough."

"What do you have planned?" Maris pushed, but the woman opened the door and shoved her toward it. Maris knew that was all she'd get out of her and acquiesced, stepping into the hallway.

"Whatever it is, it will be over soon enough," Lolly said, and slammed the door.

CHAPTER
FORTY-THREE

Back home, Maris dug in to her laptop to see what else she could find out. She understood the connection now between Dylan and Hollis, but it was still surprising she hadn't stumbled onto it sooner. She looked again at the LanTech incorporation papers. They'd formed the corporation when Dylan turned eighteen, but during his trial, they'd broken off chunks of Charter Corporations bit by bit and moved them to the less recognizable name. No wonder Hollis and Eric Charter didn't want Dylan making waves; they were trying to distance themselves from the scandal.

Satisfied she understood their motives, she turned her attention to Lolly. Who was she in all this? She knew it went deeper than a woman upset by his crimes. This was personal.

She opened her social media apps, her hands shaking, and looked for Lolly's accounts, but there were none, which was nearly impossible for a girl her age. It would have seemed less suspicious if they had been deactivated, but scrubbed altogether meant something.

Maris typed in the name of her high school and graduating year and found a Facebook alumni group, and from there she made a list of all members and started searching their individual pages. At some point, Noel made her a ham sandwich and insisted she eat it, and then he took half the list and opened his iPad.

They spent another hour bent over their devices searching for Lolly Sawyer, and it was on the seventy-third name that Maris returned a hit. She spun through six years of posts and found a reference to Slutty Sawyer and a party that had happened the weekend of their junior year. There were the usual pictures of underage kids with Bud Lights in their hands, cheers-ing each other and the camera like they were so much older than they were. In three years, Cody would be this age. The kids had set their Facebook pages to private as if that meant their parents would never see, and most of them wouldn't, but Maris had friended one of the kids with a fake profile, giving her access to the others.

She scanned the pictures, looking for Lolly, and thirty or so into a photo album from the night, there she was in jeans, Doc Martens, and a cardigan, a flannel tied around her waist. Her hair was a darker brown—what Maris guessed was her natural color—and she was flanked on both sides by two average-looking guys in T-shirts and jeans. The three of them had their arms around each other, genuine smiles on their faces. Lolly looked happy—not only like a younger version of herself but a different one. The natural hair, the lack of makeup. She didn't look anything like the different versions Maris had met.

She clicked out of the album and scrolled through the timelines and comments. Slutty on the prowwwwwwllll! read one comment.

Who all got a turn? read another.

Maris felt her gut tighten, and a sour taste filled her mouth.

Three different people posted a GIF of a woman being hit in the face with hot dogs.

And buried deep in the comments was another picture of Lolly, naked from the waist up on a bed, a man bent over her covering one breast with his body and the other with his hand. It appeared from the grainy quality to be a still of a video. Further into the comments was a similar picture with a different man. Lolly's eyes were glassy, a fresh bruise on her neck.

"Jesus," Maris whispered, and Noel asked what she'd found.

She turned the computer toward Noel, and he winced. "It's her?"

"I'm positive." She scrolled farther, and found yet a third picture—a man with curly hair on top of her, his broad back clothed in a gray T-shirt. Someone had tagged the photo: who took this shit? bball69???

Her cursor hovered over the tag for a moment, and then she took a deep breath and clicked. It took her to another page, the one she had suspected, the picture everyone knew from Dylan's signing day with Ohio State, his proud parents on both sides. It reminded her of the one she'd found on Hollis's computer, the hopeful kid at the concession stand, the same earnest grin. Early in the trial, she'd written an article analyzing news outlets that ran this photo over the mug shot, with his scraggly hair and bloodshot eyes, the look of a criminal versus a boy full of promise.

If anyone posed a threat to Dylan's future now, it was Lolly.

She sent a text to the other women, who had dispersed to their homes to catch some sleep: come now. I found the missing test subject.

Eula arrived at Maris's first since she had the shortest commute, but Janice and Karen weren't far behind. Maris was sure Dylan had been one of the boys who assaulted Lolly that night, even though she was seeing him from the back.

"She has to be the missing woman from the data," Maris insisted. "Who else would they want to be keeping tabs on?"

"But isn't she also his girlfriend?" Karen said.

Maris couldn't imagine the compartmentalization that had to go on to date your known rapist, but people were broken in complicated ways. "Yes and no. She's pretending. I think she's getting close so she can kill him."

Eula put a hand to her chest.

"But if she's the missing data point," Janice reasoned, "why would they let her get close? Why let her date him at all?"

Maris shook her head. It wasn't adding up. "I'm kicking myself for not asking her about the blackouts when I was there, but I didn't trust her enough to bring it up."

"I think we're going to have to," Noel said.

She convinced the women to sit tight while she and Noel drove over to talk to Lolly again.

"You be careful," Eula said, shaking a finger at them.

Maris hugged each woman in turn as she said goodbye, holding on tightly. She wasn't a big hugger by nature and was surprised how different each embrace felt one after the other: Eula's soft with her ample bosom and old-lady arms, Karen's firm yet quick. Janice's hug was desperate and kindred and thankful for what Maris was about to do. In a short time, this group of women had begun to mean the world to her, and it felt both daunting and humbling to hold their faith and optimism in her hands.

"I'll see you soon," she said, and hoped it was true.

◆ ◆ ◆

They drove through the rutted parking lot and climbed the two flights of stairs quickly, Maris taking short, shallow breaths against her ribs.

"Lolly?" Maris said, pounding on the door. "It's Maris. I know our talk earlier might not have been what you wanted, but I have to ask you something. It's important." She paused. "Maybe even life or death." She thought that might be enough of a clue for Lolly to open the door, but when she laid her ear against the wood she heard only silence.

"I don't think she's home," she said to Noel, who didn't look convinced.

"Or faking." He backed up and centered his shoulder toward the door to break it down, and she felt such a surge of love for him she thought it might topple her.

He paused and leaned down to kiss her. "I love you, Mare."

"I love you too," she said, and he crashed into the cheap wood, busting the lock in the process.

It looked much as it had earlier, and Maris quickly scanned the small space, sticking her head in the bathroom and pulling back the shower curtain to make sure Lolly wasn't there.

There were empty hangers on the hanging rack of clothes, and as Maris surveyed the apartment, she noticed the vodka bottles were gone. Of course she did.

"Noel," she said, and pointed to the empty counter and told him what was missing. They were the two bottles from the receipt, and it seemed like more than a coincidence they'd sat there for a week and now were gone.

"Do we wait for her to come back?" he asked, but Maris knew that tickle in her gut. She'd been outrunning blackouts long enough to know the one thing she never had enough of was time to waste.

Maris ran through the conversations she'd had with Lolly and her insistence Dylan pay *full stop*, just like the title of Maris's article. "She went to Dylan's," she said. "I'm positive." She wondered what it must be like to read article after article about your rapist and the privilege he'd amassed, rather than a focus on how to survive it. She'd always thought of her writing topics as respecting the victims' privacy, and that was certainly part of it, but had she been too focused on the problem and not the solution?

"Do you have his address?" Noel asked, but she was already opening Twitter. She'd bookmarked the picture of him in the shower shoes, one of the first taken of him back in the wild, the sloping lawn of his home behind him. All that freedom. She took a screenshot of the image, did a reverse image search, and within seconds she had the address.

CHAPTER
FORTY-FOUR

I stood over Dylan with my elbows out like Wonder Woman. He was on the floor now, laid out in front of the sofa where he'd fallen after trying to sit down. Pathetic.

I put my shoulder in his armpit and hauled him back to the couch as he moaned, a slur of red punch leaking from his mouth. Each time I touched him I had to fight a wave of nausea so strong I wondered if it might be easier just to kill him. Perhaps that should have been my plan all along, but I was in too deep now. Too many people could identify me—his family, Maris Heilman, the staff at the Treasure Club. In my darkest moods at three a.m., unable to sleep once again, I'd prowl my apartment and wonder if I shouldn't just take them all out. If they didn't all deserve to pay.

I'd shown up a few hours ago with a grocery bag of bottles in my arms and told him we were going to have a party, just the two of us. The Zolpidem had made Dylan sick, so I was back to alcohol. He said he wanted to leave that life behind, start making better decisions, but I insisted he could trust me, that like his family kept saying, this wasn't his fault. Why should he be the one to change?

And then I put my hand on his chest and told him, "I think a drink would loosen me up."

I told him, "I think I'm ready for us to take the next step."

Dylan nodded. "If you really want to."

I'd looked up punches online and found a bunch of blogs about the Mind Eraser, commonly served at college parties. Vodka was the main ingredient, with enough red Kool-Aid mix and grape cranberry to make it palatable and undetectable.

Dylan had winced at the first drink, but I promised him, "There's barely a taste in there."

After the second drink he said it was hitting him harder than he thought, and I assured him it was because he hadn't drunk any alcohol in so long. "You're a lightweight," I told him, laughing as I poured more vodka in his glass. Three drinks in, he wasn't asking anymore, just sucking it down.

I was drinking just grape cranberry and Kool-Aid, but doing my best reenactment of a drunk girl, stumbling slightly as I got up from the couch, or went to the kitchen to mix another.

When I had him back on the couch, Dylan fumbled with the remote as he sat on the off-white sofa, not caring as he wiped his mouth on a cream pillow, staining it red. How dare he live in a place like this? How dare he get to go on with his life after he'd ruined mine?

At that party all those years ago in high school, I'd gone into a back bedroom with my boyfriend, Chris, and our friend Jerrod willingly. I'd had a few hard ciders by then and thought, *Why not?* Chris and I had been doing it for a few months, and I'd always thought Jerrod was cute.

But once we were back there, bodies half-undressed and sliding across the mattress, someone else from the party opened the door, laughed, and yelled back to the living room. "Party's in here!"

Jerrod jumped up and said, "I don't want them thinking I'm queer," and told the guy who stumbled in that he was waiting his turn.

"It's a train!" Dylan yelled, laughing as he screamed back to the rest of the guys to get their asses in here, and the boys came back one by one. Chris left the party, unwilling to believe what was about to happen to me. I wasn't so lucky.

Dylan was the first, and in my nightmares still, I see him approaching, his hands on his fly. He was on top of me before I knew to react, but when I did, spitting and clawing, there were already others there to hold me down, to pour liquor in my mouth, to laugh as Dylan, their leader, curled his dirty fingers in my mouth. I had never seen him before—we went to different schools—and for many years I wouldn't be able to recall his face, only his body slicing into mine, the pain and terror as I was pinned to the bed.

When I first saw his face online, in an article Dr. Heilman published titled "Two Faces of a Rapist," it finally clicked. The article was a textual reading of his mug shot as well as his signing-day picture with his parents, his whole future in front of him. "Both of these pictures are accurate," she had written. "The boy with the bright future and the one held responsible for his crimes, and it's believing people are only one or the other that lets rape culture flourish."

Staring at the signing-day picture, his proud dad with a hand on his shoulder and his mother clutching a designer bag, my life crashed sideways. The breath left my body, and I collapsed as the floor rushed up.

The night of the rapes, I'd ended up with a dislocated shoulder, a broken tooth. Vaginal and anal lacerations. Some scars had healed, and others hadn't. I could still run my tongue over the jagged tooth and make myself bleed, the blood like welcome rust in my mouth. Once Dylan's turn was over, he started filming, laughing as he did, convincing other guys to join in to justify what he'd done.

I followed the case with Jane Doe every step. I rooted for her and her attorneys, gleeful to see Dylan finally take the fall, and when the jury came back with a guilty verdict I cheered, sleeping through the night for the first time in years. But then the judge said only a six-month sentence, later shortened to four, and I started planning my revenge, but all my plans had fallen apart.

I knew now what I had to do to make another accusation stick: physical evidence.

It wouldn't be a lie, I told myself, just late reparations on the rape he'd already committed. A second conviction on record, and surely he'd be put away for life.

"Here," I said, "have another," and put the squeeze bottle full of nearly straight vodka to his mouth. I squirted and he coughed, nearly choking as his head lolled on the seat cushion, the second vodka bottle a third gone.

"Take it," I insisted, and under half-mast eyes, he did what I said.

Tears streamed down my face as I looked at Dylan's lap. I knew what I had to do. Without semen, there would be no evidence. My hand shook as I reached for his pants' button. There were ways to do it without sex, but violation was violation, both his and mine. I told myself to go to the place in my mind where he couldn't touch me. To the void he and the other men had introduced me to that awful night that had allowed me to survive.

"Babe?" he asked, and I told him to shut up. His eyes fluttered.

I reached forward again, sobbing now.

Dylan moaned. "I don't feel good."

There was a knock at the door.

I whipped around. *Who the fuck?*

I tiptoed toward the door to see who it was. Most likely it would be Dylan's folks wanting to see if he could join them for a nightcap, still delighted to have their baby boy back home, but no matter what, I couldn't let them in.

They grabbed the knob and rattled the door, and I shot back, my hand over my heart. "Dylan? Dylan, are you in there?" a voice bellowed. I knew I'd heard the voice before, but it wasn't his father. "I can't find you."

Find you?

I stepped back toward the door, and as I placed my face against the cool wood and winked through the peephole, his uncle Hollis pulled a key from his pocket and inserted it in the lock.

PART SIX

CHAPTER
FORTY-FIVE

Noel sped past the drive-through liquor stores, fast food, and quicky marts of Lolly's neighborhood to downtown Oak Park, and eventually crossed Main from the middle-class side to the 1 percent. Lawns here expanded and sloped to the curb with crisscross patterns mowed by landscaping services.

Even though Maris had lived in Oak Park for five years, she had never been down these streets: cobblestoned and old-moneyed, with security gates at the end of most drives. The home at 306 Glendale Avenue was one of the more opulent, with a four-car detached garage supplementing the two attached to the house, although to call it a house was a misnomer. It was a mansion, no doubt, but not like the McMansions Maris was used to in the other suburbs—two-tone mullets with brick in the front and siding in the back to keep the price down. This was brick all around, a fortress.

She thought of Lolly in her myriad disguises, terrified by what she had planned.

Noel pulled to the curb and clicked off the car, unbuckling his seatbelt with the other hand as he did. Both ran to the guesthouse, Maris surprised to find the door open.

They entered through an extrawide hallway, spilling into an open kitchen with the vodka bottles—one already empty—on the counter. In the living room there was a deer head on the wall, and a fireplace with stone that reached the ceiling. Maris's heart galloped when she saw splashes of red on the white sofa, but as she ran closer, she noticed the purple tinge and knew all too well it was a spilled drink. She put her hand to her chest in relief.

Dylan was passed out on the opposite couch, his knees tucked near his belly in the fetal position, his eyes shut but fluttering. It was the first time Maris had seen him in person, and she was struck by how much he looked like any other boy his age.

Hollis entered from the back room. "What the—" he started, and he looked at her with surprise. "How did you—" He was dressed in a pair of navy pajamas with white piping and a cardigan, his face mottled with rage: a tall, angry man hovering over Maris.

"What did you do?" he yelled as he reached for her, and Noel ran up behind him and spun Hollis by the arm, slamming him into the wall with a crunch. Blood shot from Hollis's nose, so bright it looked fake as it splattered against the cream-colored wall.

Panic and pain etched on Hollis's face as he put a hand to his nose, cupping it to catch the blood pulsing into his palm.

"Sit down," Noel said, and pointed toward a chair.

"I will not," Hollis said.

Maris saw tears prick his eyes and almost laughed—so emotional! He glared at her with such unadulterated hatred on his face, she blanched at the nakedness of it. She was face-to-face with the man who had tried to take her very life away, and he had the gall to be angry with her! Why was it women had to fight so hard for what they deserved, while men could be this mad when they didn't get what they wanted? For months he'd treated her as a science subject and not a person. He'd erased whole swaths of her life. What about *her* anger? She lunged for

Hollis, catching him off guard as she smacked his chest, first with her flat palm and then her fist.

"How dare you!" she yelled, and grabbed the poker in front of the fireplace.

Noel clutched her arm to keep her from swinging, seemed to think better of it, and let her go. She held the poker at both ends and slammed it into Hollis's neck. His head snapped back, and he toppled into the fireplace and crumpled to the floor as a righteous pain flared through Maris's side.

Hollis coughed, a ragged sound, and she could imagine the bruise blooming on his neck, a black ring below his chin.

Hollis guarded his neck with his hands and crawled toward the empty sofa, cowering now. The cuffs of his pajama pants rose as he sat, his bony old-man feet peeking out from the tops of his leather slippers. Maris pressed a soft hand to her cracked ribs and wondered if she was the first woman to see him in pajamas since his own mother.

Maris stood over him, feeling her blood thrumming through her body. Was a little violence all it took to get men like this to back down? But the problem shouldn't have to be the solution.

"I'm not going to hurt anyone," Hollis said, a ridiculous statement given what he'd been doing. He cleared his wrecked throat as he smoothed the buttons of his cardigan. Grasping for an air of authority and understanding, he turned to Maris. "How were you and Dylan untraceable?" Hollis asked, his voice scratchy from the poker, and Maris dropped the poker as if it had burned her and crossed her arms. She wasn't here to answer questions.

"I know about Diane Garland and Beth Novak," Maris said. "And Carl Moore."

His eyebrows shot up in surprise. "Carl was an accident," he said, confirming for Maris that the two women were of no consequence to him.

She wanted to pick up the poker and slam it into his neck again, but playing by those rules wouldn't do her any good. She moved to Noel to steady herself and took his hand. "We have proof of everything." Hollis shot a look at Dylan on the sofa, groggy but awake. "Eula is already on her way to the police," Maris lied.

"Do you really think you can have me arrested for murder?" Hollis seemed to weigh the outcome. "If you did, I'd still go down as one of the greatest scientists of the twenty-first century."

But no, that would be Eula. They could trace everything back to her original theories, and she'd be the one to take the credit. Maris leaned closer. "What you'll end up being known as is the loser who copied his test answers from a girl."

Hollis sat up straighter with big splotches of blood on his cardigan and pajamas. His hands balled into fists, and she could read the anger in his eyes.

A door opened behind her, and Maris turned to see Lolly running from the master bedroom, knocking her attention away from Hollis as Lolly threw her arms around Maris's neck and nearly choked her. Maris ran a hand down her smooth hair, feeling the delicate bone of her skull underneath. "Oh, Lolly," she said. "Oh, sweetheart."

There was so much Maris still didn't understand, but she held the girl fiercely.

Lolly started crying. She stuttered out words, her teeth chattering. "I was going to hold him accountable, full stop," she said. "For me and who knows how many others."

"Lolly," Maris said, and held the girl's face in her hands. Had she been intimate with Dylan? How long had they been together? She wondered if Lolly had hatched this plan after she came to Maris's office hours or long before. "Breathe." Together they inhaled a deep breath, eyes locked together as the air entered and filled the four corners of their torsos. They held and then released. Maris could feel the air deflate Lolly's cheeks against her palms.

"Lolly, listen to me," Maris said. "Have you had memory blanks?" she asked urgently. "Blackouts you can't remember?" She was sure of it now: Lolly was test case #2.

"What do you mean?" she asked, and shook her head just slightly. "I don't know what—" she started as Dylan pushed himself to a sitting position on the couch, his head loose.

He stood up, unsteady on his feet. "What are you asking?" he slurred, and Maris turned to face him. A zing of adrenaline shot up her back.

"Memory blanks. Blackouts," Maris said emphatically. She couldn't find words to explain more, but could tell by the way Dylan's face paled that he understood. He was test case #2.

"If you had just shut up and accepted that none of this was your fault," Hollis said to his nephew, exasperated, "things could have continued on as they have been."

Dylan, drunk, looked confused and shook his head. "I don't think that's right," he mumbled, and tried his best to focus on Maris, recognition slowly dawning on his face. "You're the lady from the articles," he said.

"She's the one who spread those lies about you—" Hollis started, and Maris felt her body weave toward the edge of consciousness as she put a hand against the wall to steady herself. He was gaslighting Dylan with his version of the truth, preparing him for a new set of memories. Maris understood the next step in Hollis's research: to rewrite Dylan's memory so he'd believe he was innocent.

"You've had blackouts?" she asked urgently. "Moments you can't reconstruct?" Dylan nodded. "Did you lose consciousness on October 8?"

"How did you know?" he whispered.

"It happened to me too," she said, slapping her chest, her words frantic. She pointed at Hollis. "Him! He did it."

"She's hysterical," Hollis reasoned. "She's the enemy, but wants you to believe it's you." He reached into his cardigan pocket, and terror shot through Maris. Was he reaching for a weapon, his phone? Could he kill her right here?

Dylan watched Hollis's hand as well. As it reemerged with the black item gripped in his palm, Hollis pointed it at his nephew, and Dylan grabbed the fireplace poker and slammed it into his uncle's face. Red cascaded down the front of his pajama shirt, and Hollis Grant crumpled to the ground, his hand releasing the phone.

Maris, Noel, and Lolly held a collective breath for one, two, three long seconds until there was a long, wet wheeze from the middle of Hollis's chest, and then Dylan rushed over and slammed into him again. His empty face slumped to the carpet.

Lolly screamed, and it broke the spell. Dylan dropped the poker, and Maris ran to Noel, throwing her arms around his chest. She squeezed and held him for a long beat, then opened her arms to make a space for Lolly.

CHAPTER FORTY-SIX

Noel opened the front door of the guesthouse and held it for Maris and Lolly. Maris checked her watch: two a.m. She hadn't been out of the house this late sober in years, and exhaustion rested like an anvil on her chest.

They had left Dylan with his phone in his hand and told him to dial 911 in fifteen minutes. Given how drunk he still was, she wasn't sure if he'd manage, or if he'd wake up hungover to what had been her greatest fear most of her life: the consequence of her actions bloody in front of her with no memory of what had happened. But he'd proven once before what money could buy, and between that and his family's connections, he wasn't her greatest concern. If you had enough money and power, you could create your own truth.

Maris put her arm around Lolly's back to support her weight as they walked to the car, and the feel of her was so similar to Cody it made Maris's teeth ache. She would give anything right now to hold her daughter.

Noel opened the back door, and they angled Lolly into the car, her head leaning against the headrest, her eyes drooping shut. Maris imagined it was awfully tiring holding that much rage.

"Now what?" Noel whispered.

"Let's take her to our house," she said. There was no way she could send this wayward girl home. Lolly was tilted toward the door now, her cheek pressed against the glass, a thin line of drool hanging from her mouth.

"You think it's safe?" he asked, and Maris nodded, realizing that for the first time in forever she actually was. Hollis was no longer in her brain. It was like wearing a pair of earbuds in a busy city and suddenly switching them to noise canceling, the silence and peace nearly deafening. They would need to deal with his research eventually, but that was a problem for another day.

At home, Eula came out her front door, her arms crossed and holding her robe tight against her. "Everything okay?"

Maris nodded her heavy head as she climbed out of the car. "It really is. I'll fill you in tomorrow."

"Stop by," Eula said, waving. "I'll put on some tea."

Noel came around and kissed the top of Maris's head. "How are you feeling?"

"Like I could sleep for a hundred years."

"Copy that."

Maris knocked softly on the window, and Lolly's eyelids fluttered open. She wiped a hand across her mouth and stepped out of the car.

"Let's get you to bed," Maris said, and explained where they were as she led Lolly through their dark house. It struck her that she knew very little about who Lolly really was. But what she did know was that she was vulnerable and in need of someone to take care of her, and for now Maris could be that person, even if Lolly couldn't bring herself to ask for help. In Cody's room, she found a pair of clean pajamas and brought them, along with a fresh towel and washcloth, to the bathroom. She knocked on the door to let Lolly know they were outside the door—"There's a spare toothbrush in the medicine cabinet"—and said she'd meet her in the guest room to say good night.

While she waited, she texted Cody, even though it was the middle of the night. She needed to send that love out to her daughter. When Cody rolled over in the morning and reached for her phone, eyes still blurry, the first thing she'd see was a message from her mother. I love you, Cody. More than anything in this world. Her thumbs hovered over the keyboard. She didn't know what in the hell she and Noel would tell Cody about all this, but for the first time in a long time, she knew they'd figure it out together. That urgency Hollis had instilled was still there, beating in her heart like a thrilling light. You are the most amazing person I've ever known and I'm lucky to be your mom.

She pressed "Send," and to her utter shock her phone rang a few seconds later. She answered, and as she brought the phone to her ear, Code was already talking. "What's going on there? Are you dying? Why are you sending me weird texts in the middle of the night?"

Maris laughed. "I'm not dying. Very much living, actually."

"Is this menopause?" Cody asked, and honest to god, Maris would have given anything she had to hug her daughter at that second.

"Not yet. I'm fine, Cody, really. I just miss you more than you can guess." In the hallway, there was a collage of Cody's school pictures from first grade to eighth, the high school years still waiting to be filled. She had no doubt her daughter would grow to be an extraordinary woman. "I think it's time for you to come home."

Cody sniffed. "Maybe. Dad told me I have to cheer for the Huskers against Ohio State."

"We can't have that," Maris said.

There was a long pause, and Maris imagined her daughter all those miles away, so much like Maris herself at that age. Wanting to trust her parents, and weighing it against the fear she'd be disappointed once again. "Maybe I can fly home in time to be there for Halloween," Cody said cautiously, and Maris's eyes filled with tears. She was too old to trick-or-treat this year, but Cody had said she was looking forward to handing out candy to the younger kids.

"That would be great. I'll book the plane ticket later this morning."

They talked for another minute or so until Cody yawned. "Seriously, Mom. It's like the middle of the night."

"I know. I'm sorry I texted so late. Get some sleep."

"Is everything really okay?" It felt like such a loaded question, maybe even more so than Cody meant. Or maybe not.

"Better than in a long time," Maris said. "I promise." They said their I love yous and good nights, and after they hung up, Maris sent a heart emoji, side-kiss emoji, heart emoji.

A few minutes later, Lolly entered the spare room, and Maris's heart constricted to see her in Cody's flannel pj's, her face scrubbed clean and smelling of the apricot scrub Code used.

Lolly slipped her feet under the log cabin quilt, a hand-me-down from Maris's father's side of the family, and laid her head on the feather pillow. "I think I might have some anger issues," she said.

Maris swept Lolly's hair out of her eyes. "I think you're right." She pulled up the quilt and tucked it under Lolly's chin. "We'll talk about it all later," she said as Lolly smiled and closed her eyes. "For now, let's get some sleep."

◆ ◆ ◆

In their own bedroom, Noel was stretched out across their queen-size bed, shoes off but fully dressed on top of the covers. Her throat constricted. They weren't out of the woods yet.

"I'm too tired to go back to Joe's," he said. "But I can sleep on the couch if you want."

Maris shook her head. "I want you to stay here." She stripped off her clothes, threw on the Old 97's T-shirt that was technically Noel's, and crawled into bed. She moved her cold feet up against his calves, willing herself to feel the heat of his skin through a sheet, a quilt, and the denim of his jeans.

"Hey now," he said, because that's what he always said when she pushed her cold feet against him, faux complaining before turning onto his side so she could tuck her toes between his calves and warm them up.

It was still the middle of the night. In a few hours, the sun would begin to poke its rays through the window. Noel heavy-breathed out of his slightly open mouth, and her eyes began to droop, soothed by the sound.

Tired as she was, she snapped them open, fighting against the body's natural proclivity to sleep.

She didn't want to miss a minute.

Epilogue

Maris carried the bowl of ramen salad across her backyard and into Eula's, Cody trailing behind with an eight-pack of LaCroix and Noel with a package of hot dog buns. Maris had doubled the recipe, knowing it was one of those Nebraska dishes people wrinkled their noses at, then ended up coming back for thirds. She'd never serve it at a snobby faculty cookout.

Eula had debated having an end-of-summer cookout at all—her first since Carl died—but Karen and Maris both admitted they'd been looking forward to it all summer, the guest list consisting no longer of colleagues, but friends.

Noel headed across the lawn to where Karen was playing bocce with her wife, even though he'd seen her just the day before. They'd opened a general practice earlier that summer, thrilled to be home to their respective spouses by five thirty, most of their patients' ailments cured through changes to diet and exercise. When Karen first approached him, Noel had said he loved the idea and could see the sign: Hiser and Patel.

Karen shook her head. "Patel and Hiser."

Maris had also made a career shift, with official word in spring from the Board of Trustees that she would be promoted to associate professor with tenure. The social media buzz attached to #protectfemalefaculty had resulted in tens of thousands of retweets and an article by Maris in the *Journal of Higher Education*. That, along with the popularity of her latest *WaPo* op-ed about victim advocacy—"Are We Amplifying the Wrong Voices?"—had led to a book contract. Her advance and raise would help offset some of the salary loss with Noel's new position. As for their student loans? There were worse things than being in debt.

Hollis had died shortly after arriving at the hospital, where Karen had been the receiving physician, the one to announce the time of death. Eula had convinced Hollis's department chair to let her archive his research as a return favor for him archiving Carl's and had scoured all evidence of the experiments, her theories secure at least for now. Digging further into the financials, Maris had confirmed that Dylan was the heir slated to take over the Charter/Grant fortunes, but there had been concerns regarding his behavior. Not the rape itself, but his admittance of guilt. She never found a financial transaction between Hollis and Tammy Lerner and still didn't know why her chair agreed to take the scans. She might never know for sure. The real question was, Did Tammy know what she did, or did she believe it was something as innocent as taking the women's pictures?

As for Hollis's death, it was ruled an accident. The same lawyers who secured a four-month sentence for rape raised enough doubt that the charge of manslaughter didn't stick. Many sociologists wrote about the two incidents and debated whether rehabilitation was possible for a violent offender based on statistics, nature versus nurture, and access to programs, and while it was an interesting debate, it was no longer one that interested Maris. She would put her talents to other use.

Cody set the eight-pack of waters in the ice tub and pulled out a Sprite for herself, cracking the tab a millimeter for maximum slurpy-ness, a noise Maris found both unbearable and endearing. Since Cody had returned from Nebraska, their relationship had continued to evolve, and Maris worked daily to be a better mom. It had always amazed her, the biological miracle of growing another human being in her body, but it was nothing compared to the complex miracle of that person growing into herself in the world.

Noel fired up Eula's grill, because no matter how many advancements there were for women, it seemed men still cooked the meat. The sun was high in the sky, and Maris was glad she'd worn just a tank top and shorts; early Ohio evenings still felt like hot afternoon, until that one glorious moment when the air began to cool.

It was seven o'clock, and in her old life, Maris would have secured a cold glass of white wine in her hand the second she'd arrived, finished it quickly in her host's kitchen, and poured a second before anyone noticed. No one ever knew about the first glass—the coldest glass—her own little secret.

What surprised her after all this time was how much she still thought about it: the ghost-taste of vinegar on her tongue, the smell of fermentation, the rounded bowl of the glass in her hand. She walked over to the tub of sodas and waters and plunged her hand into the ice, bracingly cold and enough to clear her head. She'd tried AA for a few months, but Eula was right: it was another group of men telling her what to do. She ended up going back to her therapist instead, the one with the cute shoes, and once a week they talked through her issues with drinking, which weren't just about her drinking after all, but her dad, her mom, trust, success, relationships, and basically every other area of her life.

After the night at the Charters' house, Noel went back to Joe and Lana's to sleep for three nights while he and Maris spent the days talking, and when he moved back for good, they began the hard work of communicating. They used "I feel" phrasing and examined their relationship templates from childhood. They spoke in each other's love languages. When Maris wanted a drink, the person she told was Noel. And finally, after much discussion and openness on both sides, they agreed a baby didn't make sense for their family, and that sometimes the right decisions were still painful ones.

Lolly arrived to hoots and hugs from everyone; each of them joked they were Lolly's adoptive parent, grandparent, or aunt. After the night at the Charters', she slept for two straight days in Maris's guest room, and when she finally woke and ate a piece of toast, they sat down at the dining room table and pieced together a plan, which ended up being behavioral therapy, medications, and PTSD counseling. She found a job at a grocery store and an apartment in a safer neighborhood, with plenty of space to decide who she really was. So far, she'd figured out she liked to read feminist romance novels and looked cute in a pixie cut.

Karen tapped a fork against her red Solo cup to gather the crowd's attention. "Before we eat, I think we should hear a few words from our hostess. Eula, will you give a toast?"

"I suppose so," Eula said.

"Speech!" Janice yelled, and Cody grabbed a sleeve of cups as Lynette followed behind, pouring lemonade for anyone who didn't already have a drink. Maris took a cup and held it out as she sloshed some in.

"I feel like I'm at a kegger," Karen said, holding up the red cup.

I wish, Maris thought.

And god damn if it wasn't true. She knew that for the rest of her life, the desire to drink would be like a deep itch at the back of her throat. Just out of reach. Just short of being satisfied. Every minute would reverberate with the same question: Do I have a drink, or do I not have a drink?

But maybe that question could just be that question. It didn't have to mean, Am I a success or am I a failure? Am I worthy or am I not? Like she'd said to Noel, all she'd ever wanted was to be a person who didn't want to drink, but she was beginning to accept she was not that person. She was this one.

Eula cleared her throat. "You know, I don't think I've ever given a toast in my life," she said. "Carl was always the one who gave the toasts. I'm not sure I know what to say." She held her cup in the air. "Just cheers, I guess."

"Cheers," the others echoed as they knocked their Solo cups together, the plastic on plastic more of a clonk than a satisfying clink.

The blue sky faded to a glorious pink as the oppressive heat made way for a perfect summer evening. How many times had Maris missed ordinary moments just like this? Not just because of Hollis, but because she'd been striving for the next thing, trying so hard to prove herself. And yes, because of the drinking. What was it her father used to say? "The sun comes up, the sun goes down, and here you are." Maybe that, too, hadn't meant what she thought.

Maris held her cup up to Eula and Karen across the yard, to Noel over by the grill, and Cody, sweet Cody, smiling as she and Lynette linked elbows to take a drink.

Lolly knocked her cup against Maris's. "You ladies sure know how to party," she said.

Maris laughed, and drank the lemonade.

ACKNOWLEDGMENTS

Thanks to the Ohio Arts Council for its continued support, to the Sundress Academy for the Arts Residency for time and space, to Wright State University for an academic home, and to my students for kicking so much ass.

Thanks to Kathryn Halberg for her expertise on social media, to Dr. Tracey Steele for her feedback on the field of sociology, and to Kate Geiselman for her essay that inspired some of Maris's writing. A big thanks to Dr. Robert Fyffe for reading sections of an early draft and providing his neuroscience expertise. By the final draft, I had taken quite a few liberties with what's happening in the field of brain-stuff but still shudder to think what's possible. Any inconsistencies or flat-out exaggerations are at my feet.

So many thanks to my agent, Jill Marr, who has been such fun to work with on every level. I cannot thank Jessica Tribble Wells enough for believing in this book, as well as Celia Johnson for helping me shape it into the thing it is today. Tiffany Yates Martin at FoxPrint Editorial and Christina Consolino were also invaluable in earlier drafts, and brought so much joy to the process. Big thanks to Nicole Burns-Ascue, Sarah E., Kellie, Sarah V., Lauren W., Robin, and Sarah Shaw at Amazon Publishing, as well as everyone else I've encountered at Thomas & Mercer. It's been a big fat dream come true.

I'd like to thank all my friends for being my friends—in particular Christina, Meredith Doench, Katrina Kittle, and Jess Montgomery for keeping me sane and laughing and grounded; Carol Loranger for our regular writing meetups; Melissa Strombeck for her cute shoes and for helping me figure some shit out; and Charlotte Hogg for being the best accountability buddy a girl could ask for, as well as a daily delight.

And of course thanks to my family, which is vast and far-flung and filled with my favorite people: Doug Hansen, Andrew Hansen, Alicia Warbritton, Nat Henry, Katie Smith, Lynda and Gene Milligan, Them Sheas, and Michael Dunekacke. To my mom, Judy Flanagan, for teaching me to be a doer; to my dad, Ken Flanagan, for his storytelling; to my sister, Kelly Hansen, for understanding every one of my obsessions and always loving me for me; to my kids—Ellen Milligan, Neil Milligan, and Cora Dunekacke—for being the most amazing humans I know; and to my husband, Barry Milligan. Good cripes, I don't know how I got so lucky.

And finally, if you've suffered from sexual abuse, I hope you're being kind to yourself. If you'd like to reach out for help but don't know where to start, a good place might be the National Sexual Assault Hotline at 800-656-4673. If you struggle with alcohol, I encourage you to seek what help will work for you. If AA doesn't seem like a good fit, you might want to check out Holly Whitaker's work with https://jointempest.com or start with her book, *Quit Like a Woman*.

And to each and every person who has picked up this book, thank you.

ABOUT THE AUTHOR

Photo © 2021 Art Smaven

Erin Flanagan is the Edgar Award–nominated author of *Deer Season* and two short story collections, *The Usual Mistakes* and *It's Not Going to Kill You, and Other Stories*. She's held fellowships to Yaddo, MacDowell, the Sewanee Writers' Conference, the Bread Loaf Writers' Conference, Ucross, and the Vermont Studio Center. An English professor at Wright State University, Erin lives in Dayton, Ohio, with her husband, daughter, two cats, two dogs, and her friendly, caustic thoughts. For more information, visit www.erinflanagan.net.